WHEN YOU LOVE SOMEONE

A SWEET SECOND CHANCE ROMANCE

TINA NEWCOMB

When You Love Someone

Copyright © 2021 by Tina Newcomb

ISBN: 978-1-947786-52-3

Cover Design by Dar Albert of Wicked Smart Designs

This book is a work of fiction. Names, characters, places, business
establishments, and incidents are either products of the author's imagination
or are used fictitiously. Any resemblance to actual persons, living or dead,
events, or locations is entirely coincidental.

❀ Created with Vellum

DEDICATION

*To the late Mrs. Hepworth, for instilling the love of reading in the
4th grade.*

CHAPTER 1

⁂

*I*n the split second between hearing what his attorney said and the news actually sinking in, Jared McAlister took note of the photo of Connor's kids on his desk, how one slat on his window blinds hung crookedly, and the healthy plant on the file cabinet must be watered by an assistant. Connor would never take the time.

When the information finally registered, Jared laughed. "Are you still mad because I trounced you on the golf course last week?"

One side of Connor's mouth quirked down. That tiny motion effectively sucked all the air out of the room.

No. Jared inhaled, trying to expand his lungs. "There has to be a mistake."

"There's no mistake."

"Check again."

"I did. An assistant discovered the mistake, and I checked behind her. Twice. You are still legally wed to"—Connor glanced down at the papers on his desk—"Cecelia Chadwick." He looked up without moving his head. "I guess we need to add McAlister on the end."

Just the mention of her name set Jared's heart galloping. He pushed to his feet, strode to the window, and tried to straighten the crooked slat, which fell cockeyed as soon as he let go. Anything to buy a few moments as memories bombarded him. Connor watched him like a hawk at dinnertime. "This is the reason you insisted I come to this meeting alone."

Connor's crooked grin appeared. "Bad call?"

"No." Jared's fiancée wouldn't take this news well. They met with Stacy's attorney last week to discuss the fine points of their prenup. Her attorney and his assistants had obviously missed the "mistake" Connor's team caught.

Some telling expression must have crossed his face because Connor settled back in his chair and steepled his fingers under his chin. "Want to talk about it?"

Jared crossed to his chair and dropped into the soft leather, his mind racing to that sultry summer. "There isn't much to tell." Yet, given the chance, he could talk about those three months for hours. The long horseback rides, the lazy afternoons spent at the lake, the evening concerts, getting caught in a rainstorm, the way his pulse picked up every time Cecelia was near. "We were young and stupid and fell in love —or lust—too quickly."

Though at the time, it sure felt like love.

He left out the part that Cecelia wouldn't sleep with him until after they were married. If it had been anyone else, he would have suspected her of trying to trap him, but not Cecelia. She had specific moral beliefs on the subject of premarital sex and refused to bend. Though frustrated at the time, he'd admired her for her beliefs.

"We got married two days before I flew to California for my first year of law school, and a week before she left for her freshman year at Arizona State University. We were married for two months, exchanging emails, phone calls, and texts. I thought everything was fine. I sent her a plane ticket to visit for a long weekend and received divorce papers in reply. Uncontested, with no property or children, the divorce was finalized before Christmas."

"Is she going to hit you for back alimony when she discovers you're still married?"

"She didn't ask for alimony the first time, so no. That's not Cecelia's way."

"That *wasn't* Cecelia's way. Did she know your family's net worth?"

"Yes, she was well aware of the McAlister wealth. She didn't ask for anything in the divorce. Nothing."

"That was then, Jared." Connor shuffled through the papers in front of him. "It's been eleven years."

"She won't ask for back alimony."

"Tell me about her."

Jared jumped to his feet and retraced his steps to the window, shifting so Connor couldn't see his face, afraid of what his expressions might reveal. "Cecelia was—is younger than me by four years. Sweet, honest, book-smart, yet naïve of worldly ways.

"She never felt like she belonged in my world. Her family didn't have money. My family didn't help. Dad and Mom always looked down on her like an annoying puppy that had followed me home. Her mother hated me. She told Cecelia rich boys never married poor girls, and I was only after her for the sex."

"Were you?"

Jared twisted to face Connor. "*I* married her. *She* divorced me."

Connor nodded for him to continue.

"She raised her brother and sister because her mom and dad weren't very good parents. And when I say raised, I mean she did everything from making their lunches and dinners to doing their laundry, setting curfews, and making sure they were home when they were supposed to be. Cecelia didn't need or want my money. With a full-ride scholarship to Arizona State, she had plans and hopes and dreams for the future and a better life."

"Do you have any idea where she is now?"

"None." Jared rubbed the base of his skull where a headache threatened.

"Any idea why she wanted the divorce?"

"No. When the divorce papers arrived by courier, I lived in shock for several days while I tried to contact her. My messages went unanswered, my emails undelivered. I flew to Arizona, but she'd left school, which didn't make sense. Her family didn't have money. That scholarship meant everything to her. From Arizona, I flew to Dallas, where I hit another dead end. Her parents wouldn't give me any information, wouldn't even answer the door or my phone calls. Her brother and sister swore they didn't know where she'd gone."

He'd even threatened Cecelia's attorney that he wouldn't sign the papers until he could talk to her. Still, no word. "Eventually, I signed on the dotted line and mailed the divorce documents back."

"You mentioned her family."

"They used to live in Mesquite. I'm not sure if they still do." He paced in front of Connor's desk before retaking his seat. "So, what now?"

A million emotions warred against each other, hitting Jared's mind, his stomach, and, unfortunately, his heart all at the same time. His fiancée's parents were planning an elaborate wedding ten months from now. Flowers, photographers, caterers. The venue had been reserved two days after Stacy had a ring on her finger. She, her mom, and his, along with a wedding planner, were chin-deep in plans and arrangements.

"Since nothing was ever filed, I guess we start over."

"How is it possible that someone overlooked something so life-changing?"

Connor stood the papers on end, tapped them until they were aligned, then slipped them into a file folder. "A paralegal forgot to file it with the court before he or she quit. A clerk neglected to record it in the court records. The document fell behind a file cabinet. Any number of things could have happened. Did you ever receive the final decree?"

If he did, he'd probably shredded it upon receipt, not wanting to be reminded. "I don't remember."

Jared read the astonished *how-could-you-not-remember?* look on Connor's face.

He'd been in a dark place at the time. Maybe the decree was in a box in his guest room closet, and all this panic about still being married would be for naught. "I'll look when I get home."

"Do you want me to use our in-house investigator to find *Mrs. McAlister?*" Connor asked, his lopsided grin in place.

"You're having way too much fun with this."

"Sorry." He pressed his lips together. "I'm astonished, is all."

Me too.

"Do you want us to find her, or do you want to take care of it?" Conner asked again.

If Jared hired an investigator, his dad would somehow find out, and chaos would ensue. If he used the investigator at the law firm where he worked, again, somehow, his dad—with his far-reaching connections—would find out. "You find her. I'll tell Stacy you had to cancel our appointment tomorrow because—"

"A case came up, and I have to be in court," Connor inserted. "Want me to draw up new divorce documents and have them sent to your office to look over? Things should be pretty cut-and-dried. Like you said earlier, no property, no children."

"Draw them up, but I'll come here to get them." Though he received documents by courier all the time, he didn't want them to fall into the wrong hands accidentally.

Jared stood to leave. "Let me know when you find Cecelia."

"You don't want my investigator to serve her?"

"Not yet."

Connor quirked a brow. "Letting someone else take care of this for you would simplify your life."

Jared paused at the door and glanced back at Connor. "I've never done things the easy way. Just ask my dad."

CHAPTER 2

*J*ared stepped out of Connor's office building and into the stagnant Texas heat. Since he wouldn't be going back to his office today, he loosened his tie and shed his coat.

Looking up and down the street, he felt at a loss. His world had been turned upside down with a simple sentence. Just a few words strung together changed everything. And yet nothing at all.

Though, Stacy wouldn't see it that way.

He climbed into his car and hissed when the steering wheel burned his hand. *Stupid.*

Starting the engine, he lowered the windows and sat for a few minutes, letting the air conditioning and the sweltering outdoor heat mingle until it began to cool. Then he rolled up the windows and maneuvered through the busy streets of downtown Dallas.

The lake—a place where he could draw a deep breath, a place where he could gather his thoughts, a place filled with memories of Cecelia—tugged at him.

Pressing the phone icon on his dashboard screen, he called the office.

"Hi, boss," his assistant said after only one ring.

"I won't be back in today, Violet."

"You okay?"

He rubbed his forehead. "Yeah."

"Do you need me to do anything?"

Always one step ahead of him, he knew she was checking his schedule as they spoke. He was grateful every day that Violet had been assigned to him on his first day at Foster, Stern, and Wallace Law Offices. "Yes. I have that deposition tomorrow. Can you get sandwiches ordered?"

"Already done. I added side salads, and the deli is throwing in chocolate cake for dessert."

Again, a step ahead of him. "Remind me to get you something great for Christmas."

"I could use a new car."

He chuckled. "Something a little smaller than a car."

"I'll email you my wish list."

And she would, but it would be small things like a pair of gloves or a three-pack of golf balls.

"Stacy called. I told her you were meeting with another attorney."

"Thanks, Vi." His assistant applied her deft efficiency to every aspect of her job.

"She said to tell you she has dinner plans tonight."

Good. That would give him time to think about how best to handle his situation.

Stacy often took clients to dinner. As a financial planner, she excelled—almost to the point of cunning—at building their trust. In fact, she took pride in her ability to talk people into things they didn't want—a trait his father admired.

"Thanks. I'll see you tomorrow, Violet."

He'd driven to the lake so many times over the years that

he did it on autopilot. Instead of heading down the road to the boat ramp he and longtime best friend, Knox Chatham, used to launch Knox's boat, he drove around the east end of the lake, where he lucked out and found a parking spot. As soon as he opened the door, the sticky humidity shrouded him like a wet cloak.

He grabbed the pair of flip-flops he kept in the trunk and rolled up his perfectly pressed pants legs, wishing he'd gone home to change first. Unbuttoning the cuffs of his dress shirt, he rolled the sleeves above his elbows and headed to the crowded beach.

At the water's edge, he slipped off the flip-flops and walked ankle-deep down to the spot where everything began.

He pushed aside the anger over the way Cecelia disappeared without a word, making room for sweet recollections of their first meeting to flood his mind . . .

Home from Stanford for spring break, Jared met Knox and four other friends at the lake, their hot-weather hangout spot. They cruised close to the shore, where a nice beach always brought out bikini-clad babes. When Knox pulled his forty-five-foot mini yacht ashore, a group of girls ran over. All but one who was lying on her stomach. She glanced over her shoulder, then turned back to the book she was reading.

Jared lost interest as soon as he learned the girls were high school seniors also on spring break. He jumped off the boat when all but the one girl scrambled aboard. Her friends called to her.

"No, thanks. Have fun. Make good choices." She uttered the last sentence just loud enough that he heard.

"Come on, Jared," Knox hollered.

"I'll wait here." He almost repeated the girl's comment about making good choices as he pushed the boat off the sand so Knox could start the engine.

His best friend flashed a grin. "Your loss."

I don't think so. Jared glanced at the remaining girl. She was still engrossed in her book, so he wandered along the water's edge, passing groups and couples savoring the early spring heat.

Graduation loomed, and he looked forward to having a lazy summer break before returning to Stanford for law school. Once in California, he'd knuckle down, but this summer, his final carefree months, he planned to lay low, have fun, and do as little work as possible.

He headed back to the spot where the boat came ashore and plopped down on a towel spread out next to the girl. She didn't acknowledge his arrival, which he considered rude according to his Southern born and bred manners. Her dark hair, shimmering with red highlights, was clipped up. "What're you reading?"

She turned the book over so he could see the title.

"*A Tale of Two Cities*," he answered his question aloud.

She flipped the book back to the page she'd marked with her finger.

"Reading it for a class?"

"No. I like Dickens."

Her soft voice immediately intrigued him. He wanted to hear it again. "Dickens wrote quite a few books. Have you read many?"

"Yes."

He stretched his legs out, feeling his skin tighten under the intense rays of the sun. She seemed uninterested in helping move the conversation along, but he enjoyed a challenge. "Care to share which ones?"

She finally looked at him. "*Oliver Twist, Great Expectations, Bleak House, David Copperfield.*"

The icy blue of her eyes swirled with a myriad of emotions, none of them friendly, yet their color mesmerized him. "I read *Oliver Twist* and *The Old Curiosity Shop* in high school."

She returned to her book without comment.

He studied the curve of her shoulders, down the slope of her slender back, past the blue and white tie-dyed bikini, to a nice pair of legs. "You don't like boats?" he asked, hoping she'd look at him. He wanted to see her icy-blues again.

"I like boats." Her Southern drawl rolled over him like a fog, misty and soft.

"You didn't want to go for a ride?"

She slowly turned her head, her frosty gaze searching his face, piercing a place deep in his chest. "The boat looked a little crowded, and I figured, with it being this late in the afternoon, most of you *college boys* would be drunk. I'm not looking for the same things my friends are."

Sucked in by her comment, he asked, "What are your friends looking for?"

Her gaze flickered across his bare chest, then back to his face. "Someone like you."

"Someone like me?"

She dropped her head and exhaled with obvious irritation before she closed her book and sat up. When she unclipped her hair, it fell long and curly down her back, almost to her waist. She turned her head until those cold blue eyes met his. "Yes, someone like you. A rich college guy with a boat, who can show them a good time for a couple of days, a couple of hours, maybe a night." She stood up and adjusted the bottom of her swimsuit. "I'm not interested."

She waded into the water until she was thigh deep, then gracefully dove under the blue-green surface. When she came up for air, her long, even strokes took her about thirty yards from shore before she disappeared underwater again.

She couldn't seriously think he was attracted to a high school senior.

Minutes later, she waded ashore, making no attempt to mask her annoyance that he was still sitting where she left him. So he made no attempt to look away when she approached. Rivulets slid down her lean body as she twisted the water out of her hair.

He cleared his throat. "What makes you think I'd be interested in a high school girl?"

"I never said you were interested. I said I'm not." She lay down next to him and closed her eyes. "You're, what—three or four years older? I'm not impressed by college guys. Not even the ones who read Dickens in high school."

He grinned. This girl had no compunction about calling him out, which intrigued him. Intrigued, not interested—there was a big difference. Glistening drops of water slid down her sides or pooled in the hollow between her protruding hipbones. He glanced at her face. She was pretty in a girl-next-door way. The sun had kissed her cheeks a soft pink.

He lay on the towel and closed his eyes. They stayed that way until he heard her shift onto her stomach and open her book.

"Read aloud," he said without opening his eyes. "Please."

"Why?"

He looked at her, squinting against the sun. Instead of freezing him as she probably intended, her blue eyes made his pulse dance. "I like the sound of your voice."

So she read to him.

Eleven years later, Jared sat on the hot sand, not far from "their spot," as they called it for the three months they dated, and sat down. They came here often that summer. Sometimes with a group and sometimes just the two of them. He learned about Cecelia in this spot. She didn't like to talk about herself. Most information had to be finagled or cajoled, but he could usually get her to open up. She didn't like to discuss her dysfunctional family, but who didn't have kinfolk oddities they'd rather keep secret?

If Connor's investigator could find Cecelia and she signed the papers with no issues, maybe Stacy wouldn't have to know until after the divorce was final. He hated being dishonest, but the thought of telling his high-strung fiancée he was still married made him shudder. Better to wait until after the divorce.

Several hours and many memories later, Jared headed home. After grabbing a cold beer and making a ham and cheese sandwich, he wandered back to his bedroom and changed into shorts and a T-shirt. Glad Stacy had called to say she'd be out for the night, he went into his home office to do a little internet investigation of his own. Had Cecelia kept the name McAlister or was she using her maiden name? Had she remarried? If so, she'd be shocked to find out the marriage wasn't legal. The thought of her with another man twisted his stomach uncomfortably. Yet, the probability that she remarried after all this time was highly likely. If so, he would have to leave the investigation to someone more experienced.

He came across thirty-five Cecelia McAlisters that stretched from one side of the country to the other, but either the first or the last name was spelled differently, and only three of those were the right age. Out of ten Cecelia Chadwicks, only two spelled their name the same. One lived in Oregon and the other in New York. He couldn't imagine nature-loving Cecelia living in a huge city, so his Cecelia must have ended up on the West Coast.

He was angry that eleven years hadn't eliminated the hurt or dulled his anger. The injury felt just as raw, the pain just as fresh, as if everything happened last week.

"You'd think, after all this time, I'd be over her," he growled to his empty office walls.

CHAPTER 3

*J*ared's cell phone jarred him out of a comatose state, images of Cecelia still dancing through his mind. He grappled for the offending device before it rang again. Along with the time—one-fifty-three—a photo of Stacy with pouty lips lit the screen. "Hello."

"Sorry I didn't call earlier. I had to go back to the office after dinner with one of the company's biggest clients."

He tried to pull himself out of Cecelia's arms long enough to talk to his fiancée.

"He wants to make major changes to his financial portfolio," Stacy continued.

"Congratulations, but couldn't this news have waited until morning?"

"Yes, but I called to tell you I can't meet with your attorney tomorrow. My daddy's stable manager just reminded me about our monthly trip to Tennessee."

"He *just* reminded you at two in the morning?"

"I didn't see his text until fifteen minutes ago."

Now was the perfect opportunity to tell Stacy about his

marriage. He sucked in a breath. "I'll reschedule with Connor."

"I also wanted to remind you about Alisha and Josh's engagement party Friday night."

Again, this couldn't have waited?

The only child of very wealthy parents, Stacy usually did what she wanted when she wanted, without many consequences. As guilty as anyone for giving in to her whims, he simply found it easier than dealing with her anger.

"The party starts at eight. It will take us thirty minutes to get there, so pick me up at seven-thirty."

Jared stifled a yawn and rubbed a hand over his face, trying to focus on the conversation rather than letting his eyes slide shut. Up before dawn this morning, working on a real estate merger, then searching the internet for his should-be-ex-wife until after midnight had left him little time for sleep. And he had to be up in a few hours for an early morning meeting with the partners of the law firm where he worked.

"We need to talk about living arrangements when I get back from Tennessee, Jared. It's ridiculous to be paying two mortgages when you could sell your condo and move in with me."

"Except I don't want to live in the city."

Stacy disconnected the call without a goodbye. Jared dropped the phone on the bed and stared at the ceiling, wondering when his life ended up taking such a hard left.

He liked his condo in a rural suburb of Dallas. Stacy loved living in the heart of Dallas. His condo was nestled amid trees with a view of a pond. Hers took up the entire upper floor of a steel and glass high-rise with views of traffic and buildings and smog.

Her parents and his—both prominent Dallas families— had their own agendas surrounding his and Stacy's union.

McAlister Industries joining with Richardson Thoroughbred Farms. Money and power, marrying power and money.

His mom and dad were constantly telling him what a perfect match he and Stacy were. Stacy loved to party until the sun came up. He preferred to spend time at home or with a few close friends. She loved social engagements and dressing up in sequins and stilettos. He was most comfortable in jeans and a T-shirt. She accepted invitations to parties and receptions and fundraisers where they'd be photographed by the media for the Dallas papers' society pages. He avoided those engagements as often as possible.

Was there such a thing as a perfect match? Other than his grandparents, he saw very few people who seemed happy in their marriages. His own sure hadn't worked out. His mom and dad might have been married for thirty-six years, but they were far from happy. Thanks in large part to his dad's palpable indifference. His mom responded by scheduling "corrective" surgeries, lunching with other unhappy women, and spending as much money as possible.

Jared pulled a pillow over his head, but sleep eluded him while images of Stacy tangled with memories of Cecelia.

~

*C*ecelia Chadwick's walk to work took her through a family neighborhood where parents raised their children in the middle of a big city. The street was tree-lined, with a park and playground on the north end.

She rested a hand low on her belly. New York wouldn't be her choice of places to raise a family, but the suburbs were only a train ride away.

She turned a corner and passed shops just opening for the day. Fruit and vegetable carts were wheeled onto sidewalks, florists propped doors open with buckets of colorful blooms, and bakers filled their cases with delectable treats.

New York had managed to grow on her over time. When she first arrived in the city to attend NYU, she'd been a terrified eighteen-year-old far from anything familiar.

She pushed open the big wooden door of Winston and Associates Interior Design. Windy Conley, office manager extraordinaire—and the heart and soul of the firm—greeted her with a wave and her ever-present smile. As Arthur Winston's first employee, Windy knew more about the business side of their office than he did. She served as gatekeeper, overseer, and organizer.

Windy and her chef husband, Kevin, both natives of the city, knew all the nooks and crannies, the hot spots and not spots of New York.

"Morning, Ce."

"Good morning. It's such a beautiful day."

Windy looked at her like she'd lost her mind. "It's hot and going to get hotter. The city is in the grips of Mother Nature's introduction to Hell."

Cecelia took the messages Windy held out and flipped through them. "Who's in so far?"

"Just you. What time are you meeting with Mr. Basketball? I didn't put it on the schedule."

Cecelia smiled. Windy bestowed most of their clients with nicknames. Sometimes they were obvious, like the one for Cecelia's six-foot-eleven basketball player. But every once in a while, Windy threw the office for a loop, like the time she named a prickly-as-a-porcupine client Snuggles.

"I have to be there by ten-thirty, but I should be back before Mrs. Fredrick arrives. On the off chance I'm not, will you have her look through the fabric samples I'll leave in the conference room?"

"Sure."

Cecelia walked past Windy's desk and headed up the

open iron staircase leading to the offices. Arthur Winston's was at the top of the stairs, hers to the right. The middle of the second floor opened up to the reception area below. The offices of Winston's other two associates, Zack Bailey and Mia Scott, were on the opposite side of the opening.

Cecelia set her briefcase on the small conference table in her office and looked out one of two floor-to-ceiling arched windows to the street below. If Windy served as the heart and soul of their firm, Cecelia's office was the hub. It was an unusual day if, at some point, the staff didn't congregate here. Her kidney bean-shaped desk sat at an angle in the corner with two orange and cream chairs in front. The brown velvet sofa picked up at a clearance sale attracted more than just Zack for a nap now and then.

At her desk, she organized drawings and computer printouts for her basketball client, who'd been traded from the Dallas Mavericks to the New York Knicks two years earlier. He'd just purchased a loft that needed a complete renovation. At their first meeting, he said he wanted sleek lines with an edgy flair that would be comfortable for guests. She appreciated his ability to pinpoint a style that matched his personality. Even though the space was huge, she could deliver edgy comfort.

She loved the challenge of a loft—all that square footage with few walls. Her client entertained often, so he asked for a serviceable kitchen and bar area, plenty of seating, a great sound system, and a couple of extra-large TVs for viewing multiple sporting events at the same time.

Mr. Basketball's agent wanted publicity. Arthur Winston wanted recognition for his employee's work. After consider-able pressure, Cecelia finally agreed to be part of a national magazine spread, due out the first of September. Which meant her attempt to maintain a low profile would be jeopardized when her picture showed up in a magazine on every grocery store checkout stand across America.

After separating Mr. Basketball's plans into different areas of living space, she clipped them together. Her very visual client needed to see the plans laid out room by room.

Her cell phone rang as she put the plans in her briefcase. Her best friend's cute face popped up on the screen, a Happy New Year tiara perched in her purple hair. "Hi, Valerie."

"Hey, Ce. Is it Friday yet?"

Cecelia tucked the phone between her shoulder and ear and secured her briefcase. "I've got bad news for you, girl-friend. It's only Tuesday."

"No," Val wailed, drawing out the word. "The world is playing a cruel joke on me."

Cecelia detected an unusual note of despair in her friend's voice. "What's the matter?"

"Too long a story to tell over the phone. Besides, I don't want to drag you down into the wretchedness of my world."

Something was definitely wrong. Though prone to the dramatic, Val seldom allowed anything to get her down. "Is it work or something personal that has you sounding so low?"

"Both. I'm calling because I have tickets for *Wicked* this Saturday night. Want to go?"

"I'd love to, but what about Reese?"

"Reese and I are no longer."

That explains the down. "What happened?"

"Remember the long story part?"

"Are you okay?"

"I will be," she said, a slight catch in her throat. "I'll tell you the whole humiliating story Saturday night."

"I'm sorry."

"*Que será, será.*"

Even when upset, Val managed to add a positive spin. "Dinner before the show, my treat," Cecelia said.

"I'll take you up on that. See you Saturday."

As soon as Cecelia disconnected the call, a stocky man with black, curly-to-the-point-of-unruly hair walked in and flashed a grin, his dark eyes crinkling at the corners. "Morning, Ce. Have you got a minute? I need a wise opinion."

She glanced at her watch. "I can give you five minutes and an opinion—not sure how wise it will be."

He set his laptop on her conference table and opened up a program, then rubbed a finger under his nose, a nervous tic he had when unsure about a project. "I'm at a roadblock with this wall."

Zack had changed careers in his mid-thirties. Working on Wall Street contributed to extremely high blood pressure and a doctor's warning, so he switched gears completely. After he graduated from the Art Institute, Winston snapped him up. He had a great eye for style but remained unsure of himself when it came to the actual execution of his ideas. Once he learned to trust his instincts, he'd be one of the most sought-after designers on the East Coast.

Cecelia sidled up to him. "What are you working on?"

"A library." He pointed to a spot on the computer screen. "Nothing I put on the wall behind the desk seems right."

"I love the colors you used." Cecelia studied the design he'd worked up. "Who'll be using the room?"

"Mr. Greenwald. His wife wants it to resemble an old English library. He collects first edition books."

"Who?"

"Snookums," Zack said with a chuckle.

"Oh, right." Windy picked up the nickname Mr. Greenwald's wife had let slip once, to her husband's embarrassment.

"Mrs. Greenwald suggested antlers of some sort, but that's too predictable. Don't you think?"

"Didn't you mention in one of our planning meetings that he also collects pipes?"

"He does."

"How about a couple of shelves with those pipes displayed, or if he uses the pipes, custom-made shadow boxes that can be opened?" She pulled a chair out and sat. With a few keyboard clicks, she added several three-dimensional boxes to the wall. "What about something like this?"

He shook his head. "I knew you'd have the answer. That's exactly what I've been looking for."

"You would have figured out the answer on your own if you'd stepped away for a few minutes."

"Thanks, Ce"

Ten minutes later, she stood at the curb, signaling her Uber driver.

~

The next morning, a client took up most of Jared's scheduled time complaining about the way negotiations for a merger were going. Differences of opinion about management were causing problems between his client and his prospective partner. In Jared's opinion, his client was the unreasonable party. Jared offered several compromises for consideration before their next meeting, the one where they were to sign contracts.

Just as they concluded, his cell phone buzzed with a text message from Connor. He shook hands all around before leaning close to his client and suggesting he think seriously about a compromise if he wanted this deal to go through. After the man huffed off in frustration, Jared signaled Violet to hold his calls and shut himself in his office.

Connor's investigator had taken less than twenty-four hours to find Cecelia. A New York City address popped up on his screen, as well as a phone number. So he'd been wrong to think she would never choose to live in that concrete jungle. He had to visit the Foster, Stern, and Wallace Manhattan office every three or four months and hated the traffic, the noise, and the crush of people.

Connor also provided a work phone number, address, and a company website for Winston and Associates Interior Design. A ridiculous burst of pride swelled in Jared's chest as he pulled up the website. Against the odds, Cecelia had accomplished her dreams.

Connor followed with a line of question marks.

Jared had no idea how to proceed either. **Any indications she's remarried?**

None that we could find. She's using her maiden name. I'll get back to you.

Jared sank onto the sofa that ran along the back wall of his office. Let Connor take care of the divorce, or go to New York himself? If he went, should he go to her workplace or her home? The workplace might seem less threatening, but her home would provide more privacy.

Although he wasn't sure he wanted to be alone in a room with her. Eleven years hadn't erased the hurt or anger over her divorcing him with no explanation. Perhaps a chance meeting on the street?

Connor could explain everything in a letter, overnight the papers to her, and Cecelia could return them the next day. No contact necessary. Quick and easy.

He wouldn't have to see her.

Yet he felt the magnetic pull of Cecelia, even from hundreds of miles away. He knew if he didn't go, he'd forever wonder.

Unable to get back to sleep last night after Stacy's call, he'd gone through the box where he stored Cecelia's things years ago. Small items she'd left behind, a hair clip, a tube of lip gloss, a Jane Austen paperback, and a tiny navy-blue flower earring. The box holding the diamond bracelet he bought for her nineteenth birthday—a day they didn't celebrate because of divorce papers—still had the original bow on top.

At the very bottom, he found the final decree of divorce—still in the unopened envelope. So they weren't lost behind a file cabinet. Slowly he opened the envelope and withdrew the papers. Unbelievable. How had the decree been sent out without the judge's signature? Why hadn't he opened them to check when they were delivered? Details were a big part of his job.

Yet he knew the reason. Opening that envelope would have made the divorce real.

Anger stirred in his gut. Why hadn't Cecelia noticed the error since she initiated the divorce? He moved over to his desk, picked up his office receiver, and dialed Cecelia's home number, confident she'd be at work.

Chicken, he thought as he listened to her phone ring.

Leave a simple message . . . This is Jared. Sorry to call out of the blue, but my attorney discovered a mistake when drawing up a prenup for my upcoming wedding. Surprise! We're still married. Expect papers from Connor Gentry, my attorney. Just a simple signature is all it will take to correct the error. This time I'll make sure everything is signed and filed. Hope you're happy—No. Skip that last part. Just . . . Hope you're . . . Hope you're well. Bye, Cecelia.

What if a guy answered? He hadn't thought that far ahead.

"This is Cecelia. I'm not able to answer the phone right now. Please leave a message, and I'll return your call as soon as possible."

Jared's heart thumped hard against his ribs, stealing his breath. Even if she hadn't said her name, he would have recognized her voice with its soft Southern cadence. He opened his mouth, but nothing came out. Frustration pounded through his temples. Everything he planned to say evaporated, his mind blank.

As much as he wanted to place blame, he was just as responsible for not checking those divorce papers.

He hung up and grabbed his cell phone, quickly texting Connor. **You can handle contacting Cecelia.**

His thumb hovered over the send button a long moment before he deleted the message. If he rearranged his schedule, he could leave for New York tonight and be back in town by Friday for the engagement party. He could—

The office door opened, and his mom walked in, fluttering a hand toward Violet. "He's not too busy to talk to me."

Violet came to the door and flashed an apologetic grimace.

"It's okay, Violet."

"And I would appreciate a glass of water."

Violet kept her expression neutral at his mother's demand.

"I'll take care of it, Violet. Let me know when Mr. Hawkes arrives."

His assistant, who patiently dealt with his family and fiancée, nodded and closed the door. He moved over to a small fridge hidden in a credenza under the line of windows. "What brings you in today, Mom?"

"Stacy called. She's afraid you'll forget about Alicia's engagement party on Friday." She sat in one of the chairs in front of his desk and crossed her legs. "Alicia's mother could have found a better venue. That country club has such a tacky banquet room."

He poured a bottle of water into a glass, even though he knew Betsy Sue McAlister wouldn't drink any. She just wanted to remind Violet she was her son's assistant. He handed her the glass, which she set on his desk.

"Stacy already reminded me," he said, taking his chair.

"She says you haven't put your condo on the market yet."

Stacy loved to involve his parents in her grievances, inserting them neatly into any fights after she swayed their viewpoint to her side.

"That's because I like my condo. I don't want to live in the middle of the city."

"Jared, you need to be reasonable."

Looking for an exit to that conversation, he asked, "How's Grammy and Granddad?"

"Don't change the subject on me, young man. You'd better take care of this soon. Your father agrees with Stacy."

It didn't matter that he was thirty-three—and except for the three months between college and law school, he hadn't lived at home since he was eighteen—his dad still treated him like a disobedient teenager. "Of course he does. Stacy's condo cost seven million dollars more than mine."

"This has nothing to do with money."

It has everything to do with money. "I'll look forward to my lecture."

"Don't be smart, Jared." Betsy Sue stood and smoothed her skirt. "I have lunch plans. If I don't leave now, I'll be late."

He stood, walked around his desk, and opened the door. He kissed his mom's cheek. "Have a nice lunch."

"I will. You think about putting your condo on the market."

After she turned the corner in the hall, he glanced at Violet. "Sorry."

She batted his apology away. "Part of the job."

Jared leaned against the doorjamb. "No, it's not. You're a superhero."

"Wow, I think I deserve a raise."

"Clear my schedule for Thursday and Friday, get me on a flight for New York tonight, and I'll do my best to get you one."

She picked up her phone. "Consider it done."

In his office, he texted Connor. **Changed my mind. Can you have the papers ready this afternoon?**

Yes. What then? came back immediately.

I'll get them signed.

CHAPTER 4

*J*ared rolled over and flipped off his cell phone alarm, surprised he'd slept so hard. Violet managed to book a flight that landed in New York a little after midnight. She also got him a hotel room a few blocks from Cecelia's work address. His assistant looked at him questioningly when he gave her the address of the design firm, but she never asked questions.

When the flight landed, he grabbed his overnight bag and headed outside to hail a cab with a determination that wavered like a flag flapping in the wind as he neared the city.

I'm making a mistake. I should turn around and have Connor take care of this.

Yet he paid the driver and climbed out in front of the hotel. For closure, he assured himself. He wanted answers to the questions that still plagued him. Over the past eleven years, whenever he thought of Cecelia, "why" always followed close behind.

Why had she left Arizona State and given up the full-ride scholarship she needed? Why hadn't she contacted him about her decision? Why had she filed for divorce and vanished without first talking to him?

Behind those questions, he wondered if there might have been another man. Had she met someone to take his place? She'd been young and away from home for the first time, so he tried to understand how that might have happened. But why hadn't she told him rather than leaving him wondering?

As he stood in front of the hotel last night, the hot August air, stagnant and humid, reminded him of their last night together in Dallas. He'd held her in his arms, told her he loved her, and wiped away her tears as he fought his own.

Stupid. She'd probably laughed about that night and his choked words as he promised to fly from California to Arizona as often as possible.

Throwing the covers off, he climbed out of bed, his thoughts shifting to work. His client in the business merger had finally agreed to the terms of management in the contract, so the merger could go through the first of next month.

Most of the time, he enjoyed his job, but every once in a while, a client could make the business of helping people challenging.

Pulling back the heavy hotel curtain, he rested his forehead against the cool glass. Still early, and Manhattan traffic already clogged the intersection below. A siren wailed from some unseen street—noise, dirt, crowds.

Out of any city in the country, why would Cecelia choose New York? He didn't understand the appeal. She'd loved Texas and its wide-open sky. At least that's what she told him. Maybe he hadn't known the woman he loved as well as he thought.

He let the curtain fall into place and turned toward the shower, his determination returning with a vengeance. One way or another, he was going to see Cecelia today.

~

*C*ecelia entered the cafe and spotted her boss at their usual breakfast table. No matter how early she left her apartment, he always beat her.

Arthur Winston, a tall, heavyset man, had more salt in his salt-and-pepper hair, which only added to his distinguished looks. And a smile that lit a room. He stood as she approached the table.

"Good morning, sweetheart. I ordered the veggie omelet for you. Hope you don't mind."

"Veggie omelet is perfect." After a quick peck on his cheek, she sat in the chair he pulled out for her.

"How did your appointment with Mr. Basketball go yesterday?" he asked once he sat down.

"Wonderful." She met Winston's gaze over the table. "I like working with a client who knows what he wants and isn't afraid to throw out a few ideas of his own."

Winston and his sweet wife, Maria, treated Cecelia like the daughter they couldn't have, and they became surrogate parents for her. Winston was supportive, accommodating, and generous as an employer, and possibly the most loveable man Cecelia knew. Even though his name was Arthur, everyone called him Winston, except for Windy, who usually called him Boss.

Over breakfast, they discussed clients and the jobs they were working on. He mentioned a famous Hollywood couple, two actors relocating to New York. "They just bought two large apartments, one above the other, that they want to combine since they have several children and need the space. The project will involve a complete renovation. One kitchen will have to be eliminated, and a staircase to the apartment above added. I'd like you to take on the project."

She narrowed her eyes. "Why?"

"Two reasons. My hands are full with a couple of big jobs, and a project this big will be an excellent experience for you, Ce. I don't want to tell this couple no, but I don't have the time to devote right now. If you're interested, you won't want to take on any other big projects."

Cecelia was more than interested. She'd never done a renovation that joined two apartments on different floors. And the design would add to her portfolio. "I'd love the opportunity."

"I haven't told the couple I'm passing them off to an associate, so I'll come with you for the first meeting."

"I'm not sure I feel comfortable with that."

"Don't worry. I'll assure them I'll be with you every step of the way if need be. And I will, though it won't be necessary. I wouldn't offer this opportunity to you if I didn't think you're ready."

He took a deep breath, seeming to brace himself. "We'll do a walkthrough and get a feel for what they have in mind. If they agree, I'd like to get a before and after with *Architect and Design.* This job will get your name in print, and that magazine has a broader circulation than the one featuring you and Mr. Basketball."

"Winston." She took her own deep breath and released it slowly. "I already agreed to the first magazine and a newspaper article."

"The newspaper is to build Zack and Mia's clientele. This one's for *you.*" He tipped his head down and looked over the rim of his glasses. "Most designers would kill for an opportunity like this."

Unless they're trying to stay out of the spotlight. "I have plenty of clients. I get referrals all the time. I don't need a magazine article to build my business." She held up a hand at his raised brow. "I don't mean that arrogantly. I'm grateful for every client I have and everything you've done for me."

"What are you trying to hide from, sweetheart?"

"I'm not trying to hide. I just . . ." *would rather my mom didn't know about my success.* Winston wanted to grow his business, and she was hindering his efforts. ". . . don't want to get so busy that I can't give my clients the time they deserve."

"I'll get you an assistant."

"I don't want an assistant." She wanted to be mad at her mentor but couldn't pull it off. She was a complete pushover when it came to Winston and his wife.

"You need a social life."

Cecelia lifted her water glass. "I don't just sit around my apartment, surrounded by a dozen cats, eating ice cream and bonbons. I go out almost every weekend. Valerie and I are going to a Broadway play on Saturday. I went to dinner with Tyler last weekend."

"I know your relationship with Tyler will never get more serious than it is right now, though he would like to change that. The poor guy's in love with you."

The comment pinched Cecelia's heart. She met Tyler Beshear when the advertising firm he worked for renovated their offices. They'd been dating ever since. She enjoyed his company and easygoing manner. He planned fun, thoughtful dates, and she always had a great time, but he wanted to take their relationship to the next level. As much as she loved Tyler, she wasn't *in love* with him. They'd been dating long enough for her to know her feelings weren't going to grow more serious.

Winston shook his head. "I'm sorry. I know you'd never hurt Tyler on purpose," he said as if reading her mind. "I shouldn't have said that."

She set her glass down and dusted at imaginary crumbs on the table before meeting Winston's gaze. After eleven long years, Cecelia found herself stuck on a ledge, looking into the unknown. She met Jared McAlister on a hot spring afternoon and tumbled into first-time love too quickly, naively believing he felt the same. He said he did, professed it over and over in their three months together.

Then he shattered her heart.

How could she step off the ledge when she still remembered every moment spent with Jared so vividly? Each feeling and emotion was still embedded in her soul. She might never be able to trust another with a heart that had taken her years to repair enough to pump solidly again.

≈

*A*s an attorney, Jared prided himself in always being prepared, but his hammering heart assured him he wasn't prepared to see Cecelia again.

As he stood in front of the huge wooden door of Winston and Associates Interior Design, he wished he'd taken a cab rather than walk in the heat.

Cecelia had been on his mind every waking—and sleeping—moment since he found out they were still married. It wasn't too late to let Connor handle the details. He could jump in a cab, grab his things from the hotel, and be at the airport in less than two hours. Possibly be home before dark.

Is she married?

He wished she was.

And hoped she wasn't.

A taxi came into view. *Hold up a hand. Go back to the hotel.*

Instead, he pushed through the door before he could change his mind and looked around at Cecelia's world. Exposed brick walls, wrought iron staircase, and huge arched windows that let in lots of light despite a tree growing through a hole in the concrete right outside.

"Good afternoon." A blonde behind a reception desk stood. "May I help you?"

"I . . . uh . . ." He cleared his throat, irritated by his stammer. "Is Cecelia Chadwick in?"

"She's out of the office right now. Can I get someone else to help you?"

He glanced up at the second floor, where he imagined her office to be, and felt both disappointment and relief. "No. I'm not here on business. I'm . . . uh . . . I mean, I'm not here to see her as a client."

The blonde lifted an eyebrow.

He wanted to slap himself and ask for a do-over at the same time. He couldn't tell by the receptionist's reaction if she was enjoying his misery or felt sympathetic because of his bumbling.

His stomach twisted uncomfortably. "I recently found out Cecelia works here and thought I'd stop by and say hi. We used to know each other." He glanced around again. "Will she be back today?"

"I'm not sure. I could text her. If she's not busy, she'll text back."

He held up a hand. "No, I don't want to bother her."

"Would you like to leave a message, Mr. . . . ?"

"No. It's been a long time since we've seen each other. She may not remember me."

The woman held out a pen and paper. "Cecelia is great at remembering names."

He shook his head and turned for the door.

"She'll be disappointed when she discovers you were here and didn't leave a number."

I doubt that.

"Wait."

He stopped as the blonde came around the desk.

"Are you a scary stalker or unhinged ex?"

He wondered if his expression showed his surprise. "No," he said on a chuckle.

She eyed him for a long moment before she held out her hand. "I'm Windy Conley."

"It's nice to meet you, Wendy." She gave him a firm, no-nonsense handshake.

"No, Windy with an 'i.'"

"That's an unusual name, Windy with an 'i.'"

"I have one of those I-was-conceived stories to tell my children. My parents were stuck in Chicago during a snow-storm and thought it would be amusing to name me some-thing memorable. I've always been relieved they didn't go completely nuts and call me Blizzard or Whiteout."

Jared nodded. "I like Windy. It's original."

"Yeah, but I can never find a coffee mug with my name on it." She leaned against her desk. "Why won't you leave your name?"

She'd done a good job of calming his nerves with her friendly chatter, but he wasn't ready to reveal details. "As I said, I haven't seen Cecelia for a long time. I'm not sure she'll remember me."

One side of her mouth lifted. A smirk? "I don't believe you."

"That's not good. In my line of work, I depend on people believing me."

"What do you do?"

"I'm an attorney."

A frown creased the skin between her brows. "Oh, too bad. I almost decided to like you."

"Hey, I'm one of the good guys."

"Right. That's what all attorneys say."

He held up a hand as if swearing an oath. "Okay, the truth." *At least a smidgeon.* "I promise my intentions are good.

I'm not unhinged. I'm willing to give you the name of the law firm I work for if it will ease your suspicions."

"How will that help if I don't know your name?"

He snapped his fingers in an oh-shucks-you're-onto-me way that made her laugh.

"So, what happened? You knew each other in high school and lost touch?"

"Something like that."

She leaned behind her, picked up the HOME section of a newspaper, and held it out to him. "I have some reading material for you if you'd like to wait."

A picture on the front showed two men and three women —one Cecelia, another Windy—posed around the reception desk.

"There's Cecelia." Windy pointed her out, like Jared might have forgotten. "Has she changed much since you last saw her?"

"Her hair is shorter. She used to wear it long, almost to her waist, and curly."

"Do you still live in Texas?"

He nodded while studying the picture.

"And you're in New York on vacation or business?"

To serve Cecelia with divorce papers. "Business."

She rested her hands on the desk behind her and narrowed her eyes. "Don't make me sorry I'm telling you this."

He held his breath, preparing for the first thing that entered his mind—news of a marriage or a baby.

"Cecelia usually goes to Market City Café for dinner after her yoga class on Tuesdays and Thursdays."

Jared made a mental note of the café's name. "Is the yoga studio close by?"

"It's a couple of doors down from the café."

"What time is her yoga class?"

"Five to six."

He glanced at his watch and shook his head, deciding to keep the information that he'd be there to himself. He didn't want Windy to tell Cecelia for fear she wouldn't show. He had time to stop in at the New York office, then shower a second time before going to the café. "I'll have to see if I can catch her the next time I'm in town. Mind if I borrow this?" he asked, holding up the newspaper. "I can bring it by—"

"You can keep it. I have plenty or copies."

"Thank you. It was nice to meet you, Windy with an 'i'." He turned for the door again.

"Hey! After that long, friendly chat, and me giving you privileged information, you're still not going to leave your name?"

"Maybe next time." He winked and walked out into the New York furnace, relieved Cecelia wasn't there and disappointed at the same time. He hadn't felt this pull, this desire to see someone since he first met her. After all these years, he was right back where he started.

Yet the longer he stood in the shade of the tree in front of Winston and Associates, the more certain he was that seeing her again would be a mistake. What good could come of it?

He'd searched everywhere, desperate to find Cecelia when she disappeared. Then he tried just as desperately to forget her. She cut all ties. She knew where he was and how to get in touch, yet she never tried, so why was he here?

He probably would have lost his temper and made a fool of himself if he'd seen her. She'd put him through hell. Talking would only open new wounds when the old ones weren't healed. The answers to his questions didn't matter anymore. He'd moved on, was engaged. To dredge up all these old feelings was ridiculous.

Time to let the past go, Jared. He'd let Connor handle everything from here on out. Leaving now would be best for both him and Cecelia.

Except, the nagging hold told him he was so close. If he left town without seeing her, he'd never find peace.

Jared hailed a taxi, climbed in, and gave the address of the law firm to the driver.

As the cab pulled away, Jared felt like he was leaving a piece of himself behind.

Cecelia. He'd always wondered what happened to her. Now he knew. She chose New York over him.

*C*ecelia walked into the office, thoroughly pleased with her morning shopping trip. Mr. Basketball loved the sectional she found for his living room.

Windy wasn't at her desk, so Cecelia gathered her messages from the cubby assigned to her. The top one read, *Tall, Dark, and Devastatingly Handsome stopped by—wouldn't leave a name or number.*

The only tall, dark, and handsome client she had at the moment was the basketball player, and Tyler qualified as tall and handsome, but not dark. Windy knew both of them. Cecelia moved around the reception desk and pulled up her schedule on the office computer. She hadn't forgotten or missed an appointment.

Winston's door was closed when Cecelia reached the top of the stairs, which meant he was with a client. In her office, she sat down at her computer to check for an appointment she might have forgotten to tell Windy about, but her shopping trip was the only thing on her schedule. So who was Tall, Dark, and Handsome?

She heard Winston's door open, and his murmured

goodbye before his footsteps headed for her office. "Hey, sweetheart. How did the shopping trip go?"

She reached into her briefcase, produced a tear sheet from the furniture store, and handed it to him.

"Nice," he said, taking a seat in front of her desk. "Does he like the color?"

"He does. The sofa is incredibly plush, and the seats are deep enough for his extra-long frame."

Winston thumbed over his shoulder. "I had a meeting with Melody, and she said to tell you thanks for recommending that paint color for her daughter's room. She loves it."

"Oh, good."

"Please, tell me Tall, Dark, and Handsome got in touch with you," Windy said, walking into Cecelia's office, her arms full of fabric swatches. "Rose sent these over."

Cecelia stood, took half the swatches from her, and set them on her work table. "Who is Tall, Dark, and Handsome?"

"He wouldn't leave his name or number, and, believe me, I tried to get one. He said he has business in town and stopped by to say hi."

"Why wouldn't he leave his name?" Winston asked.

Windy perched on the corner of Cecelia's desk. "He didn't think you'd remember him."

"Did he say how we knew each other?"

"High school."

That didn't make sense. She hadn't kept in touch with anyone from high school, so how would they know she lived in New York?

"Maybe you have a stalker," Winston said. "That's very chic these days."

Cecelia held up her hand. "I don't care how chic having a stalker is, I don't want one."

"He talked like you," Windy said.

"Talked like me?"

"Yeah. He probably uses words like howdy and yee-haw." Her New York accent tripped up her attempt to tease.

Cecelia laughed. "Yes, I do use howdy and yee-haw *all the time*. What did he look like?"

Windy crossed her eyes. "Uh, hello. Did you read your message? Tall, dark, and handsome."

Cecelia picked the message off her desk. "If he stops by again, get a name because I have no idea who he could be."

The buzzer on the front door sounded, and Winston pushed to his feet. "That better be Iris Davenport. I'm going to start charging her for every minute she's late."

Windy slid off Cecelia's desk but stopped at the door. "Oh yeah. Tall, Dark, and Handsome has some killer dimples."

Cecelia's heart struck her ribs hard.

Twice.

CHAPTER 5

*C*ecelia half-jogged to the fitness center. Her one-hour-twice-a-week yoga class was a great stress reliever unless she was running late.

Images of Jared McAlister—the only tall, dark, and handsome she knew with killer dimples—dancing through her head didn't help.

After he decimated her heart, she'd been amazed and grateful for the last-minute scholarship NYU offered. She jumped at the chance to be swallowed up by the big city until she recouped a tiny remnant of her dignity and worked to get her broken heart beating again.

Though she was still very much Cecelia Chadwick, a girl from the wrong side of Mesquite's tracks, New York had allowed her to accomplish her dreams. Conveying self-confidence in both her professional and personal life had taken years of practice. She still stumbled now and then, but she was no longer the scared eighteen-year-old who'd arrived with a crushed spirit.

Ninety minutes later, she said goodbye to the people in

her class. After a quick shower, she slipped into her dress and towel-dried her hair. When Winston first hired her, she started straightening her curly locks. New life, new image. But today, she'd let the humidity dictate her hairstyle. After a quick swipe of mascara, she rushed out the door. Though the fitness center was only half of a block from Market City Café, she welcomed the relief of the air conditioner as soon as she opened the door.

Lonnie Villarini looked up from behind the counter, his brown eyes twinkling. "Hey, Ce. Missed you earlier."

"I didn't have time to place an order before—"

"Good, because someone's holding a table for you."

Cecelia turned in the direction Lonnie pointed. Her heart, under reconstruction for the past eleven years, slammed hard against her ribs, threatening to break apart. Again.

Jared.

"Hi, Cecelia."

A tsunami of sensations, from shortness of breath to tingling limbs to silent panic, crashed over her as she stood rooted to the floor. She put a hand to her stomach while ordering herself to move forward, to take a step, to stay upright, to smile. Nothing happened.

Closing the distance between them, Jared took her hand, bent forward, and kissed her cheek. The clean scent of him was so familiar, so overwhelming; her head spun in warning. He smelled exactly the same.

Jared.

"How are you?" he asked.

His rich, deep voice moved over her like the resonance of a well-tuned violin. She couldn't say she was well and mean it. Not at the moment. "S-surprised." She cringed at the tremor in her voice.

He smiled, and his dimples made an appearance, cata-pulting her into the past so quickly she felt faint. Summer walks, holding hands, horseback rides, kisses beneath a sky full of stars.

She swallowed and tried her voice again. "How are you?"

"I'm doing well."

"How did—" She stopped short of asking how he found her, hyper-aware that Jared still held her hand and wishing he'd release it because she'd started to tremble.

"I ran into a mutual friend who told me you work in New York. I happened to be in the city, so I stopped by your office to say hi. Windy said you were out, but that you came here for dinner after yoga class, so I took a chance."

She didn't believe him. Until that stupid magazine article came out, no one in Texas besides her family knew she worked here. Why not tell the truth about how he really found her?

They stared at each other for a long moment before Jared indicated a table with a nod. A very small table. "Will you join me for dinner."

Cecelia looked from the table to a chair, grateful it was only steps away. She needed to sit before her knees buckled. He must have taken her immobility as a yes because he released her hand and pulled out the chair, saving her from making a complete fool of herself.

After sitting, she folded her hands in her lap, trying to control the tremors racking her body. She bit her lip to keep her emotions at bay. In need of air, she concentrated on her breathing. In. Out. Measured breaths. In. Out.

He sat down, his mesmerizing eyes focused on her, delving into places where he wasn't welcome.

"You're Tall, Dark, and Handsome."

His grin was as dazzling and confident as ever. "Thank you. And you're as beaut—"

"No," she interrupted, embarrassed by what she just blurted out and to stop the rest of his sentence. "That's how Windy described you when you didn't leave your name. She told me Tall, Dark, and Handsome stopped by."

She left the "devastatingly" off, but it was true. Without looking around, she'd bet half the women in here were staring at him. His face and forearms were tanned, probably from being on the lake. His dark hair was shorter, but the waves that used to tempt her fingers to take a walk were still there. His deep brown eyes, lined by a thick fringe of lashes, twinkled under Lonnie's dim lighting. And his smile offered her the two details that confirmed Jared was who Windy had seen.

"I'm flattered by Windy's description. I enjoyed meeting her. She has a way of putting people at ease."

"Yes, she does." *Too bad I'm going to have to kill her for giving you the name of my café.*

"She was very careful about what she said and what she didn't. Kind of like you were the first time we met." She looked down when he grasped a half-empty beer bottle on the table. She'd always loved his hands, square, strong, yet so gentle.

"I didn't want to leave my name and number for fear you wouldn't call . . ."

I wouldn't have.

" . . . so I stumbled through an excuse, and Windy called me on it. Again, a lot like you did the first night we met."

"Windy is blunt."

"I like her." He tipped his head, his eyes traveling over her face, then her hair. "She gave me a copy of the Sunday newspaper. Congratulations, Ce. You're living your dreams."

"Yes." *Some of them.* She glanced out the window before meeting his gaze. "Are you living your dreams, Jared?"

His jaw bulged like he'd suddenly gritted his teeth. "Some of them. None that make my father happy."

Cecelia remembered Jared's father vividly. She hoped she'd never see Charles McAlister again. The mere mention of him bubbled the acid already churning in her stomach. The last time she saw him, Mr. McAlister had made sure she knew Jared would be working for their family dynasty after law school. He conveyed, in no uncertain terms, that she would not be allowed to mess that up. She wouldn't ask but still wondered how the McAlister family drama had played out over the years.

"How is your family, Jared?"

"Dad is still running the business. Granddad stays in the background now that he's semi-retired. You remember my sister, Susan?"

Cecelia nodded.

"She's being groomed to take over McAlister Industries one day."

That news surprised Cecelia, but she kept her expression neutral. "And your mom?"

"Busy with all her social circles." He sat forward, putting him way too close. "Susan is married. Her husband, Tim, is McAlister Industries' in-house attorney." His dimples winked, stealing her breath once again. "I'm an uncle, Ce. Susan and Tim have two kids."

She took a moment to digest that piece of information while pressing a hand to her chest as a fragment of her heart fell away. "Congratulations. I'm sure your parents are excited to have grandchildren."

Jared chuckled. "They're pretty amusing to watch. Mom crawling around on the floor in her linen dress and Dad trying to toss a ball in his suit and tie."

He reached out as if he might touch her, and she leaned

back. Surprise flickered across his face before he palmed his beer bottle instead.

Embarrassed by her sudden reaction, heat flared in her cheeks, but he was kind enough to glance away.

"Grams still asks about you."

Cecelia's heart throbbed as another small piece broke free. Her smile was a wobbly attempt at best. Jared's parents had barely tolerated her, and Susan had talked through her as if she didn't exist, but his grandparents had always been very kind. "How are your grandparents?"

"Grams would say they're fit as fiddles."

Lonnie set two glasses of water on the table, and she wanted to hug him for the interruption. "Some surprise, huh, Ce? How long has it been since you've seen each other?"

"Eleven years." Jared stood and held out his hand. "I'm Jared McAlister."

Lonnie pumped his hand vigorously. "Lorenzo Villarini, but everyone calls me Lonnie."

"It's nice to meet you, Lonnie."

"You must be from Texas too. At least you sound like it."

Jared nodded.

"Are you ready to order, or do you need a few minutes?"

"Do you know what you'd like, Ce?" Jared asked, taking his seat.

Cecelia ordered a salad, something she could pick at, not sure she'd be able to eat much. Jared ordered a sandwich.

"Drink?" Lonnie asked her.

"Water is fine."

He motioned to Jared. "Are you ready for another beer?"

Jared held up his hand. "I'm good for now. Thanks."

Lonnie left the table, and an uncomfortable silence fell. Cecelia glanced around the café, wondering why she'd agreed to join him for dinner. Although she desperately wanted to leave, her Southern upbringing kept her in the chair.

The only thing worse than not being over him would be him *knowing* she wasn't over him.

"How's your family, Ce? Are they still in Mesquite?"

She shifted on her chair, searching for a way to avoid talking about her family. To say the Chadwicks weren't close was an understatement. They were the epitome of dysfunctional, with a capital D.

"Mom and Dad are still there. Jenny's married and lives in Houston."

"Jenny's married?" he asked with surprise.

Her sister was twenty-six, so her being married shouldn't be so shocking.

"What's she doing in Houston?"

She straightened the silverware, aligning it with the bottom edge of her napkin. "Her husband is a computer programmer for an oil company based there."

"Is she happy?"

She, her sister, and brother had grown up in such a flawed environment that she couldn't be sure of the answer. She'd always hoped her brother and sister had been exposed to situations that allowed them to see how normal families functioned.

"She seems to be." Cecelia adjusted her placemat. "I don't see her very often. I hope she's happy."

"It's hard to imagine Jenny married. And Derrick? How's he doing?"

"Derrick joined the Navy. He's stationed in California."

"Little Derrick's in the Navy?"

"*Little Derrick* is almost twenty-three and as tall as you." She glanced around for Lonnie because this was the longest she'd ever waited for dinner. Ever. "I think he enlisted to get away from home, but it seems to have worked for him. He's doing well. We email back and forth quite often."

"Have you been to California to visit?"

She touched a fingertip to the condensation running down her water glass in rivulets. "Not yet. I did travel to Illinois for his boot camp graduation."

"I bet that was a proud moment for your parents."

He didn't seem to remember her parents very well. "They didn't make it. Neither did Jenny." As if their topic of conversation wasn't bad enough, his look of sympathy made her even more agitated. "Eleven years hasn't created magical bonds between my family members."

"Eleven years hasn't done wonders for my family either," Jared replied. "I'm close to Susan and my grandparents, but . . . Well, you remember."

Yes, she did. Jared and his dad used to butt heads every time they were in the same room. She suspected most of their feuds that summer were about her.

Blessedly, Lonnie delivered their dinner. While eating, Cecelia avoided bringing up the past and didn't delve into the future. Time moved as slowly as a garden slug while Jared asked questions about her job, and she asked a few about his. He said he worked for a McAlister family friend, Grant Stern. She remembered meeting Grant and his wife. She couldn't imagine how it happened, but it was good to know he worked for someone other than his dad.

As they talked, her tension lifted slightly, and she relaxed enough that she caught herself smiling a couple of times.

When they finished, Jared insisted on paying the bill. She decided flight was preferable to fight at this moment, so she didn't argue. *Great to see you. Thanks for dinner. Glad you're doing well. Good luck with your future. Bye-bye.*

"Can I walk you home, Ce?" Jared asked before she managed to blurt out her prepared farewell.

Her heart dropped another sliver, and she actually glanced down, expecting to see tiny shards on the floor around her feet. "I don't live far. You don't need—"

"I'd like to."

Her mind's eye had foreseen the end of this evening from several different angles—but not this one. She already knew the expanding emptiness in her chest would hurt unbearably when he said goodbye, so now or thirty-minutes from now…

She nodded.

CHAPTER 6

*A*s they walked, the humid night fairly crackled around them, buzzing with an energy that lit every nerve ending. Jared stopped himself from reaching for Cecelia's hand half a dozen times. He wanted to tuck her hair behind her ear so he could better see her profile. Why did reaching for her still seem so right after all these years? Especially after she'd ripped his heart out.

The anger he harbored for so long seemed to evaporate while they talked in the café. Or rather, he talked. She answered his questions and asked a few of her own but had been very careful to keep their conversation on neutral ground.

When given the chance to finally ask the questions dogging him for so long, he wasn't sure he wanted to know the answers anymore. If another man had taken his place, he didn't need to know the details, didn't want to think of her in someone else's arms.

Present love interests hadn't been discussed so far. She wasn't wearing a ring, and she hadn't excused herself from the table to make a phone call explaining why she'd be late.

Still, he had to ask. "Am I going to get hit by a jealous husband or angry lover when we get to your place, Ce?"

Without looking his way, she shook her head. "No. It's just me."

Her soft voice held a hint of New York accent with irritation around the edges. He waited for her to ask the same question of him and gave a mental sigh of relief when she didn't. Bringing up Stacy and his impending marriage would only make their already stilted conversation even more uncomfortable.

Before going into the café, he left a message on Stacy's cell that he planned to meet an old friend for dinner, and then turned off his phone.

"So, you aren't with anyone?" he asked, ignoring the irony of not wanting her to know about Stacy.

She stopped walking. When she looked his way, her eyes were as frosty blue as his Ice Princess of long ago.

"There's no one at my apartment, Jared."

She started walking again, and he took a couple of jogging steps to catch up, frustrated with her answer. He wanted her to admit if she was seeing someone but would rather hear, "No, I'm not with anyone." Selfish on his part, but he couldn't stop his feelings any more than he could change the weather.

He'd moved on, and she probably had too, so why probe? *Her life, her loves aren't any of my business.*

Or are they? He and Cecelia were still married.

She opened her briefcase and fished out keys as they walked up steps of what must be her building. He decided he wouldn't ask if he could come in, afraid she'd say no. Luckily, she didn't protest when he trailed her up two flights of stairs. He'd kept his hands to himself, but his eyes had a mind of their own. As much as she was the same, she was very different.

She unlocked her apartment door and walked inside, leaving it open, so he followed like a puppy, then glanced around in amazement. Her living room was larger than he'd expected and the style . . . A crazy combination of words—cozy, serene, oddly playful—came to mind. "This place is great, Ce. Very you."

She mumbled something that sounded suspiciously like, "You don't know me anymore," before dropping her briefcase near a chair. "Can I get you something to drink?"

"Water would be great."

Wanting to see every inch of her space, he tagged along behind her when she turned into a small, spotless kitchen. At some point, he'd have to tell her about the divorce papers he left in his hotel room but now wasn't the time.

She got a glass from a cupboard near the sink. When she added ice and water from the fridge, he noticed a photo strip of her and a man held to the door by a pink heart magnet. They were pulling corny faces in each shot, clowning around, having fun. Those images would burrow into his brain and make themselves at home for the rest of the night. Or forever.

She held out the glass. "Can I get you anything else?"

"No, this is fine." The two beers he had before she arrived at the café gave him the courage not to run. The third during dinner finally relaxed the knots he'd carried around in his stomach since Connor delivered the shocking news. "Will you show me around?"

A look of impatience crossed her face, but she led him through the living room and down a short hall. The first room was an office with a beautiful desk. An interesting set of Chinese doors hung on one wall, flanked by floor to ceiling built-in bookcases on either side. Her apartment was far more spacious than he'd imagined.

"What's behind the doors?"

"A Murphy bed. I also use this as a guest room." She pointed at tracks over the bookcases. "When the doors are pulled over the shelves, a bed comes down."

He stared down at her as she talked. Her simple elegance was very becoming and very different from the casual, girl-next-door Cecelia he'd known. Her cheekbones were more prominent, and her face narrower. She wore her hair straight in the newspaper article, but tonight, though shorter, her curls ruled, the red strands glimmering in the light. And her arresting blue eyes. He'd missed looking into their depths.

"Very nice way to hide a bed. I can picture you in here working, thumbnail between your teeth. Do you still do that when you're concentrating?"

His gaze dropped to her pretty pink lips. She backed away a step and then another. "No."

I bet you do.

She crossed the hall and flipped on a light in a bathroom. He glanced inside, then did a double-take. "Is that a fireplace mantle behind the tub?"

"Yes."

Another great idea. "I'm surprised by how much space you have. I've always had a mental picture of tiny, cramped" —*rodent-infested*—"apartments when I think of New York City living."

He was both amazed and impressed. He knew living in this city wasn't cheap, so Cecelia must be doing very well for herself. Against the odds, she'd done it. She'd accomplished all that she set out to do.

Or was someone helping her? The guy on her fridge came to mind as he followed her into the room at the end of the hall—her bedroom with an adjacent bathroom. Tranquil and relaxing, with touches of fun popping up in unexpected places.

This is the Cecelia I remember, the Cecelia I loved, serene with dashes of whimsical.

A set of ornate doors made up the headboard with a rough wood arbor used as a canopy. Yards of flowing white fabric draped over the weathered wood made the whole bed seem as if it was floating among the clouds, downy soft and welcoming. Antiques and unique pieces, old and new, mingled matchlessly throughout her space. "Beautiful."

So much like Cecelia.

So different from Stacy.

Or any other girl he'd ever dated.

Cecelia headed toward the living room, but he stopped her at the doorway of her office. "How did you get the desk in here?"

The corners of her mouth twitched, almost a smile. He'd only caught one or two of those during dinner. "Through the window."

"Ah, a sight I would like to see. Is that how you got your headboard in here too, through the window?"

She nodded.

He noticed three framed photos sitting at an angle on her desk. "The desk is a unique piece. Mind if I take a closer look?"

She gestured for him to enter.

He kept his back to her so he could see the pictures without her watching. A young man who had to be Derrick, though Jared wouldn't have recognized him, posing in his Navy uniform. The next was Ce's little sister Jenny and her groom on their wedding day. The third showed Cecelia cheek to cheek with a woman wearing an It's-My-Birthday headband. He ran his hand over the desk. "Is it antique?"

"Yes."

Her frosty eyes lit up for the first time tonight, making his heart thrum erratically.

"That desk was my first major purchase after I started

working for Arthur Winston. I bought it, had it delivered, and immediately threw up."

The fleeting glimpse of his Cecelia disappeared when her eyes met his, and her shield clanged back into place. He could imagine her fretting over money spent on something this extravagant after her frugal upbringing.

In the living room, he looked out the window. She had a nice view of a courtyard below. Then he glanced around for more pictures while she turned on a couple of lamps. He spotted one on a bookshelf, Cecelia on horseback, and another of her, Jenny, and Derrick as children on an end table.

"Would you like to have a seat?" She waited until he sat on the sofa before taking a chair as far from him as possible.

To her visible annoyance, he moved to the other end of the sofa, putting her within touching distance. He set his glass down on a nearby coaster.

"How often do you come to New York?" she asked, with more than a hint of impatience.

Her subtext was loud and clear. She didn't like him invading her city. "Usually three or four times a year."

When Foster, Stern, and Wallace opened the New York office—where Kenneth Wallace lived—they strongly suggested all their junior associates take the New York Bar Exam. He was one of five to follow through. Not that he wanted to live in this monstrous city, but passing the bar gave him options. He'd already taken part in several New York mergers.

She nodded, lips pressed together, perhaps holding back a retort.

"Do you get to Mesquite often?"

"I usually go for Christmas."

"Really? I'm surprised I never see you."

"We didn't exactly run in the same circle."

He watched her fidget with a silver bracelet on her wrist. She wouldn't like the new direction of their conversation, but he decided to continue. "We ran in the same circle for three months."

"Only because we were dating."

"You never see any of the old gang when you're home?"

"They were your friends, Jared, your gang. I only knew them through you."

Her statement stopped him as his mind scanned those three summer months. All the activities they participated in, all the parties they attended, all the people they hung out with were his friends. Had he been so selfish and self-absorbed that he'd never realized they'd only gone with *his* friends and did what *he* wanted to do?

To shout a denial of being anything like Stacy wouldn't change the fact that he'd done to Cecelia what Stacy did to him. His fiancée planned where they went and with who never bothering to consult him. When he dated Ce, he'd been just as used to getting his way as Stacy. Had he ever asked Ce what she'd like to do, or had he just made plans and towed her along? He couldn't remember.

He sat forward, resting his elbows on his knees. "I'm sorry, Ce. I just realized we hung out with my friends and never yours."

"You don't have to apologize. I didn't mind, or I wouldn't have gone."

He picked up his glass but didn't drink. It hurt his pride to realize how selfish he'd been back then, never considering Cecelia's feelings. She'd never complained, just gone cheerfully along with his plans. "Just the same, I'm sorry."

She looked away.

Since they'd broached the subject of the past, he decided to take the conversation a step further. "Where did you go to school?"

She shifted in her chair. "I transferred to New York University."

"And just walked away from your scholarship?"

"NYU offered a better one."

"How could it be better than a full ride?"

She moved her hands from her lap to the arms of her chair. "The after-graduation benefits were better in New York."

"What about sending divorce papers?"

She finally made eye contact. "We were silly to get married so young, especially since we were both going off to school. Long-distance romances rarely last."

"Except ours wasn't just a romance. We were married."

"Don't tell me you didn't realize our mistake as soon as you got to California."

I didn't think of our marriage as a mistake. He sat back and set his glass down. "Why didn't you talk to me first? Why didn't you let me know where you'd gone? I looked for you, but your parents wouldn't give me any information. Why?"

Brushing an imaginary piece of lint off her dress, she cleared her throat. "The scholarship here came up so suddenly. I had to move fast if I wanted to accept it. By the time I got here, the semester had already started. I scrambled to catch up. I had to find a job. Between work and school . . ." She shrugged and left the sentence hanging.

"They didn't have phones in New York?" he asked, trying to keep his tone light even though anger boiled through his system.

Not that any of her answers made a difference in their lives now. He just wanted some kind of insight as to why she disappeared without contacting him in person. "You could have called me. Instead, you served me with divorce papers, and I never heard from you again."

❦

"*I*t doesn't matter anymore, Jared." Cecelia stood, locking her muscles to keep from trembling. She couldn't do this. She couldn't answer questions with him watching her so closely. He acted so hurt, yet he'd moved on before the ink dried on their marriage license.

He said this apartment was so her, but he didn't know anything about her anymore. School, work, friends, environment, maturity—all elements that transform a person—made them very different than they'd been. She still might be a little naïve, but she sure wasn't as silly as she'd been at eighteen.

She went to the kitchen, filled a glass with water, and took a shaky sip. Leaning a hip against the counter, she closed her eyes. "Can I get you anything else?" *Please say no. Please say you have to go.*

"No, thank you."

Cecelia sagged in relief, ready to say, *I have an early morning.*

She stepped into the living room. Jared was standing in front of her bookshelves. She held her breath. The ornate box she kept his things in sat on the middle shelf, out in the open, because she'd never expected Jared McAlister to be in her home.

"I see you still read a lot."

"I do."

He turned and smiled. "I don't read as much as I used to, not for pleasure anyway. I read so much at work that when I get home it's hard to open a book."

She had no idea how to respond, so she didn't.

He emptied the last of his water glass and glanced at his watch. "I'd better go. It's getting late."

"Would you like me to call a cab?"

"I can walk. My hotel isn't far."

She took the glass from him, careful their fingers didn't touch, and set it on a nearby table. "Thank you again for dinner."

His smile reached his brown eyes. "Thank you for joining me. I wasn't sure you would."

Yep. Thanks for ruining Market City Café for me. Now every time she went in, she'd think of him.

They both walked toward the door. "I'm glad you're doing well." She hadn't asked any of the questions running through her mind, squashing every impulse to know more all night. Knowing he was going home to a wife and family would only cause her more heartache. *Best not to know any details.*

"I'm glad I got to see you, Cecelia."

The timbre of his voice dislodged another small piece of her heart. By the time he left, there would be a gaping hole. Reconstructive work would begin tomorrow.

He turned before opening the door. "Do you like New York? Living in this huge city with more than eight million other people?"

"Yes, though it took a while. At first, I was terrified, but now"—she shrugged—"it's home."

"Do you ever miss Texas? You always said you loved being able to see the horizon."

"I spent last weekend in the country with a friend. It's a short drive to open spaces and views of the horizon."

Without giving her warning, he caught her arm and pulled her in for a quick hug. Not only did he smell the same, but his body felt so familiar. How could that be after such a long time? When he released her, his gaze took over the hold. "Good night, Cecelia."

"Goodbye, Jared."

She stepped onto the small landing and watched him go down the stairs. When he reached the outside door, he turned and winked before walking outside. She slowly closed her door and slid down the wall to the floor. Hot tears came quickly, filling her eyes, and streaming down her cheeks. She didn't want to be sorry she'd accepted Jared's dinner invitation, but she knew she would be very sorry.

She put both hands to her stomach as the tears turned into wracking sobs.

~

*J*ared took his time walking to the hotel, pacified by the way the night had gone, which seemed completely ridiculous. He'd come to New York to have Cecelia sign divorce papers.

Some of his questions had been answered, but the most important ones were left hanging. At least he knew where she'd gone and why, and she was probably right to think New York could offer, maybe not more, but at least bigger opportunities. He didn't believe her reason for not telling him where she went, though. Or her reason for divorcing him. He'd seen the flicker of falsehood in her eyes.

He let himself into his hotel room, surprised the message light on the hotel phone wasn't blinking. He turned his cell back on and found two messages from earlier. First, Stacy asking why he turned his cell off and the second one telling him she was going out. *Big surprise.* Stacy was a party person. She loved to see and be seen.

He called her cell and got her voicemail. "Just checking in. I'll be home tomorrow."

After undressing, he lay on the bed with the air conditioner cooling his skin. He wouldn't get much sleep with his thoughts replaying the past three hours over and over. That and the clear picture he had of where Cecelia lived and worked meant he'd never be able to get her out of his mind.

CHAPTER 7

*J*ared reached for his ringing cell phone while towel-drying his hair. He didn't recognize the number. "Jared McAlister."

"I just called your office, and Violet said you were in New York," Stacy said.

"You didn't get my messages?" He set the towel near the sink and picked up his toothbrush.

"Oh, I misplaced my cell phone."

That settled strangely. Stacy always had her phone in hand.

"Why are you in New York again?"

"I had to take care of some business. I'll be back later this afternoon."

"Grant sends you out of town too often. You should talk to your daddy about it."

"I chose to make this trip. Did you get the horse you were looking at?"

Just the mention of a horse and she forgot his trip. Instead, she talked about the thoroughbred the Richardsons' stable manager bought, scoffed about the bridesmaids' dresses Alisha had in mind, and voiced her anger that the woman who did her nails planned to move to another state.

"I have to go, but I wanted to remind you we have brunch at the club with both sets of parents Saturday."

Can't wait.

"Another call's coming in. I have to go." And in true Stacy fashion, she disconnected the call without a goodbye.

His mom called immediately after. "Violet told me you're in New York again. I'm going to tell your dad to talk to Grant."

"I had business in New York, Mom. Grant didn't send me."

"You shouldn't be gone from Stacy so often."

Would he ever be old enough for his parents to stay out of his business? "Stacy is out of town herself. Did you need something?"

"I wanted to remind you of the brunch with the Richardsons on Saturday."

"Can't wait."

"Oh, Jared, stop being so mordant."

Mordant—his mother's word of the day. He'd have to look that one up.

"You know we have a hundred wedding details to discuss."

"The wedding is months away."

"A wedding this size takes time to plan."

His mom, Stacy, and her mom wouldn't settle for anything less than astronomical. He couldn't imagine the amount of money the Richardsons were forking over to see their only child wed.

Another call beeped through. Someone he actually wanted to talk to. "I have to go, Mom."

"You'll be back in town for Alisha's engagement party," she stated rather than asked.

"Yes, ma'am. I'll see you there."

He connected the next call. "Hey, Knox. How's it going?"

"Hot and sticky. August in Dallas is miserable as always." Knox's deep Southern drawl seemed more pronounced than usual. "Violet said you're in New York."

"Yeah, a spur-of-the-moment trip."

"Will you be back in town by the weekend?"

"Yes. Want to hit the lake on Sunday?" Jared asked.

He and Knox Chatham had been inseparable since first grade. If there was trouble around, his friend's built-in homing device found it, with Jared only a half-step behind. Charles and Betsy Sue McAlister deemed Knox a bad influence and forbade their friendship when they were caught pouring dish soap in a neighbor's hot tub at twelve, but that didn't stop them.

"I'll bring the boat. You bring the beer and brats."

"Sounds good."

"Is the old ball and chain going to let you get away after being out of town?"

Knox detested Stacy, and her feelings toward Knox were mutual. The first few redneck comments from Stacy resulted in a declaration of war. She refused to apologize, and Knox wouldn't have accepted if she had. Jared learned early on to keep the two separated. "I'll find a way. See you Sunday."

On a hunch, Jared called Stacy's phone from the hotel number.

"Yeah?" a gruff but familiar voice answered after three rings.

Tuck Powers, the Richardsons' stable manager.

"Tuck, it's Jared. I'm trying to help Stacy find her phone."

"I already told her she left it in my truck."

"Sure. Thanks, Tuck."

Too many odd occurrences between Stacy and the Richardsons' foreman made him leery of his fiancée's faithfulness. She might have a perfect explanation for why she left her phone in Tuck's truck, but Stacy usually went berserk when misplacing her phone for more than thirty seconds.

His cell rang, and he accepted the call. "Morning, Violet."

"Sorry to call with bad news. The merger is on hold again. The other attorney wants to meet with you today, if possible, about one more thing in the contract."

Time to close this one down. Jared glanced at his watch. No way would he be able to meet with Cecelia again and tell her they were still married. After seeing her last night, he couldn't bring himself to blindside her with the news by courier. Something of this magnitude deserved a personal delivery. Okay, so he'd plan another trip as soon as possible.

"See if you can get me a flight to Dallas."

"Already done. One airline has a flight that leaves from LaGuardia at one. You'll arrive in Dallas at five after four."

"Book it. See if he can meet at five-thirty. That will give me time to get to the office and change."

"The dry cleaners delivered your suit an hour ago."

"Great. Text me the details of the—" His phone dinged with the information before he finished his sentence. "—flight." He chuckled. "Thanks, Violet."

After he hung up, he picked up the hotel phone a second time and called the front desk.

"Yes, Mr. McAlister."

"Can you tell me where the nearest florist is?"

"Artistic Arrangements is around the corner on West 55th. Would you like their number?"

"No, I'll visit the store myself. Thank you."

≈

*C*ecelia spent the morning hiding her tired, tear-swollen eyes from her coworkers by visiting a woodworker who specialized in custom bedroom sets. She wanted something unique for Mr. Basketball and knew Oscar could deliver. They went over plans until she felt sure they had a design her basketball player would love. "Let me show him these plans, and I'll get back to you by Monday."

"Sounds good, Ce. I should be able to get the set made in six weeks."

"You are a lifesaver, Oscar."

Luckily she had a slow afternoon. Unlike the rest of the staff at Winston and Associates, she'd never taken a nap on the comfy sofa in her office. That might change today—if she could get Jared off her mind long enough to rest.

She was at her desk when Windy carried in a breath-taking bouquet of orange orchids. The rest of the staff flitted in like birds following a bagel cart, hoping for a tasty morsel. Cecelia knew who sent the flowers before looking at the card.

"It looks like Tall, Dark, and Devastatingly Handsome got lucky last night," Windy said.

Cecelia reached for the envelope, hoping no one noticed her shaky hand. Recognizing Jared's precise, squared-off lettering, she blinked away tears that stung the backs of her eyes. She ran a thumb over the writing before lifting the flap and tugging the card free.

Cecelia,
Thank you for joining me for dinner last night.
It was wonderful to see you again.
Jared

Cecelia looked up. Zack had stretched out on the sofa and already had his eyes closed. Winston, Mia, and Windy were watching her, eager to hear who sent the flowers. "Windy's

Tall, Dark, and Handsome's name is Jared McAlister. I dated him the summer between high school and college."

"Just how lucky did Jared get?" Mia asked, dropping into a chair.

"We had dinner together."

Windy perched on the edge of Cecelia's desk. "Were you surprised to see him?"

Surprised is an understatement. "Very."

"Good surprised or bad?" Zack asked, without opening his eyes.

Mia nodded toward Zack. "Good question. I've dated a couple of guys I wouldn't want to show up again."

"I'm not sure." Cecelia slipped the card into her briefcase. It would join the other things Jared had given her in the box on the bookshelf.

"Well, the only information I could get out of him is that he's an attorney, and he lives in Texas."

Zack opened one eye. "Why wouldn't he leave his name?"

Cecelia eased a contract from under Windy's thigh so it wouldn't rip. "He said he didn't think I'd call him back."

"Why would he think that?" asked Windy, who still believed in fairy tales because she lived in one with a handsome prince of a husband.

"Sometimes doors aren't meant to be reopened."

Windy stood and planted her hands on Cecelia's desk, leaning close. "He sent you flowers, so he'll be back."

"He won't be back for months, Windy. He only comes to New York three or four times a year."

After several minutes of speculation and Cecelia fending off their questions, Windy and Mia left her office. Winston, however, took Mia's chair while Zack snored softly in the background.

"Would you like to talk about it?" Winston asked, easing into Papa Bear mode.

"There's nothing to talk about. We dated a long time ago. He happened to find out I lived in New York and stopped by to say hi. We had dinner, caught up, and he's probably on his way back to Dallas as we speak." She stopped there, afraid if she went into more detail, tears would follow. She'd cried enough tears over Jared McAlister to last two lifetimes.

"If he's an attorney in Dallas, why was he in New York?"

"I didn't ask."

"You're not going to divulge any more information, are you?"

"I don't have any more information."

He blew out a breath. "How's Mr. Basketball's project coming along?"

Finally, something she could talk about without suffocating her emotions. She pulled Oscar's plans out of her briefcase and handed them to Winston. "He approved of the bedroom furniture this morning."

"You'll have to special order a mattress."

"Already in the works."

"The Hollywood couple is coming in next week, and they're supposed to call me this afternoon to set up an appointment. He's been filming in Vancouver and hasn't been able to get away."

"Just let me know so I can rearrange my schedule."

"I will, sweetheart." Winston stood, concern still etched across his features. "Do you need help with anything?"

"Nope. Everything's good."

After Winston left her office, she slid the vase of flowers closer and examined the gorgeous butterscotch orchids with veins of burnt orange running through the petals. Rubbing her temples, she tried to massage away the apprehension. She'd been jittery the second she saw Jared last night, and that feeling hadn't eased over the day.

She'd built a life that was highly organized and, for the

most part, predictable. With two siblings relying on her, responsibility was something she mastered when she was very young. Now her clients deserved the same. The only time her life hadn't gone according to plan were the three magnificent months she spent with Jared.

An hour later, Cecelia looked up at the knock on her open door. "Tyler, are you playing hooky today?"

"I had a meeting on this side of the city and decided to stop by to see my favorite girl."

"Your mother would be upset to hear you say that," she said, coming around her desk.

"Very true." Tyler bent and kissed her. His chestnut-colored eyes sparkled in the light coming through the window. He'd been raised on a farm in the Midwest, and that's where she easily pictured him. Riding through a cornfield on a tractor, a baseball hat pulled low against the sun. Not sitting in a New York skyscraper being saluted for coming up with the best Super Bowl commercial earlier this year.

Why couldn't she fall in love with sweet, kind, funny Tyler? If a woman made a what-I-want-in-a-husband list, Tyler Benning would be at the top.

One day she would hurt him, and that knowledge pierced her heart.

"Beautiful flowers. Are they from a grateful client?"

She leaned back against her desk. "No, they're from a guy I haven't seen since high school."

Tyler's eyebrow twitched. "A guy?"

"He lives in Dallas but is in the city on business."

She could tell Tyler had more questions but quickly countered with one of her own. "Who did you meet with?"

He looked from the flowers to her. "The head of Rory Inc. advertising. But I stopped here to invite you to a surprise birthday party a friend is throwing next Saturday."

"I'd love to come. Should I pick up a present?"

"I'll take care of it. Hawaiian theme, so wear your grass skirt and coconut bra."

"Oh, darn. I got rid of my coconut bra last week."

"Too bad for me," he said, flashing his handsome grin.

"Are you still flying out to visit your parents tomorrow?"

"Yep. Dad's surgery is scheduled for Monday."

Cecelia ran a finger between his brows where a worry line had appeared. "I hope everything goes okay. Call and let me know."

"I will. I have to get back to the office." He gave her a quick kiss. "I'll pick you up at seven-thirty next Saturday."

She waved him off. "See you then."

CHAPTER 8

*J*ared walked out of the engagement party into the sultry night air and gazed up at the dazzling array of stars glinting overhead. The sweet scent of jasmine drifted past, and he glanced around for the source but couldn't spot the vine in the dark.

Although the party was in full swing, Jared couldn't stand the loud music and claustrophobic-inducing crowd any longer. Tipping his beer bottle up, he drained the contents and set it on the deck railing.

He could barely make out the rises and valleys of the golf course. The *tsk tsk tsk* of a distant sprinkler competed with the refrain of tree frogs—Texas country life at its finest.

He rested his forearms on the weathered wood of the top rail and rubbed his temples. He wanted Cecelia Chadwick out of his head. Four days since he'd been in Connor's office, and he'd thought of little else. Two days after he left Cecelia, and he could still smell her perfume. Why hadn't he checked the divorce papers when they came in the mail? Why hadn't *she* checked? After initiating the divorce, she should have followed through.

Yet, he was the one attending law school. He should have gone over that document word for word.

He used to ask *why*. Now all he could think was *what if*. How different would his life be if they were still together?

He silently groaned at the sound of the door closing and measured footsteps crossing the deck. He should have walked out onto the golf course, where he could disappear into the shadows.

"I saw you leave, Jared. What are you doing out here?"

His father was the last person he wanted to talk to tonight. On the outside, Charles McAlister epitomized a Southern gentleman, but inside he was demanding, inflexible, and callous. Also a perfectionist, his father expected the same from everyone around him, family or not. Cold and calculating, he ran McAlister Industries with an iron fist and a heart of steel.

"Getting some air." Jared straightened when his father stopped next to him.

He hated the formality that existed between them. When Jared was a child, Charles would summon him to his office to reprimand him for the smallest infraction. Those impersonal scoldings were more principal lecturing a student than father teaching a son. Charles would glower over his imposing desk while Jared's little-boy heart pounded wildly in his chest. No matter how hard Jared tried, he never received a pat on the back or the long-coveted hug.

At one point, he stopped trying to please and, with Knox's unknowing help, started trying to get his father's attention in other ways. By the time he left for his freshman year at Stanford, he'd finally realized praise from his dad would never come, and he'd given up trying to gain his attention.

He'd always wished his dad could be more like Knox's old man. Tom Chatham was easygoing and approachable. Human. You could share a laugh with him. He praised and encouraged rather than ridiculed and criticized—the complete opposite of Charlie.

"Are you performing well at work?"

Not how is work going? Or, *Are you still enjoying your job?* A question like that might show he cared. "Yes."

His father hadn't come out to talk about work or share a friendly chat with his son. Not Charlie's style. He always had an agenda.

His dad pointed at the empty beer bottle. "How many have you had tonight?"

Not enough. "A couple." Alcohol filled the hollow in his chest that had been empty for a very long time.

"Stacy said you've been drinking a lot lately."

Stacy knew the fragile line between him and his dad, yet she constantly went to his parents with her grievances. Which only served to distance him and his father more.

"She also told your mother you've been acting distant."

Jared turned toward the golf course, angry that he allowed his father to make him feel like a kid being sent to a corner for a time-out. "You and Mom need to stay out of our business."

"Stacy coming to us makes it our business. Do you have something on the side you need to clean up?"

Jared met his father's glare with one of his own. "Something on the side?"

"Another woman?"

"No."

"You're thirty-three years old. It's time to stop running around and settle down."

His dad had no idea how many hours he devoted to work. Then he had to attend parties, social events, dinners, brunches, fundraisers. "I don't have the time or the energy to *run around.*"

A glint of satisfaction, along with an arrogant smirk,

settled on his dad's face. "Maybe you should have been wiser in your choice of workplace."

"You expected the best, and I gave it to you. I work for the top law firm in Dallas, and one of the top four in New York."

"What I expected—" His dad bit off the rest of his sentence, his jaw tightening with tension. Charles McAlister did not lose his temper in public.

"You expected me to work for McAlister Industries, under your thumb, where you could dictate my every move." *Sorry to disappoint you once again, dear old Dad.*

His father turned on his heel and stalked back into the party, probably angry because Jared had comebacks for all his points.

Jared stood on the deck for a long time after his father left, fighting the urge for another drink. He needed something strong enough to push him over the edge, to help him escape for the night. Of course, he'd just fall back into reality tomorrow morning.

Restless, at odds with the world, he moved to the darkest part of the deck, hoping to avoid another visit. Funny how he could imagine a full life with Cecelia, but he couldn't imagine a year from now with Stacy. Not the best way to start a marriage.

Seeing Cecelia again reminded him that the hollowness he felt now hadn't always been there.

Stacy's laugh cut through the music. "Where's my Jare Bear? I want to dance."

Jared went down the deck stairs and hit the path skirting the fairway. As hard as it was to admit, his dad might be right. Maybe he did have something on the side where Cecelia was concerned. He thought he'd pushed her far enough into the dark recesses of his mind that if he ever ran into her again, she wouldn't affect him. But she did, more than he ever imagined possible.

As he passed a sand trap, a memory took him to a place he didn't want to go tonight—*to a beach, where a soft, Southern voice read Dickens . . .*

When Knox returned to that stretch of beach, everyone piled out of the boat, and his ever-resourceful friend handed down a charcoal grill.

"What's this for?"

"We stopped at the marina for gas and bought the fixings for hamburgers. The girls agreed to join us for dinner."

The grill was used, so Knox had probably "borrowed" it from one of the houses along the east side of the lake. They'd have to return it before they could go home tonight.

Jared glanced at blue-eyes, who didn't look thrilled with the news of dinner together. She pulled on a pair of cutoffs and a T-shirt and got to work forming hamburgers while Knox lit the charcoal. Her friends pranced around in bikinis while she gathered wood for a bonfire they'd light once the sun went down. When the food was ready, she made sure everyone had a burger and chips before she picked up a plate. Where did her sense of responsibility come from, he wondered.

A couple of the guys tried to hit on her, but she displayed the same indifference she'd shown him. Watching the other girls giggle, flirt, and flip their hair, Jared decided she was right. Her friends were looking for a good time, and they'd found it in a boatload of college boys who were looking for the same thing.

After they ate, several from the group paired up and wandered off into the darkness. Jared glanced at the girl. She sat in the sand near the bonfire, her knees pulled up to her chest, and her arms wrapped around her legs, seemingly lost in thought.

He sat down next to her. "Thanks for reading earlier."

She turned her head toward him, her cheek resting on a

knee. "You're welcome." The corners of her mouth tipped up. Almost a smile. "I've never been asked to read to someone over the age of twelve."

She'd left her hair down after her swim, and he fought the urge to touch the silky curls. "Do you read to kids often?"

"Not as much as I used to."

To keep her attention, he asked the first question that came to mind. "Do you like kids?"

A smile flirted at the corners of her mouth again. "Doesn't everyone?"

Jared shrugged. "I'm not sure. I've never been around little kids, and I don't know anyone who has them." They sat in comfortable silence for a minute, staring into the fire. "So, I guess you want kids someday?"

She lifted a shoulder. "Sure."

"Kids, as in more than one?" This had to be the craziest conversation he'd ever had with a stranger, but he didn't care. He wanted to keep her talking, keep her looking at him so he could watch the firelight dance across her skin and flicker in her eyes. She flashed a genuine smile this time.

"More than one, but less than six."

"Six!"

They both laughed, and a strange eruption burned deep in his chest, startling him, making him think irrationally. "You want to go for a walk?"

Her smile dropped away, turning her eyes cold despite the fire. "I told you earlier; I'm not interested."

"I'm not trying to get you on a blanket in the bushes, Ice Princess. I'm just asking if you'd like to take a walk down the beach. I'm not a homicidal maniac or a serial rapist. I'll keep my hands to myself, and we'll stay in plain view—just an innocent walk."

She hadn't taken her eyes off him while he talked and,

against his will, he glanced down at her lips. He decided he'd like to kiss those lips someday. They'd been the most amazing color of rosy pink in the sunlight. Perfectly tempting. He looked back up to meet her gaze while he waited for her answer, sure she'd say no while hoping she'd say yes.

"Most serial rapists or homicidal maniacs don't go around announcing themselves."

"True." He stood and held out his hand, deciding not to wait for an answer, pleasantly surprised when her palm met his. Once she was on her feet, he released his hold and stuffed both fists in the pockets of his swim trunks. He said he'd keep his hands to himself, and he intended to keep his word. He nodded toward the beach, took a few steps, and she followed.

"I assume, by the list of books you mentioned, you like to read."

"Yes." Her reply was sweetly hesitant.

"Fiction or nonfiction?"

"Mostly fiction, but I also like to read about true-life adventures."

"Such as?"

She gathered her hair in a fist to hold it out of her face when the breeze kicked up. "Climbing Mount Everest interests me."

Surprised, he turned to look at her. She didn't seem the adventurous type. "You're want to climb Mount Everest?"

A soft laugh followed his question. "No, I'd never be brave enough to tackle something so huge, but I like to read about people who are."

"Do you travel much?"

Another laugh. "I've never been out of Texas."

In this day and age, how is that possible?

They talked about books and authors, and their tastes

were surprisingly similar. Once she let her guard down, they were able to hold a comfortable conversation. She didn't perform the usual gushy, batting-her-eyelashes type of flirting he was used to. And she definitely wasn't out to impress him. He liked her what-you-see-is-what-you-get attitude, but that didn't mean he was interested, simply intrigued.

When the beach ended at a stand of trees, they turned around.

"I heard your friends call you Ce. Is that short for something?"

She stopped and held out her hand. "Hi. I'm Cecelia Chadwick."

"Cecelia Chadwick," he said slowly, enjoying the sweet cadence of her name on his tongue. He took the hand she extended, squeezing gently rather than shaking. He imagined her firm, confident grip meant she liked who she was, despite not being brave enough to climb the highest mountain in the world.

"It's nice to meet you, Cecelia. I'm Jared McAlister."

Her genuine smile made his breath catch. "Hi, Jared. You have incredible dimples."

His face heated with a rare blush, making him grateful for the dark. "Thank you, Cecelia. You have beautiful eyes." He reached out with his free hand and tucked a strand of her hair behind her ear without thinking, surprised by the naturalness of his action, and pleased when she didn't jerk away.

"Thank you." She pulled her hand free of his grip.

He shoved both hands back in his pockets when they started walking again. The heady scents of spring and new growth hung in the air as they walked back over the sand still warmed by the sun. He was amazed at how much he didn't want to reach the bonfire and his friends waiting there. "Do you live in Dallas?"

"Mesquite."

"I live in Dallas, but I've been going to school in California," he offered when she didn't ask.

She nodded.

"You're a senior?"

"Yes."

"Do you have plans for college after graduation?"

"I'm going to Arizona State University."

"Is that in Phoenix?"

She lifted a shoulder. "Tempe, just outside of Phoenix."

"Why Arizona State?"

"I have a scholarship," she said, looking away as if embarrassed by her accomplishment.

The sweet softness of her voice was like a gentle rain washing all cares away. "Have you decided on a major?"

"Interior design, but I also want to study architecture. I don't want to just decorate houses. I want to be involved in renovations and structure. What about you?"

"I'm going back to Stanford for law school in the fall."

"What kind of law?" she asked, which no one ever did.

"Corporate. Mergers and acquisitions."

"What do merger and acquisition lawyers do, exactly?"

"Identify clients' business objectives, advise on the deal and negotiating tactics, review clients' contracts, negotiate agreements." He laughed. "I bet you're sorry you asked."

"No. I think it sounds exciting."

Another first from any girl he talked to unless she was in law school herself. She asked real questions and listened to his answers. Against his will, he found himself *interested* in Cecelia Chadwick, high school senior.

To his disappointment, they reached the group to find the guys were loading the boat, getting ready to take off. "We should keep in touch, email or call so we can discuss good books we—"

"Hey, Jared, you ready?"

He shot Knox a back-off glare. "Give me a minute."

"We're meeting the girls back here tomorrow," Knox hollered. "You two can pick up where you left off."

Jared glanced at Cecelia. "You'll be back tomorrow?"

"No, I have to work."

"You can't come after work?"

"I don't get off until late."

A herd of frustrated toddlers stomped through his chest. "You can't call in sick?"

She flashed the kind of reprimanding look a mother would give an irresponsible teenager. "No."

He didn't want to say goodbye but had no idea how to prolong their time together. He knew she wouldn't give him her number if he asked.

"I have to go. I enjoyed meeting you, Jared McAlister." She held out her hand again. "Good luck in law school."

"Thanks. Good luck to you, too, Cecelia Chadwick. Maybe I'll see you around sometime this summer. Do you come to the lake often?"

"No. I don't have a lot of free time." She pulled her hand free a second time.

"Can I call—"

"Bye." She ran off with her friends before he could finish his sentence or ask where she worked.

A week later, Cecelia had found a niche in his mind. After fourteen calls to Chadwick residences in Mesquite, he finally got lucky and recognized her soft voice the minute she answered. Though he did most of the talking, they chatted like they were old friends.

He called and talked to her almost every day for the next two months because he knew when he came home between graduation and law school, he wanted to spend as much time with Cecelia Chadwick as possible.

A sprinkler popped up, pulling Jared back to the present. He sprinted toward the raucous music and harsh lights of reality, the hollow in his chest aching.

CHAPTER 9

*T*ime spent with Valerie, a girlfriend—a best friend —was something Cecelia never got a chance to experience as a teenager. Between taking care of her brother and sister and working multiple small jobs, she rarely had time to hang out with friends.

The only way she'd be able to attend college would be if she was awarded a grant or scholarship. Luckily a high school guidance counselor helped her fill out the paperwork for both. On top of her already full plate, the counselor pointed Cecelia toward volunteer opportunities that would make a difference in how her applications were received.

She worked at a bookstore, taking any hours they gave her. She babysat and helped a neighbor with yard work, saving every dime she could to support herself when she left. Without her parents' consent, sweet Mrs. Brooks next door helped her open a savings account and allowed the statements to come to her address. If her mom knew about the account, the money would disappear overnight.

When the letter from Arizona State University arrived, she held her breath as she carefully opened the envelope.

With a gasp, she'd performed a happy dance. She'd been accepted and with a full-ride scholarship.

The most exciting news of her life, and she had no one to share it with. Her parents would destroy her excitement with a single comment. Her brother, who would be devastated to know she'd be leaving him, was at baseball practice. And her sister was probably with someone she shouldn't be with, in a place where they shouldn't be. With all she'd been doing to get ahead, she'd eliminated any friends close enough to care. So she went next door and shared the news with Mrs. Brooks and then the school counselor, two people who shared her joy.

Val took her arm as they left the theatre. "What did you think?"

Cecelia had been fascinated with the workings of Broadway ever since she came to the city, and there weren't many plays she didn't like. She'd seen *Wicked* before and enjoyed it just as much the second time as the first. "I thought it was good, but I can tell you don't think so by your expression."

"I thought it would be funnier." Val leaned her head toward Cecelia. "I needed funny."

"Are you ready to tell me what happened between you and Reece?"

"Since I got to your place too late for dinner, how about we grab some dessert instead?"

"Pie or ice cream?" Cecelia asked, knowing Val always had a hard time choosing between the two.

"Cheesecake."

"Wow. Things are worse than I thought." Cecelia steered her friend toward a café known for its delectable desserts. "Cheesecake it is." She could use some cheesecake herself, not that a slice would erase Jared McAlister from her mind.

Once they were seated and placed their order, Cecelia rested her forearms on the table. "Okay, spill it."

"Wait. We're not going to segue our way into the topic of my breakup gracefully? Just spill it?"

"We can segue if you want, but I'm not sure how to broach the subject without a lead-in."

Val squinted at the ceiling, like she was deep in thought, then snapped her fingers. "Ask me about work."

Only Val would turn the subject of her breakup into a scavenger hunt. "Okay. How's work, Val?"

Val flashed a grin, her brown eyes sparkling. "Remember my company's Memorial Day picnics?"

"Sure." Val always looked forward to their picnics. Cecelia attended once when her friend was between boyfriends. They provided tables lined with catered food from barbecue to burgers and brats, games for all ages, and prizes like gift certificates for a day at the spa, expensive bottles of wine, theatre tickets, and gift cards to fabulous restaurants.

"I took Reece this year. My boss loved him, and my work-mates all wanted him on their teams for the group games. We had a great time. We even laughed about what the office bombshell wore. I think I told you about her R-rated shorts and T-shirt."

Cecelia nodded. Val had gone into minute details about the office bombshell. "I remember."

Val slumped in her chair and tucked her short brown hair behind her ears. "Last Saturday, Reece and I had plans to go to my house, but he called at the last minute to say he didn't feel well."

By saying "my house," Val meant they were going to the house she had on her parents' property about an hour train ride out of New York City. Cecelia loved spending weekends at Val's house. She came from a big, noisy family who welcomed Cecelia like she was part of the clan. Saturdays were spent horseback riding or swimming or lounging with a good book. After Sunday morning church, the entire family met at the main house for a huge lunch before she and Val caught a train home. Val also kept a tiny apartment in the city, close to work, where she stayed during the week.

"Considerate to keep you from getting sick."

"Totally. That's Reese. Attentive, sensitive, charming, always thinking of others. But I can be nice too. Instead of going out of town, I went to the market and bought everything for homemade chicken soup."

"Very nice," Cecelia agreed. "And considerate."

"That's what I thought. I mean, perfect girlfriend, right?"

"Absolutely."

"I ring the doorbell of his apartment with my elbow because"—she raised both hands like she was holding something—"hands full of chicken soup and warm bread. Guess who answers the door?"

Cecelia shook her head. "His mom?"

Val leaned forward, planting her palms on the table. "The bombshell from *my* office. They've been seeing each other since the picnic almost two months ago."

"No." Cecelia had met the bombshell and the name fit.

"Yes. She answered the door because Reese was in the shower after their romp in the hay—so to speak."

"He wasn't sick."

"Nope. Not sick."

"Oh, Val."

She fell back into her chair. "I threw the soup in the shower with him."

"The whole pot?"

"Yep. He's lucky it had time to cool off before I got there." She shrugged in a what-you-gonna-do way. "Dumb dork. I make chicken soup, and he chooses the woman who brings store-bought Oreos to the office party."

"I'm sorry. How about the whole cheesecake instead of just a slice?"

"My head shouts yes, but my jeans groan in agony."

Cecelia sat back when their waitress delivered their order. "How did you handle working with the bombshell this week?"

"She steered clear of me," Val said around a bite of turtle cheesecake.

"Want to go on a shopping spree Friday night?" Cecelia asked. Val was an expert shopper.

"I can't. I have a date."

Cecelia about snorted cherry cheesecake out of her nose. "What?"

"My brother lined me up with one of his geeky computer buddies."

"Huh."

Why couldn't she be more like Val, who, when she finds out her Adonis boyfriend with the perfect hair and dreamy bedroom eyes is cheating on her one weekend, has a date with someone new the following one? She rants and rails and throws soup. Then it's bring on the next guy.

Cecelia dated a man for three months, was married to him for two months—eleven years ago—and still couldn't move on.

❦

*J*ared braced a hand against the console when Knox killed the boat's engine. They were in the middle of the lake with no other boats around. "What's up?"

"Actually, that's my question to you." Knox pointed at the beer bottle in Jared's hand. "You never drink like this."

"Not true. According to St-Stacy, I drink like this all the

time." His tongue felt heavy, his words tripping over themselves. "You're jus' not around to see it."

"Maybe it's time to slow down."

Jared had lost count of how many beers he'd downed, but nothing helped shake his foul mood. "Yeah, well, I bought 'em, so I guess I can drink 'em."

"I guess you can, but I'm the one who'll have to drag your butt home and then listen to Stacy sling insults about my mama and daddy raising a baboon before blaming me for corrupting you."

Jared didn't respond because Knox was right. Stacy would go off like a bottle rocket, and Knox would get the brunt of the blame. She was already fuming because Jared disappeared from the engagement party Friday night, showed up at brunch yesterday, still hungover, and then planned a day on the lake with Knox today.

"What's going on with you?"

Knox swayed with the rocking of the boat. The motion would either hypnotize Jared or make him sick, so he focused his gaze on the water-spotted window. "Remember Cecelia Chadwick?"

"That's a name I haven't heard in a long time." Knox's bare back scrunched against the vinyl of the seat when he sat down. "Whatever happened to her?"

His buddy's wind-dried short hair was sticking up in every direction.

Jared patted his own head, wondering if he looked as silly. "She left for college and poof"—he snapped his fingers—"she vanished. Gone. No phone call, no email. Never heard from her again."

"What made you think of her?"

"I found her." Jared shook his head, the motion making him dizzy. "She lives in New York of all places."

"I didn't know you were looking for her."

"I wasn't, but then I had to."

Knox looked at him like he'd lost his mind. Maybe he had.

"Did you see her when you were there?"

"Something like that." Jared snorted his disgust. "You couldn't pay me enough to live in that city."

"Good thing you don't have to. Or is the law firm pressing you to move?"

"Not yet, but they will. My fault for taking the New York bar exam."

Knox stretched his legs out. "How is Ce?"

"Great. Wonderful." He tipped his beer bottle up and took a long swallow, then held the cold glass to his neck. "Fan—*tas* —tic."

"You say that like it's a bad thing," Knox said, looking over the top of his sunglasses.

Jared pressed a thumb to his forehead where a headache threatened. "She's supposed to be in Arizona."

"You're not making a whole lot of sense, buddy. Cecelia is in New York, but she's supposed to be in Arizona?"

"Are you listening?" Jared ran his hands down his face. He knew his words weren't coming out right, probably because of the stifling heat. *Where'd the breeze go?* He heard the scrunch of vinyl against skin, Knox shifting on his seat.

"I'm listening. I'm just not following," Knox said.

Knox's you're-an-idiot chuckle grated against Jared's nerves. "She got a scholarship to Arizona State, but she disappeared."

"Still lost, so let's go back a couple of steps. You said you weren't looking for her; then you had to."

Jared wished he was sober enough to take a picture of Knox's comical expression. He patted his swimsuit pockets. Heck, he didn't even know where he'd left his phone. "Remember how we always took our first dates to five-star restaurants, wined and dined them, tried to impress them with our ordering skills?"

Knox barked out a laugh as he stood and walked to the back of the boat. "You did that. I didn't." He pulled a bottle of water from the cooler.

Right. His friend's idea of a romantic date entailed pay-per-view fights, a six-pack, and a bag of Cheetos. "I knew a five-star restaurant wouldn't impress Cecelia for a first date, and I couldn't wine her because she was only eighteen and a goody-two-shoes. Not that I minded. That was a nice thing about her. Wait— What was I talking about?"

"Your first date with Ce."

"Right." He tried to snap his fingers again, but they weren't working. Holding up his hand, he looked at his fingers. There were too many. "Anyway, I stopped at Orson's Barbecue, bought their picnic basket, and brought her here to watch the sunset." He grinned. "She loved it."

Knox nodded with a raised brow.

Jared bent at the waist and put his head in his hands as memories swirled around him. He kissed her for the first time that night—the sweetest, most innocent kiss he'd ever experienced.

Knox arranged a towel over his seat. "Let's start at the beginning. How'd you find out Ce is living in New York?"

"Connor Scopello told me."

Knox's eyebrows knit together again as he sat. "Your attorney told you Cecelia lived in New York because . . . ?"

"I asked him to find her."

"Why?"

He stood, hoping for a breeze. Nothing. He needed more alcohol to cut the headache pounding over his left eyebrow. Jared tipped the beer bottle in his hand straight up and drained the last of its contents, then dangled it by the neck from his fingertips. He fell back into the seat then hissed as the scorching vinyl seared his skin. "Unfinished business."

Knox held out a towel, and Jared fought the urge to knock the smirk off his buddy's face.

"You have unfinished business with a girl you dated a couple of times eleven years ago?"

"Yeah." Jared shook his head. "No. I don't know . . . Maybe. Yes." He rubbed the back of his neck. Knox's questions were confusing him. "And we dated more than a couple of times. We were together the whole summer." Why did he have a towel on his lap?

"Were you serious about Cecelia?"

"Yes." Jared dropped the empty bottle, raised the heels of his hands, and pushed against his eyelids until he saw red. His skin was tight from the sun, and his head whirled from beer and thoughts of Cecelia. He'd pay for his recklessness tomorrow.

"What do you mean Cecelia disappeared?"

The beer bottle rocked back and forth and back and forth, hitting the insides of Jared's bare feet. "After Cecelia left for college, we kept in touch."

He left out the married part because his best friend was already looking at him like he was crazy. He and Ce barely knew each other when they stood in front of a justice of the peace. Yet Cecelia knew him better than anyone else he'd ever dated.

They could talk for hours or sit together in complete silence. Even after all these years, he recalled how being with her felt so right. He'd never met anyone before or since who made him feel connected and present the way Cecelia did. Like they were joined . . . or something like that. He didn't believe in soulmates, but he sure felt that way with Ce.

"What happened?"

Right. Back to his story. "Out of the blue, my emails came

back as undelivered. She stopped answering her phone. I got worried, so I contacted the admissions office. They said she left school, and to protect her privacy, they couldn't tell me where she went. Her mom refused to talk to me, and her dad wouldn't go against anything her mom said."

He glanced at Knox. "I'm sure you remember how much Marybeth Chadwick hated me. She said rich boys were trouble, out to have our fun, and that we always marry our own kind."

"Which is exactly what you're doing by marrying Stacy."

Jared frowned at the truth. "When I came home at Christmas, I still couldn't get any answers from her family. If I called their house, they'd hang up. If I went to the door, they wouldn't answer. I stalked her brother and sister until I could get them alone. They told me they didn't know where she'd gone."

He looked out over the lake. The bright sun glistening on the water hurt his eyes. He wasn't sure where his sunglasses ended up. *Probably in the same place I left my phone.*

"That was the Christmas you went to the Cayman Islands. I only remember because you invited me along, but I stayed in Dallas, hoping Ce would come home and we could talk. She didn't. I sent letters to Arizona State University, hoping the school would forward them to her. If they did, I never heard back. I never saw or heard from her again."

"Why didn't you tell me any of this before? I had no idea you were serious about Cecelia. I thought y'all were just having a summer fling."

Jared glared at Knox. "How did you not know? Cecelia and I were together every day. You spent half your summer with us here at the lake or riding horses or swimming at the house."

Knox shrugged. "That was back in my selfish it's-all-about-me days." He cracked the water bottle open and downed half of it. "I remember the first day you brought Cecelia to the lake. We all thought you'd hit your head one too many times."

"You were the one who started everything that day of spring break, pulling over and loading those girls on the boat."

"All but Ce."

"Yeah." Jared smiled. "All but Ce. She was different, so unimpressed by college men."

"College men." Knox laughed. "We were morons."

"Yeah, we were." Jared put his head in his hands. "She and I took a walk down the beach that night and talked. When I got back to Stanford, I couldn't stop thinking about her."

"So you had Connor look for Ce because . . . ?"

He should have told Cecelia the truth while he was in New York. If the tables were turned, Knox would have just grabbed her, planted a big kiss on her mouth, and said, "Hey, baby, guess what? We're still married." Knox, who had the audacity of a hyena, wouldn't get his feelings hurt if she hauled off and slapped him. He'd just chuckle and hand over the divorce papers.

Jared stared down at his feet, watching the bottle roll back and forth, settling against one foot and then the other. "I wanted to see her to ask why she left without a word. I hoped getting an answer would settle the anger boiling inside me."

"And you're boiling with this anger because Cecelia left without telling you . . . What? That she met someone her own age? That she fell in love with her professor because you made her hunger after older men? That she couldn't stand your parents?"

Knox pointed his water bottle at Jared. "I'm having a hard time believing you were that serious about a girl four years younger than you. You and Ce were complete opposites. She was quiet and shy. You were anything but. You had money. She didn't. You were on your way to law school. She'd just finished high school. You only dated for a summer, so how serious could either of you have been?"

"Serious enough that we got married."

Knox spewed the water he just sipped.

"The anger is boiling because she served me with divorce papers with no explanation."

"You and Cecelia got married?" Knox coughed out.

"Yeah."

"When? Why didn't you tell me?"

"That was back in my selfish, it's-all-about-me days," Jared said, repeating Knox's earlier statement. "Her mom would have thrown a fit. My dad would have done far worse. I was selfish and wanted to keep what we had all to myself. And then it was over." Jared ran fingers through his hair. "I was stupid in love with her," he said, swallowing the catch in his throat.

"I'm sorry, Jared." Knox fell back against his seat. "I can't get past the fact that you got married without telling your best friend."

"Yeah, well, you can still congratulate me. The divorce was never finalized."

Knox's jaw dropped. "You're still married to Cecelia? Have you known all this time?"

"Connor found out when he drew up the prenup. I had Connor find Cecelia so I could serve her with new divorce papers—you know, paybacks and all. Except I couldn't do it. I saw her and—" Jared reached around the seat and pulled another beer out of the cooler.

Knox snatched the bottle out of his hand. "I know you bought 'em, and you're a big boy, but drinking yourself into oblivion isn't going to solve your problem, my friend."

Jared raised his head and blinked at the two Knoxs floating in front of him.

"How'd Ce look?"

"The same. No," he said, shaking his head. "She's not eighteen anymore. She looked . . . professional. Like a New Yorker. Like she belongs there instead of here with us." Jared pointed at the deck of the boat. He imagined Ce in front of him, and his heart kicked his ribs hard for several beats. "Beautiful. She looked beautiful."

The boat rocked when a speedboat shot past, and Jared closed his eyes. The violent motion made him sick, so he opened his eyes and watched the water roll toward shore after lapping at the side of the boat. Those ripples would change the face of the lake for a while and maybe even alter the shoreline in some significant way. Would that change make a difference in the long run?

All actions came with consequences. What would the consequences be if he went to see Cecelia again? Would those consequences make a difference in his life in the long run? What about her life?

"So Cecelia doesn't know you're still married?"

"Not to my knowledge."

"Does Stacy know?"

Jared shook his head. "Not yet."

"If she's the problem, I'd be happy to stuff her in a closet, lock the door, and lose the key."

Snorting, Jared pushed to his feet, but the cooler with water looked a million miles away, so he dropped back down on his seat.

Knox got up, retrieved a bottle, and handed it to Jared. "I take it Cecelia didn't remarry, or this mistake would have been discovered. Is she seeing anyone?"

"She's not living with anyone. We had dinner at a café, and I walked her home. The only trace of another guy I saw was a strip from one of those photo booths hanging on her fridge. She and a man were in all the pictures together. I asked her about a husband or boyfriends, but she didn't really give me an answer."

"You have to tell her the truth, Jared. Or have Connor break the news. Keeping her in the dark isn't fair."

"I want to be the one to tell her; I'm just not sure how." He finally glanced at Knox. "What do you think I should do?"

Knox's slow grin spread from ear to ear. "I don't know, but *please* let me be there when you tell Stacy."

CHAPTER 10

Cecelia woke early to the crack of thunder, followed closely by another that shook her bedroom window. Then the storm hit. She lay in the semidarkness for a long time, listening to the rain beating down. Memories of a day she and Jared got caught in a rainstorm wafted through her mind. Funny how a smell, a taste, or even a sound conjured memories from long ago. Rain, croaking tree frogs, pulled pork sandwiches, and now butterscotch-colored orchids were all reserved for Jared.

She dreamed of him last night. They were at a party, and she tried really hard to capture his attention, but in the end, he went home with someone else. She rolled over and pulled a pillow close, wishing she could erase the time he chose another.

Three hours later, Mia and Windy were coming out of the kitchen when Cecelia entered the office. Both women laughed as she peeled off her trench coat.

"Why do you walk when it's raining so hard outside?" Mia asked.

"I don't mind the rain, and I enjoy the walk. Besides,

traffic is a nightmare on stormy days. I'd just as soon skip the hassle of trying to hail a cab."

"We were just going to check your schedule. I need some help if you have a few minutes today," Mia said. "I have a new client who wants traditional, and you know that's not my area of expertise."

After Cecelia hung up her coat, she headed for the stairs. "I have an appointment this morning, but I'm free after lunch."

"Are you nervous about meeting the Hollywood couple?" Windy asked.

"No, I got over my nervousness about meeting famous people my first six months working with Winston. I am a little nervous about them accepting me as their designer when they expected Winston, but he assured me they were fine with the change."

"I'm glad it's you and not me," Mia said in a tone that indicated the opposite.

Windy picked up the ringing phone. "Winston and Associates, this is Windy." Her eyes widened, and she waved her free hand in the air. "Well, hello, Jared McAlister."

Cecelia stopped halfway up the stairs and put a hand to her stomach. She hadn't expected to hear from him again.

Is he calling from Dallas, or is he still in New York?

Please be in Dallas.

"Yep. Your identity has been revealed. Beautiful flowers, by the way." Windy mouthed *Oh, my gosh, it's Jared* like Cecelia missed that little tidbit. "No, she didn't seem embarrassed that you sent them. Of course, we all had to congregate in her office and try to get details."

She paused, and Cecelia started up the stairs again. "No, she didn't give out much information, just that you two dated years ago." Another pause. "As a matter of fact, she just walked through the door. When are you coming back to New York?"

"Windy!" Cecelia hissed, glaring over the banister.

"The flowers gave you away," Windy continued as if Cecelia hadn't spoken. "You wouldn't have sent them if you didn't plan on coming back." She laughed. "Hold on just a minute while I transfer you."

Cecelia's phone buzzed before she made it to her desk. She shut the door, set her briefcase on the floor, and took a steadying breath before picking up the receiver. "Cecelia Chadwick."

"Your voice could calm the savage beast."

The comment surprised her because hearing his voice made her heart race like a jackrabbit trying to outwit a predator. "Does the savage beast need calming?"

"This one does. Life is a little crazy at the moment."

"Professionally or personally?" The instant she asked, she wanted to grab the question back with both hands. She spent the weekend fighting the urge to do an internet search on Jared. Not knowing anything about his personal or professional life would be a huge plus for her peace of mind and well-being.

"Both."

Jared's answer came hesitantly, and she hoped he'd stop with that while she wound CLOSED FOR CONSTRUCTION tape around her chest. "Thank you for the orchids," she said quickly, hoping to divert the conversation to safer ground. "They're really beautiful, but you shouldn't have."

"You're welcome, and yes, I should have. I hijacked your café without warning. But I'm glad I did. It was really great to see you again, Ce."

She clutched her aching chest. "It was good to see you too, Jared."

"Do you have a busy day?"

"Very."

A long pause followed. He might have been waiting for her to ask the same question, but she didn't trust her voice.

She heard him exhale into the receiver. "I'll let you go. I just wanted to say thanks again."

He was ending the call too quickly—but that was a good thing. Disappointing, but good. So many conflicting emotions swirling around at dizzying speeds made her sick to her stomach. "I hope your life loses a little of the crazy."

"It already has. Bye, Cecelia."

"Goodbye, Jared," she said, tears springing to her eyes.

Another piece of her heart ping, ping, pinged as it bounced along the floor at her feet. *Please, don't come back to New York, Jared. Please, please, stay away.*

~

*J*ared hung up, amazed that talking to Cecelia could make his life feel so settled when it seemed anything but. He needed to tell her they were still married, and he needed to tell Stacy. Keeping the information from either of them wasn't fair, especially if Cecelia had a serious relationship with the guy in the pictures on her fridge.

Just the thought made his stomach hurt.

Violet leaned into his office. "Mr. Stern is here to see you."

"Thanks, Violet." Jared stood and buttoned his suit coat to greet one of the senior partners and a family friend of the McAlisters.

A tall man with gray hair and warm brown eyes walked into his office and smiled. "How are you, Jared?"

"Hey, Grant. Doing well." Jared indicated one of the chairs in front of his desk. "What can I do for you?"

"I heard you went to New York last week." Grant sat and propped a foot on the opposite knee.

"A personal trip."

"To the Big Apple?"

"I know. Not my favorite place."

"I keep hoping you'll change your mind about that. Though I'd miss you here, Ken Wallace would love if you transferred to his neck of the woods." Grant wrapped his hands around his ankle. "Speaking of New York, Robert Levine just fired an attorney working on a communications merger and asked if you're available."

Jared's heart jumped. "In New York."

"I can recommend someone else."

Jared shook his head. He'd been in on another deal with the communications mogul last year, and they worked well together. "No, I'll take it."

"You sure? You might be there for a week or more until the deal gets rolling."

"I'll go."

"The corporate apartment is available for you to use while you're there. Better than staying in a hotel. You have two weeks to get up to speed."

"I just closed the deal I was working on here, so I'm good to go. I'll stay as long as I need to be there."

Grant lowered his foot and sat forward. "You're putting in a lot of hours lately. Don't get me wrong. Foster, Stern, and Wallace appreciate all the hard work, but you can't have much of a life outside the office."

"I just got back from two days of personal time in New York, and I spent a day on the lake with Knox yesterday."

"How is Knox?" Grant asked with a smile.

Being a long-time friend of the family, Grant knew Knox well. "Crazy as always."

"Good. He wouldn't be Knox without some crazy." He ran

a hand down his tie. "I hope you aren't trying to appease your father by putting in all this extra time." He met Jared's gaze. "You're a good attorney, and you don't have to prove yourself to him or this firm."

Jared nodded at the man who looked so much like his father in stature, though Grant didn't exude the same air of arrogance as Charles. The men's friendship went back to grade school. Both lettered in basketball, served as best man for each other, attended Stanford together.

They were the best of friends until Jared chose Foster, Stern, and Wallace over McAlister Industries. Charles blamed the decision on Grant. The families had stopped seeing each other on holidays and special occasions. No more barbecues in the Sterns' backyard, which made Jared feel guilty. Grant assured him the break had been bound to happen sooner or later.

"I quit trying to please my dad years ago."

"Do your long work hours have anything to do with Stacy?" Grant quickly held up a hand. "Sorry, that question is out of line, but I think of you as a son. I know your parents and Stacy's are pushing this wedding, but this is *your* life, too, and who you marry should be your decision. Using the office as an escape is no way to nurture a relationship."

Grant had always been observant. He knew Jared better than his own father. "Can I tell you something that stays between us?"

"Always."

"Do you remember Cecelia Chadwick?"

Grant smiled. "Of course I do. She was a lovely young woman. Where did she end up?"

Jared couldn't have set up the question any better if he'd planned it. "New York."

Grant tipped his head, the information registering across his face. "Really?"

Jared nodded. He didn't tell Grant about their marriage. He'd find out soon enough.

His boss stood, a smile playing at the corners of his mouth. "Okay, then. Let me know if you need anything for your meeting."

"Will do. And thanks for the offer of the apartment."

~

*C*harles McAlister clicked a few keys on his keyboard to transfer money into James Decker's account. "I'd like you to start immediately, and don't use one of your employees. I want you to tail Jared yourself. Something is going on with that kid, and I want to know what before the situation gets out of hand."

"I'll get right on it, Mr. McAlister. Does he have any travel plans?"

"Not to my knowledge."

The private investigator stood and turned for the door. "I'll be in touch as soon as I have—"

"No." Charles stood. "I want a daily report this time. I want to know when he arrives at his office, when he leaves, and who he's with."

"I can't be there twenty-four/seven."

Charles gave a curt nod. "Do what you have to, but I want to know every move he makes."

"Yes, sir."

After the PI left, Charles turned toward the wall of windows behind his desk to watch the rainstorm sweeping through downtown Dallas, but instead of relieving the heat, the humidity would skyrocket.

He placed the palm of one hand against the glass and performed the exercise in self-control he taught himself in high school. Starting with his thumb, he'd press it quickly, lightly, then his index finger, middle finger, and so on, picking up speed as he went. His wife Betsy hated when he did this on her arm or her back, but the training calmed him, and he needed calm where Jared was concerned. His son was a wild card, impossible to rein in, especially when Knox Chatham was involved. Though he'd tried, he'd never been able to sever Knox and Jared's friendship.

Jared, who couldn't commit to anything, had finally proposed to Stacy. A marriage between the McAlisters and the Richardsons would benefit both families, but Charles had begun to worry that Jared would change his mind before he and Stacy made it down the aisle. Planning the wedding of the year—though great for the publicity—was taking too long. But the Richardsons insisted on giving their only child and everyone in Dallas society a night to remember.

As far as Charles was concerned, a quick trip to Vegas, though uncouth, would be preferable for sealing the deal. Maybe then the kid would finally settle down and realize working for his family was a better choice.

Jared's sister had a head for business, and she learned quickly, but being a woman, Susan didn't belong at the head of a company the size of McAlister Industries.

~

*C*ecelia followed a few steps behind the Hollywood couple as they walked through the two apartments, scribbling notes while Winston snapped pictures with her digital camera for later reference.

Her tumbling stomach had nothing to do with meeting two actors. Mr. and Mrs. were as nice as they could be and arrived with ideas about how they wanted their space to look. After going through her portfolio and talking to a couple of her clients, they were happy to let her take over the renovation.

Mrs. Hollywood already contacted the international design magazine Winston suggested. The editors were thrilled with the idea of a before and after story. Although unhappy about another article, Cecelia consented because once she saw the space, her mind spun with a million ideas.

Back in her office, she hooked her digital camera up to her laptop and started scrolling through the pictures. She'd worked with Winston long enough that he knew exactly which pictures she'd want.

She glanced up at the sound of footsteps. Tyler appeared in her doorway.

"What are you doing on this side of town again so soon?"

Tyler flashed his gorgeous smile. "I had to meet a client and finished early, so I came by to see if you're free for lunch."

He came around her desk when she stood and ran knuckles down her cheek, his eyes drinking her in. Why, oh why, couldn't she fall in love with sweet, kind, happy Tyler?

"I am free. How's your dad doing?"

"Mom said he's getting stronger every day."

"That's good news."

Minutes later, they climbed into a taxi. "How's your day going?"

"Eventful. How about yours?" she asked.

"Crazy. I presented the jeans campaign I've been working on for months. The client didn't like any of it."

"That *is* crazy." Cecelia took Tyler's hand. "I loved the campaign you showed me."

He lifted a shoulder in a you-win-some-you-lose-some shrug. "I'll go back to the drawing board after lunch. Now tell me about your eventful day."

"Winston wants me to work with a Hollywood couple

moving to New York. Their renovation will entail some things I've never done before, so I'm a little nervous."

"You? Nervous? You don't give yourself enough credit. Winston would never turn over a job he didn't think you were capable of handling."

"I know. I did see the space this morning, and the possibilities are endless."

"Do I get to know the names of this Hollywood couple?"

She shook her head. "Confidential, but you'll get to read about them in the magazine article Winston is setting up."

Tyler chuckled. "My famous little designer in another magazine article. Are you going to worry about this one the way you did about the last?"

"Of course."

He raised her hand to his lips and kissed her knuckles. "Want to tell me why national publicity scares you?"

She inhaled and held her breath a moment. "It doesn't scare me. I just . . ." her excuse faded on her exhale.

The cab stopped in front of the restaurant. Tyler must have called ahead because a table awaited them. She added thoughtful to his very long list of attributes.

After they ordered and the server moved on to another table, Tyler cleared his throat and shifted on his chair. "The friend of a friend asked me to accompany her to a wedding in two weeks."

She felt it like a bee sting, quick and shocking.

Then realization moved over her like a fog. This was the beginning of their end. Though she'd been expecting it, the pain of knowing she and Tyler didn't have a future still cut deep. Looking down, Cecelia wrapped her hand around her water glass. Tyler wanted her to protest, to get angry, to be jealous. Instead, she felt relieved that he'd decided not to wait around any longer for her feelings to change.

"I thought you should know," he added.

She blinked away the sting of tears while praying their friendship would survive, though she had her doubts.

And just like the clap of thunder that rumbled over the city, Jared McAlister and his devastating dimples appeared front and center in her mind. After years of attempting to move past the hurt, she found herself right back where she started as a teenager. He'd etched a permanent place in her heart that threatened to haunt her forever.

She reached across the table and took Tyler's hand. "I'm sorry."

He took a deep breath, his smile sad. "I know, Ce."

CHAPTER 11

*W*hen Jared got home from work, Stacy's car was taking up three-fourth of his two-car garage. He backed out and pulled into the visitor's space while wondering why she was here. She very rarely came to his condo, preferring her spacious penthouse.

Inside, he went straight to the kitchen for a beer. His bedroom door was closed. He could hear her talking—he assumed on a phone call—but couldn't make out her words.

After a swallow of his cold medicinal liquid, he walked into the living room, slumped into his recliner, and kicked off his shoes. Thanks to the upcoming meeting in New York, his workload in the office was lighter. For the first time in weeks, possibly months, he hadn't brought any work home. He leaned back and closed his eyes, propping the beer bottle on the arm of his chair.

"You can't tell me when you get home?"

Jared opened his eyes. Stacy stood in the doorway, looking appetizing in a red dress that appeared to be plastic-wrapped around her body. Her soft blond hair cascaded over her bare shoulders. "Sorry. You were on the phone, and I didn't want to interrupt."

"How long have you been here?"

"About five minutes."

Her glance flashed to his hand. "I see you had enough time to get a beer."

He ignored her comment and held out his free hand. "Come here."

"We don't have time. We're meeting Alisha and Sam for dinner."

He wiggled the fingers toward her. "Let's stay in tonight, just the two of us, snuggled on the sofa. We can order a pizza and listen to music or watch a movie."

"I've already made plans, Jared, and you know I don't eat pizza."

"Stace—"

"We have to be on the other side of town by eight-thirty."

He dropped his hand.

When he didn't move, she flung a small clutch, hitting him in the chest.

"We can't be late, or we'll lose our table. Get up. Wear the tie I gave you for your birthday. That one"—she glared at his chest—"looks like something Grammy picked out."

He was tired of her demands, tired of her never asking first, tired of fighting. And he liked this tie because Grammy *had* picked it out for him. "Just once, could you ask me before you make plans? Just one time in your life, could you consider someone other than yourself?"

"If I left decisions up to you, we'd never go out. Get up and change, Jared. We have to leave in fifteen minutes."

She said she loved him, but he couldn't see any sign of affection in her blazing brown eyes. She did love his money. Though she made plenty of her own, she liked to use his to satisfy her excessive spending habits. She loved him when he bought a ridiculously-priced purse or a pair of shoes she ordered custom-made in Italy. She loved him when he took her to expensive restaurants or fundraisers where the media could get pictures of her in a ballgown and jewels. But her love never felt as true or sincere as Cecelia's love for him.

So why were they getting married?

He closed his eyes, thoroughly disgusted with almost every aspect of his life. His relationship with his parents would always be strained because he didn't bend to their every whim. Stacy would never change. She'd always be a spoiled rich girl. Neither of them would change. Fancy dinners and his picture in the society pages would never be important to him, and she'd always need those things.

"Name one day this week we've stayed home, Stacy. Name one day in the past month when *you've* stayed home."

She walked over and kicked his chair. He opened his eyes to meet hers, glaring down at him, her nostrils flared. She didn't look very appetizing anymore.

"I'm not going out tonight." He held up her clutch, and she snatched it out of his hand. "As a heads-up, I invited Knox and his new girlfriend to meet us at the club Saturday night."

"Oh no, you didn't," she ground out between gritted teeth. "You're the most selfish person I know, Jared."

Jared couldn't stop a snort of disbelief. He leaned forward. "You want to talk about selfish, Stacy? Are you sure you want to go there tonight?"

Her jaw cocked to the side. "Are you saying I'm selfish?"

"That's exactly what I'm saying. You never consider anyone but yourself. Everything is about you and what you want. We go out every night of the week with *your* friends, and I never say a word. I invite Knox to join us one time, and you call me selfish."

Stacy's eyes narrowed dangerously. "You know I can't stand Knox. That's the only reason you invited him."

"I invited him because he's my friend."

"He's disgusting, and he's rubbing off on you."

Her slam went in one ear and out the other. "I'm not going out tonight. If that makes me selfish, I'll take my turn." He leaned back in his recliner, raised the footrest, and closed his eyes.

The slamming of the door on her way out didn't faze him.

~

Friday night, Cecelia arrived at the grand opening of Valerie's cousin's new pizza parlor. Valerie's big, noisy, wonderful family filled the whole back room. After all the cheek-kissing and hugs were exchanged, Cecelia and Val found a couple of chairs at a table topped with a bright red and white checked tablecloth and a canning jar of fresh daisies in the middle. Scents of yeast and Italian seasonings filled the air, and unexpected alternative music played in the background.

"Joey has been wanting to open his own pizza place since we were kids," Val said.

"Based on the crowd outside, I'd say his dream will be a success. Thank you," Cecelia added when they were served salads. She smiled at Val. "Have you gone out with your brother's friend yet?"

"We didn't go out, but he did survive his test of courage when he came to Sunday dinner at Mom and Dad's," Val answered around a cherry tomato.

"That's good to hear. What did you think?" Cecelia asked, pointing at the dollop of salad dressing on the corner of Val's mouth.

Rather than use a napkin, Val licked the spot. "He held his

own. We had a good time. I thought he'd bore me with talk of computers like Teddy does"—she pointed her fork at her brother who sat at the next table—"but he didn't bring up computers once. We like the same kinds of movies, though he's a Trekkie, and I'm not." She popped another cherry tomato into her mouth. "And we did have to agree to disagree on politics."

"Cute?"

Val bounced her eyebrows. "Clark Kent, black-framed glasses and all."

"Tall?" Another of their standard questions, since they were both taller than average.

"A head taller than me with heels."

"Nice." Cecelia could tell Valerie had already moved past the hurt of her Adonis boyfriend cheating with the bombshell in her office. She wouldn't hold a grudge because that wasn't Val's style. Her easygoing, kind parents raised their kids to let go of the things they couldn't change. "When do I get to meet him?"

"Let's plan a double date."

"Thank you," Cecelia said when a server arrived with their pepperoni-veggie pizza. They suspended their conversation while slices were plated.

"What do you think?" Val asked once the server left. "You, me, Tyler, and Aaron. We could meet at that new—" She narrowed her eyes. "Did you break up with Tyler?"

"No. We're going to a surprise party tomorrow night for a friend of his."

"But you're going to. I can tell by your face." Val shook her head. "I don't get you, Ce. Tyler is like the perfect guy."

"I know."

Val knew her better than anyone. They met freshman year in college when their eyes connected during a particularly boring lecture. Valerie crossed her eyes, and Cecelia laughed, attracting the attention of everyone in the lecture hall, including the professor. They'd been fast friends ever since.

"You're still hung up on *your first love*," Val said, using air quotes with one hand because she held her slice of pizza in the other.

"He found me."

Val stopped mid-bite. "What?"

"He was in New York on business."

"When?"

"Last week."

"And you're just telling me now?"

"He was waiting for me at Market City Café, thanks to Windy telling him I go there after yoga."

"Wow."

"Yeah, wow. I probably looked like a koi at the Chinese Scholar's Garden with my mouth bobbing open and closed."

"So you talked?"

Cecelia peeled a mushroom off her slice of pizza. "He did most of the talking."

"Is he married?"

"I didn't ask." At Val's *you're-nuts* look, she added, "I don't want to know."

"If you knew, you could stop obsessing."

Cecelia glanced around, but everyone was too involved in their pizzas and conversation to pay attention. "I'm not obsessing."

She'd never told Val anything about Jared other than they dated the summer before she came to New York.

Val flashed another of her you're-nuts looks as she set her slice of pizza down, wiped her hands, and pulled her phone out of her purse. "What's his name? I'll look him up, and then we'll either celebrate with dessert if he's single or commiserate over dessert if he's married."

Cecelia shook her head.

"Come on, girl. I'm curious."

Cecelia cut a piece of pizza with her fork, careful to get a mushroom in the bite.

"Until you know, you'll never move on."

Cecelia shrugged, her mouth conveniently full of pizza.

"Ce, you have a nice man. They don't come any nicer than Tyler. He's like every woman's dream."

Val had a point. Tyler had all the qualities any normal woman looked for in a man. Except he wasn't Jared. And she couldn't force feelings that weren't there. "Maybe I'm destined to be single." Cecelia peeled a green pepper off her slice of pizza and bit it in two. *Maybe I had my shot and chose the wrong man.*

"I don't believe that, and neither do you." Val selected another slice of pizza and set it on her plate. "Where does your first love live?"

"Texas."

"How did he find out you live in New York?"

"He said a mutual friend told him."

"You don't believe him?"

No, she didn't. "One, we didn't have any mutual friends, and two, I haven't kept in touch with anyone from Texas."

"He was looking for you."

That's what she thought, but— "Why?"

"Maybe he's just as in love with you as you are with—"

"Stop, Val. It's been eleven years. I'm sure he's moved on. If he's not married—"

"Was he wearing a wedding ring?"

"No." She held up a hand when Val opened her mouth. "That doesn't mean he's not married. And if he's not, then he's dating a very rich, extremely gorgeous socialite." His parents wouldn't allow it to be any other way.

CHAPTER 12

*C*ecelia walked into her apartment and set her keys on the console before she realized Tyler was standing just inside the door. She went back to him. "Do you want to come in?"

He put one hand on her hip and ran the knuckles of his other hand down her face from temple to jaw. "Not unless I can stay for breakfast."

She wrapped her fingers around his wrist. "Tyler."

"I know. Forget I said that." He shook his head and glanced around without making eye contact. "Thanks for coming to the party with me. Your Hawaiian dress was perfect for the occasion." He looked down into her eyes before pulling her close. "I still would have liked to see you in that grass skirt and coconut bra."

Cecelia smiled.

Tyler dropped his forehead to hers. "Someone really did a number on you, and I think it was the guy you had dinner with last week."

Focusing her gaze on his throat, she pressed her lips together.

"Your non-answer is answer enough." He lifted his head and framed her face with his hands. "I'm crazy about you, Ce. I know you don't feel the same, so don't say anything. I just want you to know I'd never hurt you."

"I know you wouldn't." She wrapped her arms around him, hugging him tightly, resting her cheek against his shoulder. His arms enveloped her in familiar comfort. "Besides Winston, you are the sweetest man I know, Tyler. Please believe me when I say it's not you. I know that's so cliché, but it's true. It's all me. I'm so sorry I've hurt you."

He tipped her face up and gently pressed his lips to hers. "Bye, Cecelia."

An aching loss filled her as she watched him go down the stairs to the street door. He walked out without looking back.

～

Knox and his girlfriend moved on the dance floor like they'd been together forever. They hadn't been dating long, but Jared liked Abbey. She settled Knox down, balanced him out, and they looked good together. Friends used to say he and Cecelia looked good together. He'd never thought much about the comment until now. How he and Cecelia fit, how they felt when they were together, that's what was missing with Stacy.

Where was Cecelia tonight? At some big New York City party with the guy pictured on her fridge, or were they curled up on the sofa watching a movie and enjoying each other's company?

Where would *he* be right now, at this moment, if Ce hadn't walked out of his life? He imagined they'd be in their home with one, maybe two kids snuggled safely in their beds. He'd have his head in Cecelia's lap, and she'd be playing with his hair while she read to him in her soft voice.

He couldn't picture that scenario with Stacy. There would be no kids or reading aloud. There wouldn't be—

"This is a great club, Jared. Thanks for inviting us," Abbey said, interrupting his thoughts.

"Glad you and Knox came." He tipped his beer up and took a long pull. He was already drunk and planned to get even more so before the end of the night.

He tried to focus on Knox, who watched him with a raised brow.

Stacy bounced over and grabbed his arm. "Jare Bear, come dance with me."

"Hello, Stacy." Knox drew out her name, complete with his deep Southern drawl.

Stacy shot him one of her ominous glares.

Knox laughed.

"Stacy, th's is Abbey Wil-ams. Wil'ams. Wil-li-ams."

"You date Knox on purpose?" Stacy asked Abbey with a sneer.

I need another beer.

Knox slung an arm over Abbey's shoulder. "Ignore Stacy, darlin'. She's been a selfish, self-absorbed witch since birth."

Stacy rolled her eyes and yanked on Jared's arm. "Let's dance, Jare."

Jared set his empty beer bottle on the bar too close to the edge. Abbey caught it before it hit the floor. He tried to smile his thanks, but his face seemed to be numb. Or lopsided. He wiggled his jaw, which felt strangely loose.

The image of his head in Cecelia's lap fogged his mind, and he closed his eyes. He could hear her voice over the pulse of the music, feel her fingers in his hair, on his face. He could smell her perfume. She smiled, and he couldn't breathe.

His eyes popped open when he stumbled. Stacy moved in

front of him. Exotic. Sexy. He tried to keep up with her, to follow her moves, but his legs weighed too much. Stacy grabbed his hands and rested them on her hips. He shuffled lead feet. At least he thought he was shuffling. He glanced down. *Yep, feet are moving.*

"Why did you invite them, Jared?" Stacy hissed near his ear. Her face weaved in and out of view as she moved around him while jabbing him in the chest with a long fingernail. But she knew why. They'd discussed this. Or had he just imagined their conversation?

He glanced toward the bar and spotted Cecelia standing close to Knox, watching him, frowning. Blinking brought her into focus. He smiled. Waved. Blinked once more, and Cecelia vanished. Again. Gone without a word. Instead, Abbey waved back.

I need another drink.

Yanked from behind when he turned for the bar, his shirt buttons rained onto the floor. He tried to gather the white material together where it gaped open, but his fingers wouldn't work. "Stace . . . you ruined my sh-shirt."

The weight of an arm on his shoulder almost toppled him. "Come on, buddy. Give your keys to Stacy, and I'll drive you home. You've had enough to drink tonight." Knox swiped a cut-off sign when the bartender stopped in front of them.

Jared held up his hand to stop the guy, but he walked away. "Hey!"

"I don't want to drive home alone."

Knox smirked at Stacy. "What's the matter, *princess*? You don't know your way?"

"Shut up, you country hick."

"Oh, ouch." Knox put a hand to his heart, but his expression turned hard instantly. "As you can see, Jared can't drive, so you'll have to either drive his car home, find another ride, or come with us."

She stuck her chin out and jammed fists on her hips. "It's not even midnight yet."

Knox pulled his wallet out of his pocket and handed it to Abbey. "Give princess, here, fifty bucks for a taxi ride home, will you, baby?"

Jared tried to step between them, but Stacy shoved him aside, so he leaned over the bar and snapped his fingers. Then he lifted his hand to his ear and snapped again. *Yep, fingers are working.*

A strong grip pulled him away. "No, buddy. You're done for the night."

Stacy held out her hand. "Give me your wallet, Jared."

Jared reached for his back pocket, but Knox stopped him. "Either you take my money or get a ride with a friend."

Looking back and forth between Stacy and Knox made him dizzy. They were arguing about money, but he had money. He reached for his wallet again.

"I've got this, Jared," Knox said.

"I need 'nother drink." *Why can't I get a drink?* Jared leaned over the bar. "Hey! Am I invis- in . . . Can you see me?"

Someone spun him around, and he lost his balance, hitting the floor hard.

*W*hen Jared blinked, dashboard lights—*his* dashboard lights—hurt his eyes. He couldn't remember getting into the car. He rolled his head on the seat and squinted, focusing on the driver. Knox. *But where is Ce?* She'd been reading to him. "Where's Cecelia?"

Knox chuckled. "You mean Stacy? Your fiancée? Or maybe you do mean your wife. I'm having trouble keeping up with you lately."

Jared closed his eyes, trying to clear his clouded mind. The picture of Cecelia reading to him had been so clear. But she was in New York with someone else.

"Why are you—?" His tongue weighed two hundred pounds. He stuck it out to look but could only see the tip.

"You're an idiot. You can't keep this up, buddy. You're going to turn into a version of me or die trying."

Jared tried to laugh but coughed instead.

Knox cast a worried glance. "Are you going to hurl?"

"No-o."

"You sure? Do I need to pull over?"

"No." He swallowed to get the next words out. "I haf'ta go to New York in a week."

"Yeah? You going to break the we're-still-married news to Ce?"

"I should." Jared rubbed his burning eyes. "I don't wanna divorce."

Knox blew out a low whistle. "Maybe you should get away for a few days to clear your head. Take a vacation."

"Maybe." *A vacation away from Dad. And Stacy.*

"We could fly down to the gulf and do some fishing."

He blinked one of the Knoxes away. "We haven't gone fishin' in a long time."

"See if you can get away next weekend. We'll rent a house and a boat for a few days. I'll call a couple of the guys and see who can come with us."

Blinking didn't help, so Jared squinted. "You serious? Could you get 'way for a long weekend?"

Knox chuckled. "I'm the boss. I can take a vacation any time I want. Let me make some calls, and you find out if you can take off Friday and Monday." Knox glanced over and shook his head. "Are you going to remember this tomorrow?"

"Yeah, I'll 'member." Jared let his lids slide shut over his burning eyes.

"Jared." Knox pushed on his shoulder. "Stacy is *not* invited."

"Not 'nvited," Jared mumbled, relieved by his friend's command.

~

*S*crolling through the pictures James Decker sent didn't ease a father's suspicions. The PI knew what Charles wanted from him. He'd been on and off Jared duty since the kid left for college.

Decker sent several videos of Jared downing beer after beer, stumbling around a bar with his shirt open to his navel. Luckily the media hadn't been out to capture that image for the Dallas papers. The kid might manage to ruin the family name yet, and Charles couldn't think of any way to stop him other than getting him married.

In his opinion, Knox wasn't upper class in the brains department, but he'd been smart enough to stop his very drunk friend from driving home on Saturday night. One picture revealed Jared on the floor of the bar, the next showed Knox almost carrying him to the car. The last was Knox helping Jared from the car to his townhouse.

The report said Knox and an unnamed female went inside for about ten minutes. Then they left in the car Decker identified as Knox's. The girl must have followed them. Stacy stayed behind with a group of her friends.

Stacy called this morning, upset because Jared had decided to fly to Mobile with Knox and a few buddies for a long weekend and then was headed back to New York with no return date.

Her fury stemmed from a double standard, in Charles's

opinion. She often traveled for work and pleasure, and if Jared had something on the side, he wasn't the only one. Decker had taken plenty of photos of Stacy with her daddy's stable manager on more than one occasion.

Charles wouldn't hesitate to go to her with those pictures once she and Jared were married if she continued. A cheating scandal *would not* disgrace the McAlister family name. Her relationship with a stable hand was as inappropriate as the one Jared fell into with that gold-digging Chadwick girl.

He sent a quick email informing Decker of Jared's travel plans, with the order to stay on him. He wanted to know everything his kid did on this long weekend with his so-called buddies.

After saving the PI's report and photos to a private folder, he pressed the intercom button on his phone.

"Yes, Mr. McAlister?"

"Polly, call for a town car. I have to go out."

"Would you like me to reschedule your eleven-fifteen meeting?"

"No, I'll be back before that, but call my wife and cancel our lunch reservations." His impromptu meeting would relieve him of listening to Betsy's incessant, meaningless chatter about wedding details. He didn't care what color the napkins were or whether they served artichokes or carrots with the chicken. He'd just be glad when the wedding was over, and Betsy's life could go back to pink or purple pillows on the sun porch sofa.

His intercom beeped. "Yes?"

"The car will be here in five minutes, Mr. McAlister."

"Thank you." Charles stood and buttoned his suit coat. *Time for a long-overdue chat with a former friend.*

CHAPTER 13

*C*ecelia jumped when a hand touched her shoulder.

"Sorry." Winston chuckled. "I didn't mean to scare you, sweetheart."

She put one hand to her heart while she pulled out an earbud with the other. "I didn't hear you come in."

"You must have had the music up loud to miss my heavy steps."

Cecelia had been in the zone. She rolled her neck and glanced at the time on the antique mantel clock. She'd been sitting at her work table for a couple of hours without a break. "We missed you yesterday."

"I spent the day in Montauk with Binky."

Cecelia couldn't call Winston's oldest and dearest client, Barbara, by the nickname given to her in infancy. A stylish philanthropist, she finagled Winston into decorating the venues for her many benefits—not that he minded donating his time and talents for a good cause. "How is she?"

"Agitated when she called and asked me to come to her house. She saw a couple of pillows in a magazine and insisted she had to have them. When I arrived, she'd forgotten all about the pillows but had several other projects saved up for me." He lifted a shoulder in a half shrug. "She's lonely. You'd think with all the family she has, one of them could spend a little time with her. I'm sure when she finally meets her expiration date, her drawing-room will be overflowing with long-lost relatives."

"That's sad."

He nodded and pulled a chair close. "I see you've started on the Hollywood couple's renovation."

She turned to her work. "I have. What do you think?"

"These look great. I like the built-in bookcases in the den. Has Mrs. Hollywood decided when they can sit down with the architect?" Winston flipped the top computer printout to look at the next one.

"They're working around her husband's filming schedule. She said she should know something by next week."

"Did you enjoy the surprise party with Tyler?"

Her throat tightened. "We had a nice time."

"But?"

She felt Winston's eyes on her before she glanced his way. Her feelings were still tender after the finality of Tyler's goodbye. "But nothing. It was fun."

Winston flipped another computer printout. "You know, I've been thinking, before you get all caught up in this renovation, why don't you and Val take a girls' trip? Go to some exotic beach for a week, or go visit your family in Texas. You must get homesick."

Cecelia never felt homesick for the house she grew up in, but she did miss Texas. She also missed her brother and sister. Despite her parents' neglect, they had a good childhood. Countless nights they'd curled up together on Jenny or Derrick's bed and read bedtime stories.

When spring storms rolled in, with thunder crashing and lightning flashing, she'd lie awake, waiting to hear Derrick's little footsteps running down the hall to her room. Well before morning, Derrick *and* Jenny would be snuggled under the covers of her twin bed, and she'd be on the floor where she could comfort them if the thunder started again.

"I'll go home for Christmas. My brother can't get leave until then."

He studied her for a long minute before he pushed to his feet. "You should call Val and get away for a few days."

"I'll think about it."

"Which means no," he said, raising a brow.

He knew her too well.

After he left her office, her thoughts returned to her brother and sister. She used to babysit neighborhood children to earn enough money to take Derrick and Jenny to the small carnival that passed through town once a year. She'd buy them ride tickets, popcorn, and cotton candy. She could never quite satisfy Jenny, who always wanted more, but Derrick was completely thrilled in his wide-eyed, little-boy way.

Cecelia forever felt like she could have done more. She remembered the agony of leaving them behind when she went to college. Sixteen-year-old Jenny stood at the curb, angry because she wasn't the one leaving. Derrick, at twelve, had decided he was too old to let her see his tears. Scrubbing his eyes, he complained of a sudden allergy.

Jenny had stalked into the house, leaving Derrick alone. Cecelia hugged him tightly. He held on while stifling a sob. As the shuttle pulled away from the curb, she watched him shrink in the distance until the driver turned the corner. She'd sobbed all the way to the airport.

When her phone rang, grateful for the interruption of her thoughts, Cecelia pushed away from her work table to answer. "Cecelia Chadwick."

"Good morning, Cecelia."

The unexpected voice on the other end almost caused her to drop the receiver. She put a trembling hand to her stomach, completely shaken, because of her delight at hearing from him. "Good morning, Jared."

"How are you?"

"I-I'm doing well." She sat down behind her desk. "How are you?"

"Busy." He waited a beat. "It's good to hear your voice."

"It's good to hear your voice, too." She put a hand to her mouth. The words had come so naturally.

His chuckle floated over her, warm and familiar. "I'll be in New York next week, and I'm calling to see if we could have dinner."

Another piece of her heart tumbled out of her chest, the hole growing too large to putty over. "Uh . . . I'm not sure it's a good idea."

"Why?"

A million reasons.

"Come on, Ce. Two exes getting together for a friendly dinner? We'd be poster material for a therapist."

A smile tugged at the corners of her mouth before reason kicked in. *Absolutely not a good idea.* "I'm busy at work."

"I'm not coming tomorrow."

Her heart screamed *NO!* while the rest of her body whispered *Yes.* Again, reason reared its sensible head. "Let's see how things fall when you're here. I don't want to say yes and then not be able to get away."

She heard him blow out a breath. Had she frustrated him? *Good. Still, doesn't come close to what you did to me eleven years ago. Or what you're doing to me now.*

"Do you have anything fun planned for the weekend?"

Neutral ground felt safe underfoot. Cecelia glanced at the bouquet of orchids. Several of the flowers had fallen off the stems, but she couldn't bring herself to throw the petals away. Instead, she'd wrapped them in a tissue and stowed them in her desk drawer. How pathetic could she get? "I'm going to an antique show."

"That sounds interesting."

"What about you?"

"I'm going to the gulf for some fishing."

A weekend getaway. "That sounds fun."

"It will be nice to get out of town. Dallas is like an oven."

She could relate. New York was still hot.

"I better let you get back to work. Please, think about dinner, Ce."

"I will. Have a great vacation."

"Thanks. You have fun at your antique show."

As soon as Cecelia disconnected the call, Windy appeared at her door.

"Jared is so nice."

Cecelia took a deep breath to settle her quivering stomach, wishing she could control the thrill and trepidation that settled like oil and water, coexisting but not mixing well. "He is—was. I don't really know him anymore."

"Seems he'd like to change that." Windy held out a contract needing a signature.

"No matchmaking, Windy."

"What?" Windy asked with wide-eyed innocence. "I'm just stating the obvious."

"You're wrong, so leave it alone."

When Windy left her office, Cecelia pushed out of her chair and walked to the windows. For some reason, the Fourth of July she and Jared spent together drifted through her mind. They went to the lake with a gang of his friends, and after a cookout, they sat on blankets looking skyward as fireworks were shot from a barge.

Jared had been subdued at first but finally admitted he and his father fought earlier that day. When she asked what the fight was about, he redirected her attention to the shower of sparks raining through the dark sky. She knew then that they'd argued about her.

Charles McAlister's dislike of her was blatantly obvious. He judged her by where she lived. He judged her by her parents' jobs and by their small house. She worked in a bookstore, couldn't afford designer clothes, didn't have her hair done at an expensive salon. She was a nobody in his eyes.

She wondered how Mr. McAlister would react if he knew she and his son had dinner together.

～

*C*harles McAlister took the elevator to the eighteenth floor. When he stepped out, the glass doors of Foster, Stern, and Wallace were straight ahead. He entered the offices, and a receptionist sitting behind a large wooden desk looked up.

"Can I help you?"

"I'm here to see Grant Stern."

She turned to a computer. "Do you have an appointment?"

"No. Tell him Charles McAlister is here."

She picked up the phone and called someone, probably Grant's assistant. He waited at the floor to ceiling windows. He didn't like coming here to ask rather than tell.

A woman appeared at his side. "Mr. McAlister? Mr. Stern can see you."

He followed her down a hall. Grant waited for him at the door of a big corner office. He held out his hand. "Charles, come in. It's good to see you."

They shook hands.

"Please hold my calls while Mr. McAlister is here, Anita,"

he said, then waved Charles into his office. "What brings you in this morning? You need a good merger and acquisitions attorney?"

Grant's attempt at humor didn't amuse Charles. At one time, perhaps, but not anymore. "I had some business near here."

Grant indicated a chair in front of his desk. "How's Betsy?"

Charles ran a hand over his tie before he sat. "She's fine. Busy with all her little committees. They make her feel useful." Actually, his wife continued to drive him crazy in her usual ways. His mother mentioned sprucing up her dining room, and, not to be outdone by her mother-in-law, Betsy suggested she might need to do a little sprucing up herself.

Although not here for idle chit-chat, he felt obliged to mention Grant's wife. "I trust Jessie and the girls are well." Grant had married beneath him, and then he hadn't been able to produce a son, so he'd seen fit to seize Jared. By doing so, Grant had destroyed their longtime friendship.

"Jess and the girls are fine," Grant said, taking his chair.

"How's Jared doing at work?" he asked, moving on to the reason for his visit.

"Excellent."

"Stacy is having a hard time getting him involved with wedding planning."

Grant propped his elbows on the arms of his chair and steepled his fingers. "I think it's pretty normal for a man not to care about the wedding favors."

"Still, he should be more concerned. Jared's always been erratic and undependable. I've had to clean up his messes since he was a boy. And that Chatham kid has been a bad influence since they were kids—still is, in my opinion—and Jared just follows along like a puppy instead of being the leader he should be."

Charles hated the smug look on Grant's face as he tapped his fingertips together. "It's probably not wise to tell one of the senior partners of the law firm your son works for that his employee is erratic and undependable. Lucky for you, I know Jared."

Charles leaned forward. "You, of all people, should remember how many times I've had to bail Jared out of trouble."

"Those were childhood troubles, Charles. Jared isn't breaking into abandoned warehouses or egging people's houses anymore. He's a responsible, hardworking adult."

"He's making too many trips to New York to help his fiancée plan their wedding. Why?"

"Jared is Foster, Stern, and Wallace's best junior attorney. One of our New York clients requested him over any of our other attorneys. Your son is building an excellent reputation for himself. You should be proud, Charles. He followed through with the senior partner's request to take the New York State bar exam, which made a substantial difference in his salary and will influence the senior partners' decision when advancement positions open up. I'm sorry, but I'm not going to stop him if he chooses to go to New York."

Charles stood. He'd wasted enough of his time trying to talk sense into Grant. He'd have to take matters into his own hands. "Then I'll stop him."

∼

*G*rant waited just outside Jared's office while Jared finished with a call. "Hey, Grant," he said as soon as he hung up

"Have you got a minute?"

"Sure." Jared indicated one of the chairs in front of his

desk. He could tell Grant had something on his mind when he ran a finger under his lower lip. "What can I do for you?"

Grant sat on the edge of his chair and blew out a breath. "Your father just left my office. He isn't happy about your New York trips."

Jared wiggled his jaw to keep from grinding his teeth. He wouldn't be free of his father's meddling as long as he lived in Dallas. After graduation, he'd considered taking a job in California. Maybe he should have. He inhaled, then exhaled slowly to calm his anger. "I'm sorry he bothered you."

"I can handle your dad. I told him I wouldn't stop you from going if that's what you choose."

Jared looked down at his desk, then met Grant's gaze. "I just found out I'm married."

Raised eyebrows were Grant's only response.

"Cecelia and I got married before I left for law school. She filed for divorce shortly after. When I went in to talk to Connor Scopello about a prenup two weeks ago, he informed me the divorce had never been filed."

"Huh," came out on a huff.

"Yeah. I haven't told anyone but Knox. I went to New York to serve Cecelia with divorce papers, but I didn't."

"She doesn't know?"

"Not that I know of, and I'm not sure how to tell her. Or Stacy."

"Does Stacy know you were previously married?"

"No. She's going to explode."

Grant uncrossed his leg and sat forward, a frown settling over his face. "How did this happen?"

"I was shocked when I received divorce papers from Cecelia's attorney. I tried to contact her, but she'd disappeared. After trying to find her, without any luck, I signed the papers and sent them back." He held up a hand to stop

Grant's next question. "Yes, I had an attorney look over the papers. Cecelia wanted nothing from our brief marriage."

Grant nodded like he might have expected that news.

"When Connor told me, I went home and found the final decree, in the same envelope in which it was mailed, unopened. The judge never signed the paperwork. I never thought to check. I guess Cecelia didn't check either."

"I assume your family doesn't know."

Jared rubbed the back of his neck. "No."

"I remember your dad didn't like Cecelia."

"Hence the reason they never knew. Dad would have done everything in his power and beyond to have our marriage annulled."

"Why did Cecelia file for divorce?"

Jared swiveled his chair to stare out the window. "The divorce papers didn't come with an explanation, so I have no idea."

"You didn't ask her when you saw her?"

"She said we were silly to get married so young, especially since we were both going off to school. When I asked why she didn't talk to me first, she said NYU offered her a full-ride scholarship after the semester started, and she had to rush to catch up and find a job." Jared glanced toward Grant and nodded at the look of skepticism that crossed his face. "Yeah, sounded like a quickly made-up excuse to me, too."

Grant stood and, with hands in pants pockets, slowly paced in front of Jared's desk. "She hasn't remarried, or the mistake, more than likely, would have been discovered."

"She's not married, and she lives alone."

"You know you have to tell her, Jared," Grant said, making eye contact. "It's not fair that she doesn't know."

"I plan to take divorce papers to New York with me."

CHAPTER 14

*J*ared flipped the bumpers overboard, hopped onto the dock, and tied a few hitch knots to secure the boat to the hot metal cleats. He also secured the bow and stern lines since they wouldn't be back until morning.

They had a good day on the water, caught a few fish they let go. Tomorrow they'd catch dinner. This group of high school friends hadn't gone on a fishing trip together in years, mostly because all but he and Knox were married with kids, making it hard for them to get away.

"When are you going to New York?" Knox wasn't one to duck and elude. He went straight for the jugular.

"Tuesday."

Knox pulled the keys from the ignition and pocketed them. "You going to tell Ce you're still married?"

"I'll take the divorce papers with me."

"So you've decided."

"I don't have a choice. She deserves to know the truth."

He jumped aboard and started collecting trash into a

plastic bag, then held the bag open for Knox to drop some things inside. "I can't let her go on thinking she's divorced."

"Have you ever considered that your dad might have had something to do with Cecelia's disappearance? You know the only person he hated more than me was Cecelia."

Jared snorted. "No. My dad's reach is long, but . . ."

Knox raised his brows when Jared's reply dwindled. "I could get you into trouble, and I usually did"—Knox said with a smirk—"but Cecelia would have meant more than just casual trouble for the McAlister Empire. If Charlie suspected you two were serious, he'd step in."

"I wouldn't put it past him, but Cecelia would never have been involved with my dad." Even as he made the comment, his mind screeched to a halt. "He didn't know we got married."

"Just something to think about," Knox said with a shrug. "You know, still being married could be advantageous."

"Not if Cecelia doesn't want to be married, and not if I have a fiancée." They climbed out of the boat and headed for Knox's truck, stuffing the trash in a can at the end of the dock.

"There's an easy remedy to that second problem. Get rid of your fiancée. In fact, why do you have a fiancée?" Knox asked, pointing the remote to unlock the doors.

They'd dropped Troy, Mateo, and Brock at the dock of a restaurant to hold a table, so Jared felt free to talk. "I won't after my granddad's birthday party next weekend."

"That's the smartest thing I've heard you say in a very long time, buddy." Knox slung an arm around Jared's neck. "That encounter won't be pleasant."

Yeah, he wasn't looking forward to telling Stacy he couldn't marry her.

. . .

*T*he next night Jared gazed out the window of their rental house. A storm had moved onshore, and rain came down so hard it obscured the coastline. Lightning flashed against the black sky, and thunder cracked and then rolled for a solid thirty seconds before the next flash of lightning. Reports said the storm would blow through quickly, and blue skies were in the forecast for tomorrow.

Laughter from the guys around the poker table behind him echoed through the cathedral-ceilinged house. After a dinner of fried grouper and hushpuppies, they'd settled in the dining room with cigars Knox picked up in Cuba and several bottles of Wild Turkey.

He hadn't thought about Stacy much since his talk with Knox yesterday, which shot a twinge of guilt through him because he'd thought about Cecelia plenty.

When he told Stacy about this trip to the gulf with friends, they fought like demons before she ran to his parents to intervene. His dad called, demanding he cancel. His mom called, insisting he take Stacy along. Stacy accused him of taking a woman with him. Jared bit off a sarcastic, *Women are exactly what I'm trying to escape.*

Thoughts of Cecelia invaded his quest for peace. He knew he needed to tell her the truth, but over the past week, his need for answers circled back around. He wanted closure. He wanted to find a reason to forgive.

Knox's suggestion that his dad had been involved in Cecelia's disappearance left him tossing and turning last night. Charlie would have done everything possible to end his and Cecelia's marriage if he'd known. Now that Knox had planted the idea in his mind—like the frozen images of Cecelia and the man held to her fridge by a magnet—he couldn't seem to shake it free. If Charlie *was* responsible, how had he managed to make it happen?

And again, Cecelia and that man cheek-to-cheek in those photos ran through his head. Why did seeing her with another man hurt like a knife to the gut? He wouldn't want her to be unhappy. She'd chosen a life in New York, and she'd chosen to live it without him.

That was the killer.

He'd deliver the divorce papers when he was in New York next week, even as maybes and what-ifs rolled through his mind. She was four years younger, just graduating from high school, with her whole life ahead of her. Leaving Texas and all her family responsibilities had to be freeing. Though, deep down, he knew she'd never disappear on her brother and sister. They were a responsibility she'd never walk away from.

The scholarship thing still niggled like an itch just out of reach. Something just didn't seem quite right with her story.

"Ready for another hand, Jared?"

He put the cigar between his lips, inhaled deeply, and puffed out a cloud of smoke. He'd smoked a cigar at a pool party that summer long ago. Cecelia had wrinkled her nose in distaste and refused to kiss him.

He walked over to the table and snuffed the cigar out before sitting down to the cards he'd been dealt—both then and now.

~

*C*harles moved his jaw back and forth to release some of the tension before slowly opening the envelope of pictures the courier delivered earlier. Meetings all morning had kept him away from his desk.

He slipped the photos out and spread them over his desk in the order Decker had stacked them. Decker had blown the pictures up, enhancing details as much as possible.

The private investigator's report said no women were present, and the pictures showed none. Just Jared and four other men, all of whom he recognized as his son's derelict high school friends. Pictures of them getting on and off a boat, pictures through a window—five of them playing poker, smoking cigars, and passing around the Wild Turkey. Lots of empty beer bottles in a shot of the outside garbage can. It had been a harmless weekend getaway for five men, nothing he would have to clean up after.

He slipped the pictures back into a manilla envelope, turned to his computer, and typed a simple, *Thank you, Decker,* before hitting send.

Then he opened his bank account and transferred funds into Decker's account.

Charles knew from Stacy that Jared was going to New York in two days. After looking through these pictures, Charles didn't see any reason to have the kid followed.

Leaning back in his chair, he set his hands on the desktop and closed his eyes. One by one, he pressed his fingers against the leather blotter, searching for calm. He had needed calm when dealing with Jared ever since the kid met Knox Chatham, a friendship Charles wished he could sever as neatly as he'd severed his own friendship with Grant.

Pushing away from his desk, he opened his office safe. The photos joined stacks of others.

CHAPTER 15

After her yoga class, Cecelia showered and dressed in a white wrap skirt and a cropped baby blue top. Lunch had come and gone while she shopped with Mia's traditional client. Then she stopped at Mr. Basketball's loft to discuss a problem with the electrician, who didn't think a *woman her age* knew anything about outlets and regulations. By the time she finished, she had to rush to her yoga class with no time to order dinner.

She ran down the stairs of the fitness center. Pushing the door open, she squinted against the bright sunlight.

"Hi."

The familiar voice stopped her. She whirled around as all breath left her lungs. Jared flashed his dimples like waiting for her outside the fitness center was an everyday occurrence.

She put a hand to her stomach as nausea washed over her. "You're here. In New York."

He took a step closer. "I have business meetings this week, so I thought I'd surprise you."

"You succeeded." Though he said he'd be back, she'd expected a call before actually seeing him.

He wore jeans and a polo, his arms tanned. She wanted to touch him, feel his sun-warmed skin to make sure he wasn't a mirage brought on by the heat and hunger—while also wishing he'd disappear with the blink of an eye.

"Are you free for dinner?"

A silly thrill buzzed up her spine—one she wanted to punch with a fist and then stomp flat. She wanted to be busy, to have a date, to be able to think of an excuse why she couldn't. Instead, she nodded. "I-I'm free."

"Do you want to go to the place on the corner?"

"No," she responded quickly. She loved Market City Café. Now it would be forever tainted with memories of their one dinner together. Better not to make it two.

He held out his arms. "This is your city. Where would you like to go?"

Somewhere close. Somewhere they could walk so that she wouldn't be enclosed in a taxi with him. Somewhere that served food quickly, keeping their conversation short. Somewhere she could sit to get off her shaking knees. So much for her yoga relieving any stress. "There's a pizza place around the corner."

"I love pizza."

I remember.

"Which way?"

Cecelia pointed in the opposite direction of Market City Café, and they set off. Her mush brain searched for something—*anything*—to discuss. "You never told me how you came to be working for Grant Stern rather than McAlister Industries. I remember meeting Grant and his wife, Jessie, several times that . . . summer." Ack! She hadn't meant to mention the past. "They were very nice people."

"They still are. Grant's more like a dad to me than my own father."

"Isn't it strange we both have someone in our lives like that? Winston, my boss, and his wife are like surrogate parents to me."

"Not strange. Lucky," he said with a grin.

Agreed. "Extremely lucky."

"To answer your question, I never had any intention of working for McAlister Industries."

"Your dad told me you'd agreed to be the in-house attorney."

Jared's eyes narrowed. "When?"

His reaction surprised her. "I don't remember exactly. Sometime before you left for law school."

"I'm sure he told you a lot of things to discourage our relationship."

More than she cared to remember. She'd never liked Charles McAlister, but she'd never taken him to be dishonest. Another wave of nausea washed over her. What other lies had he told?

"I almost took a job in California when Grant called with an offer too good to pass up."

She stopped in front of an Italian restaurant. "Do you like working for Grant?"

"I love it," he said, pulling the door open.

They were lucky enough to snag the last table in the compact basement restaurant. When selecting a place close and fast, she didn't take into account how tightly packed they would be. The table was so small, Jared had to sit at an angle, so their knees weren't banging together every time they moved.

"This place is busy."

"They make a great pizza."

His expression softened. "How is it your smile makes the day better?"

She hadn't realized she was smiling. Suddenly self-conscious, she attempted a neutral expression. "Has your day been so bad?"

"Not bad, just long, but I can't complain. My meeting went well, and I expect tomorrow to be as productive."

"I imagine joining two companies together can be complicated."

"It can be at times."

She felt her cheeks heat under his scrutiny. He touched the bridge of her nose with the tip of his finger. In their tight quarters, she couldn't have moved away, even if she wanted to.

"You still blush."

When he folded his hands on the table, the memory of their wedding night flashed through her mind. His gentle hands running over her waist, along her hips, quieting the fears of her first time. The way he kissed her like she was the most precious thing in the world.

That didn't last long.

"Tell me what you're working on," he said.

She glanced at the couple sitting next to them, two people in love by the way they were looking at each other. "In a way, I'm working on a merger too. A family bought two apartments, one over the other, and I'm joining them together."

"Sounds complicated. Have you ever done anything like that before?"

She shook her head, feeling connected in a merger sense. *So silly.* "First time."

"Congratulations, Ce."

The waitress stopped next to their table, and Jared picked up the menu. "Do you still like pepperoni with veggies?"

"Anything is fine."

After Jared ordered, he turned to her and exhaled, his shoulders sagging slightly. He flashed a tight smile. "The merger isn't the only reason I'm in New York."

~

"*W*hy else are you here?"

He'd missed her expressive eyes, wanted to reach out and smooth the little line that suddenly appeared between her eyebrows. It would never occur to Cecelia that he would be here to see her. How could she still be so naïve, especially after living in a city like New York for so long? "I came to see you."

He watched the puzzled expression fall from her face, replaced by surprise. "Why?"

You have a calming effect on me, Ce. After a long flight and a busy day at the office, I needed more than just hearing your voice. I needed to see you, to be near you. "You make me smile. You calm my racing mind."

Another blush touched her cheeks as she shook her head. "There's something else. I see it in your eyes."

"You were always good at reading me." He looked down at his hands, wishing they were alone. "There is something else, but I'd rather wait until we aren't surrounded by a crowd."

When he glanced up, her little line of worry had returned. "Are you okay?" she asked.

Of course she'd be worried about him rather than herself.

"I'm fine," he replied. "It's nothing terrible."

Life-changing, but not terrible.

"And you expect us to eat dinner like this elephant isn't sitting between us now?"

He chuckled. "Wasn't there already an elephant sitting between us?"

Their drinks and salads were delivered. Cecelia spread a

napkin over her lap. "Tell me about the two companies you're merging"—she glanced up—"if the information isn't secret."

She'd separated herself from the present, the elephant set aside for now. She was an expert at doing that early in their relationship. Perhaps a quality she'd acquired when dealing with her parents' neglect.

She asked about his job, something his fiancée never did. Stacy couldn't be bothered with his everyday details unless it benefitted her in some way. Although comparing Cecelia and Stacy was unfair. They were two very different people who'd been raised in two very different worlds. Still, that Cecelia asked about his day was nice.

He needed to tell her they were still married but decided to keep Stacy's name out of the conversation. No reason to reveal the mess he'd gotten himself into.

"No. I'd rather hear about your day."

She picked at her salad, again, not making eye contact. "I had a good day."

"How was it good?"

"I have a client who's happy with the way his loft is turning out." She set her fork down and picked up her water glass. "And we're ahead of schedule, which makes him even happier."

He swallowed his bite of salad. "A happy client is a good thing. Mind if I ask a personal question?"

Her eyes narrowed. "You can ask, but I don't promise to answer."

The defensive answer made him smile. "It's nothing bad. I was just curious how often your clients ask you out."

He watched her physically relax. What question had she been expecting?

"Why would you ask that?" She moved the salad she

hadn't touched so the waitress could set their pizza on the small table.

"Thank you," he said, handing his empty salad plate to the waitress. "If I were one of your clients, I'd ask you out."

She plated a slice of pizza and held it out for him. "I've only dated one client, and we didn't go out until after he wasn't a client anymore."

"Are you still dating him?"

"Time to change the subject. This one's making me uncomfortable."

Jared chuckled. "Okay. Tell me what you did for this client who isn't a client anymore instead."

~

*I*n her opinion, his question didn't change the subject because they were still talking about Tyler in a roundabout way. "I redecorated the suite of offices where he works."

"Was he happy with the results?"

Cecelia took a sip from her water glass while fighting a smile. Was this an ex-husband inquiring, or Attorney Jared McAlister keeping the witness slightly off-balance? "He asked me out, so I guess he was happy enough."

Jared flashed his dimples, then turned, bumping his knee against hers, his expression conveying an air of confidence she'd always envied. "Will you take me sightseeing the next time I'm in town?"

Another piece of her heart dropped away. She took a bite of pizza and chewed slowly, formulating her answer. "I'm really busy at work. I just started the *big merger*, and I'm in the middle of another, so I don't have much free time."

He laughed. "This conversation is so déjà vu. The day we

met on the lake"—he tipped his finger and thumb between them—"same exchange."

On the pretense of wiping her mouth, Cecelia hid a smile behind her napkin.

"I'll make it easy for you. I'll come prepared with a list of things I'd like to see." He leaned forward. "Show me some reasons to like this place. Grant would love it if I moved to the New York office."

Her stomach dipped. Would he actually consider moving here? "They have guided tours for people with lists."

"Cecelia, I came to New York to spend time with *you*."

The tiny corner of her heart that was left ached. "Why?"

His beautiful brown eyes softened as he stared at her. "Why do you think?"

"I don't know, but I . . . I don't think it's a good idea," she whispered, wishing he'd stop looking at her the way he used to when they were young and stupid.

"What isn't a good idea? I'm asking you to be my guide. You know this city, and I'd rather spend time with you than a stranger."

Cecelia looked away. He destroyed her once. She hoped she was strong enough, wise enough, not to let it happen again

Placing a finger under her chin, he tilted her face toward him. "Please, Ce?"

"I'll see what my schedule looks like once you're back in town."

He grinned. "I'll settle for that."

CHAPTER 16

After Jared paid the bill, Cecelia led the way up the stairs to the street level door. Outside, an ambulance's siren blared, making conversation impossible, which gave him a minute to think.

"On my way to the fitness center, I passed a school or church, something that had a small park on the side. I noticed a few benches near a playground," Jared said once the siren blended into the other city noises. "Can we go there to talk?"

"Okay," she said, her tone touched with a hint of suspicion. She started back the way they'd come.

He wanted to slow her hurried pace, but apparently, she wanted to get the information from him and be on her way.

He wanted more time with her, though. For that reason, he left the divorce papers on the kitchen counter of the corporate apartment because once she signed, there would be no reason to see her again.

He should have told her before he filled up on pizza because suddenly, he felt nauseous.

Cecelia turned at the school entrance and found a bench

on the far side of the playground. She sat down in her no-nonsense way, then looked at him expectantly.

He sat next to her, resting his elbows on his thighs, and stared at his laced fingers.

"What is it, Jared? You're starting to scare me."

Say it. He turned his head to look her in the eye. Her pretty blue eyes were icy at the moment. "Our divorce was never finalized."

"What?"

He straightened and rested both arms on the back of the bench. "We're still married."

"No. I have the final decree. It was mailed to me."

"Did you open the envelope and check for the judge's signature?"

"I must have. I . . ." Her brow wrinkled as she looked past him. "I don't remember."

"The judge didn't sign the decree. After I was told, I checked mine, and there was no signature. Our divorce was never finalized."

She huffed out an unexpected laugh, then covered her mouth with her hand. "How could this happen?"

Shrugging, he shook his head. "Lost paperwork, negligent clerk, busy judge, who knows?"

Mouth closed, her shoulders shook with laughter. Then she doubled over, laughing into her hands.

Her reaction shocked him. He'd expected anger, even tears, but not uncontrollable laughter.

Lifting her head, she patted his thigh, still laughing too hard to speak.

Her amusement was contagious, and he smiled.

She opened her mouth, but a snort of laughter came out instead.

"You okay?"

Waving a hand in front of her face, she nodded. "I'm j-just imagining your d-dad's face."

"He never knew we were married." He covered her hand with his. "I didn't tell anyone. Not even Knox."

Her laughter fell away, replaced by an expression he couldn't identify. "You didn't?"

"No," he replied, squeezing her hand. "We agreed not to. Remember?"

"I remember."

She slipped her hand out from under his, took a deep breath, and exhaled slowly. "How did you find out?"

This is where he would lie. He flexed the fingers that had held onto hers. "I had a background check done by a company I was working with and received a copy of the paperwork."

Two kids ran past on their way to the playground. Cecelia smiled. She'd been good with children. Every time people brought their kids to a party at his parents' house, she'd get down on the kids' level and play games to entertain them.

Stacy never played with kids. Not even his niece and nephew. Ever.

At that moment, he realized he and Stacy had never discussed having a family, but he couldn't imagine her in the role of mother.

"What now?"

Cecelia's question brought him back to the park bench, where he sat next to his wife—a nice place to be. "I had my lawyer draw up divorce papers."

"Oh."

Her soft voice held a hint of . . . He decided to go with ego-building "disappointment."

"Do you have them with you?"

"I left them in the corporate apartment I'm using."

"I guess I should have an attorney look them over."

He nodded. "I can have them delivered to your office tomorrow."

She looked back at the playground where the two kids were swinging on the monkey bars while singing *Five Little Monkeys Jumping on the Bed*. Cecelia smiled again.

He leaned forward and rested his forearms on his thighs. "Other than the night we met, having a family is something we never discussed. Do you think if we had stayed together, we'd have a kid or two by now?"

Her icy blue eyes studied him for a long moment before she nodded.

"I think so too. Boy and girl? Two boys? All girls?"

"It wouldn't matter," she said, looking away.

Agreed. He watched an ant struggling along the sidewalk in front of them. The piece of chip or bread was bigger than the ant, but he carried it along at a steady pace.

"Where do I send the papers after I sign them?"

"I'll include my attorney's information." He swallowed around the tightness in his throat. "Or I can pick them up from you. I'll be back next week to continue negotiating this merger. Will that give your attorney enough time to look the papers over?"

"Yes. I'll text you," she said, pulling her phone out of her bag.

He drew his phone out of his pocket, and they exchanged numbers.

"I'm sorry about this," she said. "I hope it hasn't caused you any problems."

He shook his head. "I'm as much to blame. I should have checked for signatures when I received the paperwork."

A woman walked past and called the kids to her. "Time to go home."

Cecelia stood and looked skyward. She'd left her hair down, and it hung straight to her shoulder blades.

Dusk had fallen, the hour between light and dark. The time of day when lines were blurred, and the world appeared softer somehow.

Jared pushed to his feet. "When did you start straightening your hair?"

She circled her hair between thumb and middle finger and pulled it over her shoulder, away from him. "A few years ago."

It looked nice. Professional. But he preferred her natural curl.

"Thank you for dinner, Jared."

"I'll walk you home."

"I can make it on my own."

"Ce—"

"I'll get the divorce papers back to your attorney as soon as I can."

He didn't want to leave things between them like this. "I can't let you—"

"You can't *let* me?" she asked with raised brows.

"You know what I mean. I would rather walk with you or put you in a cab, so I know you get home safely."

She shrugged in what he assumed to be consent, and they set off toward her apartment. They didn't talk much on the way, but his mind worked overtime, still searching for answers. "Cecelia? Why did you file for divorce?"

"Didn't we have this conversation?" she asked in a clipped tone.

"Appease me."

"We were young and reckless."

"We were in love."

"We *thought* we were in love."

He took her arm to stop her. "So you weren't in love with me?"

She looked everywhere but at him. "We were married a long time ago. Why rehash the past?"

"I guess because I'm still confused. I thought we were *both* in love. I thought we were *both* happy."

When she pressed her lips together, he knew she'd said all she planned to say.

He held out his arm. She stared at it for two heartbeats. He could see her trying to decide whether to touch him or not. Finally, she slipped her hand into the crook of his elbow, and they started for her apartment again. Her hand felt nice on his skin. It felt nice to have her beside him.

~

*J*ared kissed her cheek at the street door rather than come up, for which she was grateful. After knocking her flat with the news that they were still married, he expected answers to his many questions. She had an excellent reason for filing for divorce. He should be glad she hadn't filed on the grounds of infidelity rather than incompatibility. Heaven forbid the McAlister name be tarnished with the truth.

She let herself into her apartment and dropped her bag on a chair. Stopping in front of her bookcase, she took the carved wooden box off the shelf and sat cross-legged on the floor. Setting the box beside her, she opened the lid and lifted out all the contents. On the very bottom, she found the envelope that held her divorce decree. She slipped the papers from the envelope and flipped through them. The language was pretty straightforward since they didn't own any property and had no children together. Jared was right. The document hadn't been signed.

She leaned back on the palms of her hands and stared at the blank line. They had so many plans, or at least she had.

They'd talked about spending every holiday with each other, discussed the style of house they'd eventually like to buy or build, and they even decided where they'd spend their honeymoon when they could finally take one.

She thought back to the night they met and carried on the strangest conversation. He said then that he wasn't sure he wanted kids because he'd never been around them. But after seeing him play with little ones at a pool party, she knew he'd make a great father.

And the memories kept coming—days at the lake, fireworks, lunch dates, and drives in the country. Her sister had been too busy with her friends, but many times, they brought Derrick with them to get her brother out of the house.

Picking up a small velvet bag, she untied the knot and tipped the contents into her palm. She slipped the simple gold band onto her left ring finger. Holding her hand up, she studied the ring. She wouldn't have married Jared if she hadn't been certain he loved her.

Obviously, she couldn't trust her instincts in that area. She used the excuse that she'd been young and naïve. And Jared was her very first boyfriend. She didn't know a lot about love or relationships, but Jared taught her a quick lesson about ignorant trust.

She reached for her bag, pulled out her cell phone, and scrolled to her best friend's number.

"Hi, my friend," Val answered, with a smile in her voice.

Cecelia blew out a breath. "Where are you?"

"At my apartment."

"I know it's late, but can I come over?"

"Uh-oh. Are you okay?"

"Yes, I just really need to talk to someone with a level head on their shoulders."

"How about I come to you? I'll be there in twenty."

"Thanks, Val."

Cecelia knew Val would bring an overnight bag, so she went into the guest room-slash-office, lowered the Murphy bed, and pulled clean sheets out of the linen closet. In the kitchen, she whipped up Val's favorite shrimp dip and arranged some crackers on a decorative plate. Just as she finished setting two glasses of water on the coffee table, the buzzer at the street level door sounded.

She let Val in and opened her apartment door, smiling as she heard Val bound up the stairs.

"Hey, girlfriend," she said, swinging the door shut and setting her overnight bag on the floor. "Oh, shrimp dip. You want my undivided attention."

"Actually, I want— I'm not sure what I want. Maybe just a listening ear without too much judgment and are-you-crazies."

Val plopped down on the sofa and ran a cracker through the dip. "Madam Val, all-knowing and giver of valuable advice, is at your service."

Cecelia settled on the other side of the sofa.

"Lay it on me. What's going on?"

"The name of the guy from high school is Jared McAlis-ter. He and I got married when I was eighteen."

Val coughed, and bits of cracker flew onto the coffee table. "You what?" she choked out.

"He was twenty-two," she said, finishing her thought.

"You got married?" Val picked up a napkin and wiped her chin.

"I was in love, and Jared said he was too. Before he left for law school, we got married." She leaned forward and put her head in her hands. "Really—and I'm not proud to admit this —I forced his hand, but not intentionally."

"Forced his hand? Where you pregnant?"

"No. But I wouldn't . . ."

"Aww, you wouldn't put out until you had a ring on your finger."

Cecelia's cheeks heated. "It's just—"

Val scooted close and put a hand on Cecelia's back. "You don't have to explain it to me. After ten years, I know you. We all have our quirks. Yours is premarital sex." She winked. "Still, I can't believe you've never told me you were married to this guy."

She turned her head and looked at Valerie. "I've never told anyone. Well, my mom knew, but not until after the fact. Jared and I were only together two days before he left for law school in California. I was young and dumb and so in love." She huffed out a laugh. "He didn't feel the same."

Val quirked an eyebrow. "How do you know?"

"Turns out our marriage vows meant something different to him than to me."

"Are you sure?"

"Positive." Cecelia waved her hand. All this was history. She didn't hold a grudge. Jared had turned the heads of women, no matter where they went. He still did. Plenty of women took a second or third look tonight when they entered the restaurant. Even the mom on the playground had flashed an inconspicuous glance.

She sat up and took a sip of her water. "There's more. Turns out, we're still married."

Val's mouth fell open.

"Yep. Jared met me after my yoga class to tell me our divorce was never finalized. I checked the papers I got in the mail, and he's right. The judge didn't sign the final decree." Saying it aloud made her furious at herself. How had she not noticed? Why didn't she check every page of that document? Stupid oversight because of a disillusioned, shattered heart.

"What are you going to do?"

"Jared brought new divorce papers with him. He's having them delivered to the office tomorrow."

"Are you okay?"

Am I? She felt the hot sting of tears. "No. But I will be."

"At least you didn't own asparagus tongs you both loved or have to decide who got the glass poodle great-grandma sent as a wedding present."

Just the thought of signing those papers a second time made Cecelia sick to her stomach. She didn't want to sign the first time, but the pressure she got, and then the proof that Jared had been unfaithful were enough motive to put pen to paper. "True. It should be quick and easy."

CHAPTER 17

⬧

he look on Windy's face when she glanced up from her computer was worth his trip to Cecelia's office. She jumped up and ran around her desk with a grin. "Jared! Does Cecelia know you're in town?"

Jared returned Windy's warm hug. "I had dinner with her last night."

"She didn't say a word."

Not surprising. Especially after the bomb I dropped. He held out a brown box.

"What's this?"

"A present."

"For me?" Windy took the box and untied the orange ribbon with wide-eyed delight. She lifted the lid, pulled the engraved mug out, and squealed with delight. "I can't believe you did this. I've never had a mug with my name on it."

"I'm trying to buy my way past the sentry. Is it working?"

"Yes. Except not today. Ce's in a meeting with a couple about a project."

She glanced over his left shoulder, and he turned. Ce sat in a glassed room on one side of a conference table. A man and woman sat opposite her. He willed her to look up. Instead, she pointed to something on a stack of papers. The woman nodded.

"Can I ask you something?" Windy asked.

He turned to face her. "Shoot."

"Are you serious about Ce, or just looking for someone to spend time with when you're in New York?"

Jared chuckled at her candor. "I'm not just looking for someone to spend time with."

"You didn't answer the serious about her part."

How to answer? "You're asking an unfair question. I live in Dallas, so getting serious would be a little hard."

"New York is a great place to live."

He shook his head. "I understand you're concerned about Cecelia, and I appreciate it, Windy. She and I are just two old friends getting reacquainted right now."

She walked around her desk and straightened a bouquet. "Too bad. She has a pretty cute guy wanting to be more than friends."

That got his attention. "Yeah?"

Glancing pointedly at the flowers, she nodded. "I'm just throwing that out there for you to think over."

"Did he send those to her?"

Windy mimed turning a key at her lips.

"Is he the same guy whose picture is on her refrigerator?"

Lifted brows were the only answer he got.

"Is he a former client?"

Windy bit her lip. "Maybe you should ask Ce these questions."

"Can you, at least, tell me if she's serious about him?"

She pressed her lips together.

Frustration pressed down on his chest. "Does the answer rhyme with dress?"

She laughed. "I already got in trouble for giving out the

name of her favorite café. You're not getting any more information out of me."

He felt like he'd swallowed a tennis ball. He had no right to ask these questions. Or maybe he did. Cecelia was still his wife, which reminded him. He held out a large manila envelope. "Can you give this to Cecelia when she gets out of her meeting?"

Windy took the envelope. "Sure, but flowers would work better."

Probably not.

"Her birthday is coming up."

"I know."

Windy's expression softened. "You know when her birthday is?"

He nodded.

"We always have a party in the conference room." She pointed to where Cecelia sat.

He glanced that way. Cecelia was still engrossed in conversation. He had the feeling she knew he was out here. "If I'm in town, maybe I can stop by. Does flower guy know?"

"Nope. It's just a party for coworkers. And you. Two o'clock."

"Thanks, Windy." He turned for the door.

"Should I tell Ce you dropped by?"

He chanced one more glance toward the conference room. "She knows."

~

*C*ecelia shook hands with her clients. She'd be organizing and decorating a home office for this husband and wife real estate agent team. The space was large, but an easy job. They came prepared with several ideas, and they liked what she'd shown them.

She walked them to the door, well aware that Jarred left only minutes before. He'd been on her mind since the moment he showed up at the fitness center yesterday. She'd hoped talking things out with Val would help. It didn't.

"So, Jared's in town. He brought me a present." Windy held out a coffee mug with her name printed on the side. "He and I are pretty tight."

"Is that right?"

"He dropped this off for you."

Cecelia stared at the end of her marriage in Windy's hand.

Mia leaned over the banister. "Ce, have you got a minute? I need some advice about a couple of *very* traditional fabric choices."

"Sure."

"Mia, Tall, Dark, and Handsome is in town."

"Really?" Mia looked from Windy to Cecelia. "Is this getting serious?"

Cecelia took the envelope Windy held out. "No."

"You sure?" Windy asked.

Pretty sure. "Jared lives in Dallas. I live in New York."

"Trivial detail," Windy said.

"Trivial? Texas is what—nine or ten states away?—and you think that's trivial?"

"Could be worse," Mia said. "I once had a long-distance relationship with a guy who lived in Arizona."

"And how did that work out?" Cecelia asked to prove her point to Windy.

Mia wrinkled her nose. "It didn't. Too much bother, and he wasn't worth the expense of flying back and forth."

"I rest my case. I don't know anything about Jared anymore. He probably has a dazzling model girlfriend."

"You haven't asked?" Mia asked at the same time Windy interjected. "He doesn't."

Cecelia looked pointedly at Windy. "Did he tell you that?"

"No, but he wouldn't be stopping by if he had a girlfriend."

"I've had married men hit on me," Mia said, tapping the metal banister with her dagger-pointed fingernails.

"Windy, you don't know anything about Jared's private life," Cecelia said, wanting to believe Windy really did know everything and could reassure her. Silly on her part since he'd just dropped off divorce papers for her to sign.

"I know he isn't married. He would have told me," Windy responded.

Cecelia stifled a manic laugh. *Actually, he's very married.*

"By the way, Mr. Basketball sent flowers." Windy pushed the bouquet forward.

Pulling the envelope free of the little plastic pitchfork, she slipped out the card.

Thank you for making my new loft feel like home. The space turned out better than I hoped.

So thoughtful. Mr. Basketball had been very easy to work with. She positioned the bouquet at the end of the reception desk. "I'll leave them here to brighten up the reception area."

She went into Mia's office and quickly helped her with the fabric choices, then closed herself in her office. Instead of sitting at her desk, she settled onto the cushy sofa and took out the divorce papers. Her chest tightened painfully, and her throat closed up. Would there ever be a day when her heart didn't throb like it might stop beating forever?

Jared's attorney, Connor Scopello, had placed little stickies in the places that required her initials or signature. She opened the contacts on her phone, scrolled to Novalene Hillyard's number, and hit the phone icon. Her roommate during college was now a high-powered New York city attorney.

"Hillyard attorney at law. This is Melissa. May I help you?"

"Melissa, my name is Cecelia Chadwick. I'd like to leave a message for Miss Hillyard to call me at her convenience."

"Are you a client of Miss Hillyard's?"

"No. We went to college together."

"Can you hold, please?"

Cecelia listened to elevator music for about thirty seconds.

"Oh my gosh, Cecelia! Is that really you?"

"It is. How are you, Nova?"

They spent ten minutes catching up with each other. Novalene had been the party girl of their small group of friends. She loved going out every night and could still pop out of bed, bright-eyed, as soon as the alarm went off the next morning.

"So what can I do you for?"

"I was hoping you might have time to look over some divorce papers for me."

"Divorce papers? I didn't get invited to a wedding."

"Long story."

"I'm free tonight. Want to meet for dinner?"

"I'd love to."

They made a plan, and she disconnected the call just as a text from Jared came in.

Leaving for Dallas tomorrow. Can we meet for dinner tonight?

She said a silent prayer of thanks that she'd made plans with Novalene. **Sorry. I have plans with a friend. Windy gave me the papers. Thanks for dropping them off. I'll get them signed and sent back as soon as possible.**

The conversation bubbles rolled in the corner of her screen, then disappeared for a long minute.

Sure. Sorry I missed you, finally popped up.

Have a safe trip home.

Another long pause. She thought he'd finished texting, but her phone chimed a message a minute later.

Thanks, Ce. Have a nice night.

She didn't reply.

Later that night, Cecelia sat on her bed, staring at the divorce papers. After a leisurely dinner and some catching up, Novalene said the divorce decree was standard and straightforward.

"No loopholes. You just sign and send it back, all neat and tidy." She took a sip of her cocktail. "I've heard of this happening before, but never to someone I know."

Cecelia shrugged. "Lucky me."

"The ex is back in town, huh?"

"Not permanently." A man sitting at the bar made eye contact and nodded. Cecelia turned her full attention to Novalene. "He's a merger and acquisitions attorney and comes to town on business."

"How'd he discover you two are still married?"

"A background check of some sort."

Novalene swirled the brown liquid in the bottom of her glass. "Is he rich?"

"His family is. I imagine he'll inherit part of the McAlister kingdom."

"You know, we could get some of that money," Novalene said, lifting a brow toward the man who was now looking at her.

"I don't need his money, Nova. I make a good living."

"Still, some extra—"

"No."

Novalene looked at her. "You don't seem very happy about this impending divorce. Is there something you're not telling me?"

"No," Cecelia repeated. "Just him showing up and divorce papers has dredged up a lot of memories I'd rather forget."

"Men have a way of leaving a trail of bad memories."

Cecelia studied her college roommate. "You didn't use to be cynical. What happened?"

"Two divorces. And neither ex-spouse was as kind as you. They married me for money and wouldn't let go until my dad paid the leeches off."

Novalene came from a family as affluent as Jared's. Two brothers who built an empire from shipping and railroad trade during the gilded age. Her grandmother still lived in a Newport Mansion. Cecelia visited with Novalene over spring break one year, and she remembered being in awe of the gaudy splendor. Nova's grandmother, a tiny woman, had looked down her nose at Cecelia, much as Charles McAlister did. One long weekend proved to be enough for Cecelia. She was sick of feeling less-than enough around people who thought they were better simply because they inherited loads of money.

"Jared's dad said I married Jared for his money."

"Did you?"

"This will be my second divorce from him, and I haven't asked for a cent."

Her cell phone ringing yanked Cecelia back into her bedroom, centering her attention on the divorce papers in front of her. Novalene said she could take care of the details, but what details were there? Sign and send—she could take care of that herself.

She connected the call when she saw Val's cute face on her screen. "Hi, Val."

"Hey, girlfriend. How are you doing?"

"I'm okay." Cecelia tossed the comforter over the papers so she didn't have to look at them.

"You don't sound okay."

"Guess who I had dinner with?" Cecelia asked.

"The ex-husband."

"Nova Hillyard."

"You had dinner with my arch enemy?"

"I needed a lawyer to look over the divorce papers."

"Please tell me she didn't charge you."

Nova blatantly stole Val's boyfriend in college. They'd remained enemies even though the guy turned out to be a jerk who cheated on Nova too. "I bought her dinner and several drinks."

"Sounds like she's still a lush. How'd she look?" Val asked flatly.

"Eleven years older."

"Come on, Ce. You've got to give me more than that."

Cecelia stood and walked to her bedroom window. The sun had disappeared behind the building across the street long ago. Cotton-candy colors now softened the evening sky. "She looked the same, except her hair is short. In a bob."

"Fat?"

"No."

"Darn it. Is she married?"

"Divorced. Twice," Cecelia added, wandering into the kitchen for a cup of tea.

"At least she's been married."

"Why so down?"

"Adonis came into the office today to take Bombshell to lunch. Before I could react, he hugged me. Man, he smelled so good. Aaron smells like peanut butter."

"Maybe you could gift him some cologne for . . ." Labor Day was the next holiday. "When's his birthday?"

"I haven't asked."

She set the teakettle on the stove and lit the burner. "Other than smelling like peanut butter, how is he?"

"Great, actually. He takes me on fun, thoughtful dates.

Places Tyler used to take you. I wonder if Tyler is dating anyone yet. He doesn't smell like peanut butter. Would it be against girl code to ask him out?"

"It might be, but it wouldn't be against Cecelia code," she said, opening the cupboard for a teacup.

"But then we could never double date."

Cecelia laughed. "When do we ever double date?"

"Never, but we *really* couldn't then. Would you feel weird coming to our wedding?"

This was the Val she knew and loved. "I would love to come to yours and Tyler's wedding. I'll buy you a waffle iron. You can name your first daughter after me."

"I love waffles," Val moaned. "You are the best friend ever."

"No, that title is reserved for you."

CHAPTER 18

⁂

*J*ared scooted close to his nephew, who was lying on the floor, and drove a toy car over his belly. Little Charlie's giggle caught his sister's attention, and she crawled onto Jared's lap. Snuggling close, she grinned up at him, her angel face inches away. "Me wuv you."

He kissed her forehead. Her dark hair smelled of sunshine and lavender. "Me wuv you too, Chloe girl."

"Don't use baby talk when speaking to her, Jared. She'll never learn to pronounce words correctly."

Jared looked across the room, where his dad sat erect in one of Susan's chairs near the fireplace. His mom sat in the matching wingback, her legs crossed, her eyebrow raised.

"How about we let her be two for a while longer, Dad?"

Jared turned his attention back to the kids. Family celebrations meant he got to spend time with his niece and nephew. With his work schedule, he didn't get to play with them often enough. After a great meal, the family settled in Susan and Tim's living room, sated and lazy. At least on his part.

His mom wanted to have a big, catered party at the

country club for Granddad's eightieth birthday party, but, at his grandfather's request, his sister had gone low-key with just immediate family. Granddad and Grammy were down-to-earth people who'd worked hard to build McAlister Industries from a small oil enterprise Jared's great-grandfather started into a multi-billion-dollar company with hundreds of employees.

He didn't want the fuss and had laughed at the idea of champagne and a five-tiered cake. Instead, he asked Susan to make his favorite dish—chicken fried steak with creamy gravy, mashed potatoes, and green beans. After they spent a little time visiting, he'd cut into another of his favorites, Grammy's blue-ribbon chocolate cake.

While Jared played with Charlie and Chloe, Stacy flipped through a magazine from the safety of the sofa. He couldn't tell her about Cecelia before dinner. She would have ruined the celebration for everyone. He'd tell her when he took her home. That would give him the weekend to deal with his parents. And possibly hers.

"Jared, why don't you get the kids up on the sofa so Stacy can play too," his sharp-as-a-tack grandmother said. She sat on a loveseat next to his grandfather, who was looking through the book on exotic birds Susan and Tim gave him.

"That's okay, Grammy. I can see them just fine from here," Stacy interjected quickly. She sent Jared a warning glare before clearing her throat. "I think I'm coming down with something and don't want to get the kids sick."

More like, she didn't want them to transfer anything to her.

"Anyone ready for dessert?" Susan asked. She was sitting near Stacy, occasionally glancing at the magazine when Stacy flipped to another page.

Tim pushed off the carpeted floor and joined his wife on the sofa. "I couldn't eat another bite just yet, sweetheart."

"Jared," Stacy held up the magazine. "Isn't this the basketball player who was traded from the Mavericks to the New York Knicks? Remember the big controversy surrounding that trade?"

Only half listening, Jared pulled a silly face that sent both Charlie and Chloe into fits of giggles.

"Jared, don't scare the children," his mother reprimanded.

He glanced at his mom, a vision of propriety. "It's called playing."

"Yeah, that's him," Tim said, leaning past Susan to see the image Stacy held up.

Susan took the magazine from Stacy. "Hey, little brother, he's with that girl you dated in college."

"You'll have to be more specific," Jared said.

Tim snorted. "You dated a lot, huh, Jared?"

"Enough of that talk," Betsy said, disapproval dripping from each word. "The children don't need to hear about Jared's college"—she glanced at Charlie and Chloe— "escapades," she whispered like it was a dirty word.

Jared laughed. "Yes, let's not taint the children's image of their favorite uncle by talking about his *escapades*."

"I'm serious, Jared. This is the girl who lived in Mesquite." Susan's gaze locked with his as she held up the full-page photo. "Cecelia Chadwick is in this magazine."

Jared jumped off the floor and set Chloe between her great-grandparents. Walking behind the sofa, Jared looked over his sister's shoulder. Cecelia stood several stairs up in the Winston and Associates reception area, her face lit with her beautiful smile. The basketball player in question stood below her, putting them at eye level.

"You dated her?" Tim flashed Jared his crooked grin. "She's hot."

"Hey, I'm right here." Susan elbowed her husband in the ribs.

"Cecelia was a very nice young lady," Granddad said without looking up from his book, too busy showing pictures of birds to Chloe.

"When did you date her?" Stacy demanded.

"May I see that magazine?" Grammy asked.

Jared plucked the magazine out of his sister's hands and flipped to see the cover before handing it to his grandma.

"Jared, when did you date her?"

He met Stacy's glare, amazed that the subject of Cecelia came up on the very day he planned to tell Stacy he had a wife. "The summer before I left for law school."

Grammy tapped the page of the magazine. "Cecelia was a natural beauty."

"Beauty?" Charles suddenly inserted himself into the conversation. "She ran around here all summer in shorts and flip-flops, her hair hanging wild. She probably didn't own a tube of lipstick."

"That's exactly why she was a natural beauty, Charles. She had a fresh-faced glow. She didn't need lipstick."

"She had stunning blue eyes. Very nice young lady, always so polite and cordial," Granddad added.

Jared's grandmother flipped to the cover and looked pointedly at Jared. "She's obviously successful. I don't think a magazine of this caliber would feature someone who hadn't made a name for themselves."

Charles pushed out of his chair and held out his hand. "Can I see that, Mother?"

She held out the magazine. "Yes, but I'd like to read the article when you're finished. I told Betsy the other day I wanted to spruce the dining room up a bit. Maybe I'll call Cecelia for a consultation."

"No, you won't," Charles pronounced. "I'll get the name of a decorator if you think you need to make any changes."

For the first time, Granddad looked up from his book.

"Excuse me. You will address your mother with respect, son. You'll also remember she doesn't need your permission. If she'd like to redecorate, she can call whomever she wants."

Jared relished his dad's brief moment of embarrassment, a rare occurrence.

"Of course. I apologize, Mom. But there are plenty of decorators right here in Dallas. There's no need to fly this woman in from wherever she lives now," he said, giving the magazine a shake.

Jared wondered if Knox had been right as he watched his dad's face twist in disgust when he glanced over the article. Could he have had something to do with Cecelia's disappearance? There were a lot of things he believed his father capable of, but did he have the power to accomplish that? And if so, how had he persuaded Cecelia to go along?

Grammy caught his eye and winked.

"How long did you date— What did you say her name was?" Stacy asked Susan.

"Cecelia Chadwick." Susan leaned against her husband. "Dad, I remember you and Mom didn't think Cecelia would amount to anything. I guess she proved you wrong."

"How did she prove us wrong, Susan? She fluffs pillows for a living." Charles handed the magazine to his mother.

"How much did you and Betsy pay to have your house redecorated the last time, Charles?" Grammy asked. "Debra Delaney spent months at your house. If I recall, she took a trip to Europe when she finished."

They all listened to a few tense ticks from the grandfather clock in the corner of the room. His grandmother smoothed the grin off her face.

Charles glowered.

"Jared, how long did you date this, Cecelia?" Stacy demanded in her I-want-an-immediate-answer tone.

Jared scooped Chloe off the loveseat and kissed her cheek. "Three months."

While the family enjoyed Grammy's famous chocolate cake, Stacy pored over the article, then studied the picture, picking apart Cecelia's makeup, hair, and wardrobe. She fired questions about Cecelia from Susan's driveway to the parking garage of her condo.

"You've never asked about any other woman I've dated," Jared finally shot back, wheeling into her guest parking space. "What's with your fixation about Cecelia?"

"I saw your reaction when Susan mentioned her name. You jumped off the floor like someone set a firecracker off under you—all to get a look at that picture." She slid out of his car before he could open the passenger door. "I also saw your mama and daddy's faces. Betsy looked like she'd swallowed something sour, and your dad's expression was even worse. So, you tell me, Jared, why did they react that way?"

Truth. "They didn't like her."

That stopped Stacy in her tracks. "Why didn't they like her?"

"They saw her as a threat. They were worried my relationship with her would take my mind off my studies at law school. Her parents lived on the wrong side of town. Take your pick." They thought the Chadwicks were beneath the McAlister name.

She jabbed the elevator button, then turned to him with a fist on her hip. "Did you love her?"

"Yes."

"How much?"

"How much did I love her? I don't even know how to answer that." Except he did. *Time for the first big reveal.* "I loved her enough to marry her."

"You what?"

"Cecelia and I got married a couple of days before I left for law school."

"And you're just telling me now?" she said, her tone low and ominous.

The elevator opened, and she stomped inside. He followed.

"I didn't tell you before because I didn't think it mattered. I didn't tell anyone—not even Knox knew until a couple of weeks ago."

She slowly turned to him. If looks could kill, he'd be a pile of ashes she wouldn't even bother to sweep up. "You told Knox before you told me?"

The elevator stopped on her floor, and they got off. He held the door for a couple getting on, and when he turned, she'd already gone inside her condo. He stuck his foot next to the jamb just as she flung the door to slam it shut.

"You can leave," she shot out, trying to kick his foot aside.

"I will, but first we have to talk."

"I don't want to hear anything you have to say."

"You'll want to hear this, Stac. What I have to say is important."

She stepped back and crossed her arms, her glare firing darts. He tried to take her arm, but she yanked out of his grasp. So he walked into her spacious living room with a view overlooking the city and gestured to the sofa. "Please, come sit down."

Stalking into her own space, she sat, back rigid, on the sofa.

"I don't blame you for being mad, but I didn't mention my marriage because it happened long ago and only lasted a couple of months before Cecelia filed for divorce."

"She filed?"

He sat beside her. "Yes."

"So you'd still be married if she hadn't."

He'd stepped right into that one. "Stac—"

"You would. I can see it in your face," she spat out. "Why did she divorce you?"

"She won't—" He stopped short of saying *She won't say*, but not soon enough.

Stacy's mouth dropped open, and her eyes narrowed dangerously. "The article said she lives in New York. You went to New York to see her."

"I did, but—"

She reacted so fast he didn't have time to duck before her palm connected with his face, jarring his head sideways.

"Get out!"

He put a hand to his stinging cheek. "I need to tell you—"

"That you slept with her? You did, didn't you?" she snarled.

"No."

She jabbed a long-nailed finger in his chest. "Liar."

"Would you please listen?"

"Get out!" She jumped to her feet and pointed at the door.

He stood. "I've seen Cecelia twice, but nothing happened. I wouldn't do that to you—or her."

"You said you met an old friend for dinner, but you were with her!"

"Cecelia and I are still married," he blurted out, or he'd never have a chance to tell her.

Several emotions crossed Stacy's face; then tears flooded her eyes.

"You asked me to marry you, and you're still married to someone else?" She shook her head violently, flinging her blond hair from side to side as she stared at a point behind him. "This isn't happening," she choked out between sobs. "Things like this happen in movies. Not in real life. And not to me."

Before she could slap him again, he grasped her wrists.

"It's a fluke. The judge never signed the decree. I found out the divorce was never finalized, and I went to New York to tell Cecelia. Nothing. Happened."

She stared up at him, her pretty eyes already puffy. Pools of mascara had collected under her lower lashes.

"Can we please sit and talk?"

Yanking from his grasp, "We have nothing to discuss. Fix this," she snarled.

"We do have something to discuss. Come sit down."

She allowed him to lead her to the sofa and pull her down beside him. "How long have you known?"

He ran his thumbs over her knuckles. "A couple of weeks."

"I can't believe you didn't tell me. Honesty is the foundation of a good marriage."

They'd been down the honesty road before.

She jerked out of his grasp again. "You're doing this because you can't let what happened between Tuck and me go. I was completely innocent that night."

That's not how he heard the story, but that didn't matter anymore. "Let's get back to us."

"Us?" She flapped a hand between them as if swatting at gnats. "There *is* no us until you're divorced. How quickly can Connor resolve this issue? I don't want anyone to know about this, Jared. If the media gets ahold of this information—"

She jumped to her feet and started pacing. "Maybe we should move the wedding up. A Christmas wedding would be perfect. I'll order red and white roses, and we can have Christmas trees decorated with thousands of tiny white lights and—"

"Stacy, we need to call off the wedding."

"No! We need to move the date up. Call Connor right

now. You have his cell number. Ask him how quickly he can push the divorce through."

He rubbed the back of his neck. "We need to call the wedding off."

"Why?" Stacy's head snapped around as if he'd hit her.

"Let's talk about kids?"

"Kids?"

"Yes, kids. I want two, three, maybe even four."

Her jaw clenched, then relaxed. "Sure. Eventually. Down the road, we can have a kid. We'll hire a nanny."

He shook his head. "I don't want my children raised by a nanny."

She crossed her arms and cocked a hip. "So you expect me to give up my career and stay home with a baby?"

"Neither one of us has to give up our careers to raise our children, Stacy, but we wouldn't leave them in the care of a nanny all the time either. Having children would mean changing diapers and midnight feedings, baseball games and ballet lessons, all the things that come with raising a family. We would have to make sacrifices, stay home at night, make dinner, help with homework, tell bedtime stories, search for shoes under beds, and lost teddy bears. Kiss boo-boos."

He watched the subject send her into a tailspin of emotions. She knew she wouldn't win this battle, and she didn't like losing.

"You know what?" she said. "Let's forget about your divorce, getting married, or kids. I'll get you a beer, and you can relax while I change. Crystal texted earlier. The gang's meeting at The Stampede. We can dance and forget all this craziness."

She would try to distract him with drinks, parties, and fun until she could figure out a way to get what she wanted. That's how Stacy rolled. "Let's finish this discussion."

"No."

He inhaled and blew out a breath. "I'm calling off our wedding."

"No, you're not. We *are* getting married."

Jared shook his head.

"We are not canceling all the plans I've made. You tell Connor to push your divorce through as quickly and quietly as possible. We can't let this news get out."

Exhausted by her endless orders, he pushed to his feet. "I'm sorry, Stac. We don't want the same things out of life. In fact, we have very little in common." She opened her mouth, but he held up a hand. "You talked about honesty earlier, so be honest right now. You love the idea

of being married, but your dream husband isn't me—a homebody who wants kids. You want someone who loves so go out every night. Someone who would love living in this high rise. I'm not him."

Her face twisted with defeat. "Okay, you want honesty? I hate kids. I hate your condo. And I hate you. Get out."

Kicking him out meant she was calling off their wedding rather than him. He didn't have a problem with that. He stopped at the door. "I didn't mean to hurt you. I'm sorry."

"You didn't hurt me," she sneered. "I've got men lined up. You'll be replaced by tomorrow."

"Bye, Stacy."

She slammed the door behind him.

Instead of an elevator ride, Jared took the stairs, anxious to be away as quickly as possible.

His mind traveled to Cecelia. He still didn't know why she divorced him. Maybe her mom pressured her. Marybeth Chadwick had disliked him as much as his dad disliked Cecelia. If that was the reason, how did Marybeth find out? Cecelia was the one who wanted to keep their marriage quiet.

Fate was a development of events beyond a person's

control—something that happened by accident. He wanted to believe his divorce hadn't been finalized because the universe was possibly giving him a second chance with Cecelia, and he planned to grab hold with both hands.

He hoped Cecelia would be willing to take that chance along with him.

CHAPTER 19

As soon as Jared and Stacy left Susan's house, Charles hustled Betsy out the door. That article mentioned Cecelia lived in New York—the city Jared had visited twice very recently.

Had he seen Cecelia? Jared kept his eyes on his grandmother the whole time she droned on about the girl's *natural beauty* and needing a decorator, which she'd said just to rile him. He'd noticed Jared flip to the cover of the magazine, and in case his son had missed it, his mother made sure he saw it a second time.

"Why are we in such a rush to get home?" Betsy asked as soon as he slid behind the wheel of the car and shut his door.

He started the engine. "I have urgent work I need to finish."

"You can't do it over the weekend?" Betsy fastened her seat belt. Something she refused to do on the way over because she didn't want to wrinkle her dress. "Why tonight?"

"I have a mess to clean up before Monday," he said, pulling around Susan and Tim's circular driveway.

"Don't you have employees in place to clean up messes?"

"Betsy, stop badgering. This is something I need to take care of personally."

His wife smoothed a hand over her lap. "I can't believe Cecelia Chadwick is in a national magazine. She's still very pretty."

"Anyone can get their name in print."

"I guess that's true." She fiddled with her air conditioner vent. "The basketball player and her boss said some very nice things about Cecelia in the article."

"Of course they did. The article was about the basketball player, so he had to say nice things, and it would hurt her boss's business to say otherwise." Charles turned out of his daughter's neighborhood.

"Did you read the article?"

"I have better things to do than read some silly article about a girl who probably slept her way to the top."

"Charles, that's a little harsh. Maybe she worked hard to get where she is. According to the article, she's worked with some pretty prestigious clients. She's decorated a senator's home."

He glanced at his wife, who'd be impressed by any name she recognized from the news or society pages. "Yes, the girl is very accomplished at painting rooms and hanging pictures."

Betsy rolled her eyes. "You're impossible to talk to when you get in these moods. I'm just saying, maybe we judged her too hastily."

"We didn't. Believe me, Betsy. She'll turn out no better than her crass-mouthed mother."

His wife settled back in her seat and stared out the passenger window. "I never met her mother."

"Well, I did. She's a vulgar, unpleasant woman. She and Cecelia are two peas in a pod. Why work when I can get my hands on someone else's hard-earned dollar? Cecelia Chadwick was out to catch a rich husband, but her plans backfired."

"Did you notice Jared's reaction when Susan said Cecelia's name?"

Everyone had, including Stacy. "Jared's engaged. He'll be married soon." He glanced at Betsy. "Maybe we should consider moving up the wedding a few months."

"Don't be ridiculous. We can't possibly finalize all the details before the date Stacy set."

He could tell by his wife's tone she wouldn't even consider his suggestion.

At the house, he went straight to his office and pulled up the webpage for Winston and Associates Interior Design. Each of Arthur Winston's associates had their own page, and he clicked on Cecelia's. He hated admitting her portfolio and list of clients were impressive.

He did an internet search and scoured through everything he could find on the girl. She'd made quite a name for herself. Well, she could thank him for that. She'd been nothing but a money-hungry teenager. It took him about ten seconds to see through her charade and realize exactly what she was after—his son's inheritance.

He tried every inducement he could think of to split up his son's relationship with her. The kid turned down a trip abroad, a diving expedition off the coast of Chile, and flat-out monetary bribery. Nothing worked. Jared was determined to spend the summer lazing around the lake with that freeloading Knox Chatham and the gold-digging tart.

Cecelia had been out of their lives for a long time, but she hadn't been forgotten.

Now, the million-dollar question. Had Jared found Cecelia? And if so, how much had transpired between them? Jared would never tell him, so Charles dialed James Decker. His call went to the PI's voicemail.

"Decker, I need you to meet me at the office first thing Monday morning."

He disconnected the call and sat back. One hand on the desk, he performed his finger exercise. Jared was the cause of his graying hair. That kid could get into trouble faster—

Charles reached out for the ringing phone. "Yes." He sat straighter in his chair. "Slow down, Stacy. I can't— What do you mean?"

He tried to make sense of Stacy's hysteria. Two sentences stood out in her rantings. Jared saw Cecelia in New York, and he called off the wedding.

~

Cecelia rubbed her tired eyes. Tomorrow was her brainstorming meeting with Mr. and Mrs. Hollywood. She had a pretty good idea of the style they were going for, based on the magazine and internet pictures they sent her.

At her request, they also visited furniture stores and took pictures of things that inspired them. She would show them where she thought the stairs would work best and how she could rearrange the kitchen so they could take advantage of every square inch of space.

An architect she worked with would join them right before lunch so they could formulate a plan and begin to build a relationship with each other.

When her stomach growled, she realized night had fallen, and she hadn't eaten dinner. She went into the kitchen and pulled a container of leftover lasagna out of the fridge. Winston's wife, concerned that Cecelia didn't eat proper meals, regularly sent him to work with containers of food for her.

The whir of the microwave sounded loud in her quiet apartment.

Earlier in the evening, she realized she'd been married for twelve years this month and had never celebrated an anniversary.

When the buzzer sounded, she pulled the lasagna out of the microwave, grabbed a fork and a napkin, and sank into a kitchen chair just as her cell rang.

She looked at the screen and what was left of her heart squeezed at the sight of Jared's number. Taking a deep breath, she accepted the call. "Hello."

"Hi, Ce. I hope I didn't wake you."

"No, I just warmed up some dinner. Are you back in New York?" she asked. Her question sounded too hopeful to her own ears. What would Jared think if he noticed?

"No, Dallas. We celebrated Granddad's eightieth birthday tonight."

"How nice. Was it a big celebration?"

"Just family."

"Did you get a chance to play with your niece and nephew?"

"Absolutely. My favorite part of the party."

She could hear the smile in his voice. She poked her fork in the lasagna, then her finger. The middle was still cold. She got up and put it back in the microwave. "Tell me about the celebration."

"Dinner was great, and the cake was delicious, but our evening got interrupted by a beautiful woman."

Cecelia sank into the kitchen chair a second time. "Since when is an interruption by a beautiful woman a bad thing for a man?"

"Oh, it wasn't a bad thing. My brother-in-law was quite impressed that I'd dated the—and I use his word, but not because I disagree in any way—*hot* woman in the design magazine sitting on my sister's coffee table. He especially liked the picture of her standing on the stairs in Winston and Associates reception area with a tall basketball player."

She'd be forever grateful that Jared couldn't see her burning cheeks right now.

"Why didn't you tell me, Ce?"

"I hoped it would go unnoticed."

"Why?"

She hesitated to tell him the truth. Part of the reason she tried to stay out of the public eye wasn't important now that Jared had found her. The other part was her mother, who constantly badgered her for money despite the healthy check Cecelia sent her every month. "Mom."

~

*A*hh, Marybeth Chadwick must be taking advantage of her successful daughter. The summer they dated, Cecelia caught her mom ransacking her room for money more than once.

"You got some good publicity at Susan's tonight. Grammy wants to hire you to redecorate her house. I bought a copy of the magazine for myself after dinner, and I'd be surprised if Grammy doesn't pick up a copy too."

"You did not."

"I did. When I left Susan's, Grammy was reading the article and saying what a—and again, I'm using her words —*natural beauty* you still are. Granddad talked about your stunning blue eyes."

"If you don't stop, I'm going to hang up."

Jared laughed. "No. Please, don't hang up." He could imagine the blush flooding her face. "Everything I've said is true, but I don't want you to hang up."

"Tell me about your niece and nephew."

In true Cecelia fashion, she turned the subject from herself to him. Not something Stacy ever did. Stacy also *never* asked about Charlie and Chloe. Cecelia had never met them, yet she wanted to know.

He debated whether to tell her about Stacy. With their engagement broken and the wedding called off, he didn't see any need to tell Cecelia. At least not yet.

After he told her about Charlie and Chloe, she asked about his work. "Enough about me. Tell me what you're working on, Cecelia."

"My Hollywood clients are flying in from LA tonight. They have to go back to California on Sunday, so I'll be holed up with them for most of tomorrow."

He leaned back in his recliner and listened to her soft voice, which had changed over the years. Now her Southern accent coexisted with a bit of New York brusque, unique like her. "This is a complete renovation?"

"Yes. Movie stars who've decided to relocate."

"Anyone I know?" he asked, intrigued and impressed at the same time.

"Probably, but I don't discuss clients with friends."

Friends echoed through Jared's mind, but what else could they be? Soon-to-be-ex-spouses sounded hollow and awful. He described Cecelia as a friend the night they had dinner at Market City Café. "Are we friends, Ce?"

"I . . . hope we're friends. Am I wrong?" she asked.

"No. You're not wrong." He wanted to see her face when he asked the next question. He wanted to be looking into her eyes. "Are you sorry I came to New York, Cecelia?"

"No," she said quietly. "I'm not sorry."

A gentle relief settled over him.

CHAPTER 20

*C*ecelia spent nine hours in the office conference room going over the renovation plans with the Hollywood couple. The architect, who walked the space a week earlier, confirmed that Cecelia's placement of the staircase would be the best choice if they wanted to make a statement and get the best use of their available space.

Major changes were made to her kitchen design when the couple decided to add a butler's pantry for dinner parties. They also wanted the master bedroom and bath extended and a sitting room added. In total, three walls would be knocked down completely, and four would be moved.

Zack delivered lunch at one and stuck around for a couple of hours to watch the process of working with an architect. Despite the mental energy of working through construction details, Jared slipped in and out of her thoughts all day. Only after they hung up did she realize he never gave her a reason for his call. After a few minutes, talking to him became easier. She didn't like that he was already stealing his way back into her fractured heart.

*J*ared expected his father to call immediately upon hearing he'd called off the wedding. Instead, the dinner invitation issued two days later wasn't a request. Tempted to turn down the summons, Jared decided airing his feelings and reasons for the action would be best. The weekend seemed never-ending, and he was looking forward to Monday.

He pulled through the gate of his childhood home and wound his way up the long drive to the house that was more museum than a home. Standing tall and grand as seen through a lane of live oaks, twelve southern columns and a wide veranda graced the front. The inside was opulent, untouchable, a showplace where children couldn't run and play, rooms with white carpets and silk furniture, heirloom vases, and priceless works of art.

Growing up, he spent more time at his grandparents' house, just a half-mile farther down the twisting driveway, hidden in a grove of trees rather than showcased. Even now, their door was always open to him and his friends, complete with an endless supply of fruit on the kitchen table and homemade cookies in a jar on the counter.

His grandparents' home reminded him of Cecelia's apartment, comfortable and relaxed. No wonder her place appealed to him the minute he stepped inside.

He pulled to a stop at the bottom of the front steps, tugged his cell phone free of a pocket, and called Cecelia.

"Hi, it's me," he said after her soft greeting.

"Hi, me."

His breath caught. She used to say the same thing eleven years ago. "Just hearing that voice of yours makes me smile."

"You mean you've had nothing to smile about all day?"

"No. Knowing I'm having dinner with the parents tonight

sucked any joy I might have had right out of the day. So I'm pretty sure your voice is responsible for the smile."

"I hope your dinner goes well."

"Thanks," he said while wishing he was with her. Though their conversation was a little on the stilted side, it still felt good to talk to her. "What're you doing tonight?"

"I have a date with a good book."

Relieved to know her date was with a book and not another man, Jared's smile grew. "I'd better go. Mom is peeking out the window, wondering why I'm sitting outside."

"Put on a happy face and enjoy your dinner."

He waited until she disconnected the call before he climbed out of his car. Like a man with a death sentence hanging over his head, he trudged up the porch steps. Before he could knock, the door flew open.

"Jared, when did you get married to that girl? Stacy is beside herself, and her mother says she won't eat a thing."

Stacy probably called his parents before he reached the elevator in her building. He bent to kiss his mother's cheek. "Stacy never eats anything, Mom."

"Your father is furious."

"The story of my life," he muttered.

Their footsteps echoed across the marble floor of the foyer, then turned whisper-soft when they entered the carpeted great room. His grandfather stood and wrapped Jared in a bear hug. "Hey, young man. It's good to see you."

The greeting surprised him since they'd just seen each other two nights earlier. "Hi, Granddad." He nodded at his dad, who remained standing near the fireplace.

His grandmother patted a place next to her on the sofa. He sat down and kissed her soft cheek. "Hi, Grammy."

"How could you, Jared?" His mother plopped down in a chair opposite the sofa, another surprise. Betsy wasn't a plopper.

"Give him a moment to settle in, Betsy," his grandmother scolded. "He'll tell us the story."

He decided to start with the still-married part of the story. "Cecelia and I got married before I left for law school. She filed for divorce shortly after. My attorney recently discovered the divorce was never finalized."

Betsy pressed her index fingers to her temples. "Why would you get married without telling us?"

"As for the broken engagement," he continued, not wanting to talk about Cecelia with his dad in the room, "Stacy and I want different things. I realized I don't love her enough to get married. And if she were honest, she'd admit she feels the same. She's in love with the idea of a big wedding, stacks of presents, people swooning over her dress, and a nineteen-layer cake, but she doesn't want to take on the role of a wife. At least not in the traditional sense. Our engagement was a mistake—my mistake. I shouldn't have proposed."

"You are the most irresponsible kid on the face of the earth," his dad huffed.

Grammy turned on the sofa to face her son. "How is Jared responsible for something out of his control?"

"Marrying that teenage gold-digger was not out of his control."

"And breaking up with Stacy is the responsible thing to do if he doesn't love the girl," she continued as if her son hadn't spoken. "You and Betsy have your priorities skewed." She took Jared's hand between hers and squeezed. "I'm very proud of you, Jared. No one should have to live the rest of their life being called Jare Bear."

Jared winked at his grandmother. A petite, white-haired, loveable woman, Grammy's brown eyes twinkled with mischief most of the time. How she'd borne such a controlling, starched son mystified him.

"That being said"—his grandmother tried to look stern—"you should have told us about your marriage to Cecelia."

Charles stalked over, stopping in front of Jared, eyeing him like a coiled snake ready to strike. "I asked you once before if you had something on the side that needed cleaning up."

"And I told you once before that I don't. My still being married has nothing to do with my broken engagement."

"You being married has everything to do with your broken engagement," his mother cried. "Stacy told her mother you're having an affair with Cecelia."

"I'm not having an affair. Again, canceling the wedding has nothing to do with Cecelia or any other woman. I'm sorry I hurt Stacy and her family, and I'm sorry if I hurt any of you because of my decision, but it is *my* decision."

"The Richardsons have already put down deposits on the venue and pre-paid the caterer."

"I'll reimburse them any money they've spent."

"That will come out of your money and not mine," his dad said.

"When have I asked you for money, Dad? Not since high school. I didn't even use *your* money to go to college or law school. I used the trust Granddad set aside for me."

The McAlister housekeeper announced dinner. Grateful for the interruption, Jared held out his hand to help his grandmother up, and they made their way into the dining room.

"What brought this on so suddenly, Jared?" his mom continued to badger.

"The decision wasn't sudden. I've been unhappy with our relationship for a long time. Stacy and I fight all the time. She's angry about my hours at work. She spends double the money she makes. I've tried talking to her about expenses, and she ignores me. She wants to party every night until all hours, which doesn't interest me." Jared shook out his napkin and spread it over his lap. "All that aside, our biggest difference didn't come up until recently. Stacy doesn't want children."

His mom waved her hand, swatting away his remark. "That's silly. Of course she wants children."

"Have you ever seen her play with Charles or Chloe? She doesn't acknowledge them. Never even says hi when they enter a room. She talks around them as if they don't exist."

"That's not true," Betsy said.

"Yes, it is," Jared's grandfather said. His disappointed gaze traveled from his son to his daughter-in-law. "Stacy is a spoiled woman who does whatever she wants or needs to do in order to get her way."

"We're veering off the subject," his dad said. "This has to do with Jared's responsibility to Stacy and this family."

Jared's grandfather held up both hands. "Enough. Jared and Stacy have split. Jared said he would reimburse Stacy's parents. There is nothing left to talk about." He glanced at Jared. "Your grandmother and I support your decision."

Charles went from frowning at his father to glaring at his son. "So, what are your plans, Jared?"

"What do you mean? Other than calling off the wedding, my plans haven't changed."

Betsy's fork clattered to her plate as she covered her face with her hands. "What is Stacy going to do?"

Jared wiped his mouth, though he had yet to eat a bite. "Stacy will be dating someone else by next week. She's not one to stay single for long."

Charles snapped his napkin open. "I'm not happy about this, Jared."

Jared had all he could take from his overbearing father. He stood up and planted his palms on the table. "And I'm not happy about you coming into the office and talking to Grant about my work, Dad, so I guess we're even."

"Jared," his grandmother reprimanded. She didn't tolerate disrespect, deserved or not.

"Grant and I had a private conversation. He had no business coming to you."

"He had every right. It's *his* law firm. I don't appreciate you using your friendship with Grant to manipulate my work environment."

"You ruined any friendship we had when you accepted a job with that firm."

"No. You ruined your friendship with Grant because you didn't get your way. Grant has put his trust in me, and he's happy with my performance. If he weren't, he'd come to *me* because that's the kind of relationship I have with my boss. We talk. Something you and I have never done."

Jared pushed his chair in, patted his grandfather's shoulder, and kissed his grandmother's cheek. "You'll have to excuse me. I've lost my appetite."

CHAPTER 21

When Cecelia walked into the office after an onsite appointment, she noticed two women sitting on the sofa in the reception area. Both stopped rifling through magazines and looked her up and down.

She glanced at Windy, who stood up at her desk. "These two women are here to see you. I told them you have a full schedule, but they insisted on waiting to talk to you."

Cecelia set her briefcase down next to Windy's desk and walked over to the sofa. Both women stood. The one with shoulder-length brown hair pasted a false smile on her face and held out her arms. "Cecelia Chadwick. It's Crystal. Crystal Summers from high school." She teetered on her stilettos, her navy dress a little too tight, her lipstick, along with her voice, a little too bright.

"Crystal Summers," Cecelia repeated, trying to recall the name or the face. Neither were familiar.

Crystal dropped her arms. "We had social studies together. Or maybe science." She lifted a fisted hand in the air. "Mesquite High! Go Rams!"

Cecelia had no memory of Crystal, but to move things

along, she feigned recognition. "Of course. It's good to see you again, Crystal."

The other woman, a blonde, stared at her in what Cecelia could only describe as distaste. She also wore a skin-tight dress and very high heels, but she looked more at home in the outfit than Crystal. Her long hair fell in soft waves around her shoulders, her makeup model-perfect.

Crystal flapped her hand, like a nervous twitch. "Oh, I'm sorry. This is one of my best friends, Stacy Rich—"

The blond shot Crystal a killer glare.

"Riddick. Stacy Riddick."

Right. "It's nice to meet you, Stacy."

Stacy nodded but didn't return the greeting or a smile.

"How on earth did you end up in New York?" Crystal asked.

"I went to design school here."

"Oh, wow. Do you ever get back to Texas?"

Something was up, but Cecelia couldn't be sure what. "Occasionally."

"Well, it's so great to see you." Her eyes grew wide as she looked around. "And look at this place. You must be doing really well."

Cecelia didn't respond.

Crystal shot a nervous glance at Stacy, who showed no emotion. "So, do you ever see anyone from Texas? Like old classmates or . . . I don't know . . . old boyfriends?"

If Crystal actually remembered her, she'd know Cecelia didn't have any boyfriends.

"Nope."

Crystal glanced at her left hand. "No ring. You never married?"

That question stopped her heart. Who were these women? The dialog sounded preplanned, and Crystal's enthusiasm, phony. They were on a fishing expedition, but why? She glanced at her watch. "I'm sorry, but I have another appointment soon. What can I do for you?"

The blond stepped forward, crowding Cecelia's space. Her immediate impression—Stacy wanted to intimidate her.

"Crystal just moved to New York and saw your picture in a magazine. Once she gets settled, she'd like you to give her some decorating tips."

Cecelia forced herself not to take a step back. "I'd be happy to take a look, though I'm booked until after the holidays." Cecelia walked over to Windy's desk, picked up one of her business cards, and held it out to Crystal. "You can call Windy and set up an appointment for some time in Janu—"

"Sorry, that won't work," Crystal's friend snapped. "She needs someone before the holidays. We assumed, since you're an old friend, that you'd be happy to work her into your busy schedule."

Cecelia flashed a tightlipped smile. She'd been railroaded by better than this blonde. "I'm sorry too. Windy can give your name to one of the other associates here at the firm, or I'd be happy to recommend a couple of other designers in the New York area. You'll have to excuse me." She picked up her briefcase. "Good to see you again, Crystal."

She winked at Windy as she crossed the reception area and jogged up the stairs.

An hour later, she answered her ringing phone. "Cecelia Chadwick."

"Hi, Ce. How's your day?"

She'd asked Windy to tell her before transferring Jared's calls. In one ear and out the other, which wasn't like Windy.

"Interesting. How was dinner at your parents' house?"

"Anything but interesting."

"Sorry."

"Nothing new. What's made your day so interesting?"

"I had a strange visit from a girl I supposedly went to high school with."

~

"*R*eally? Did I know her?"

"I don't think so. Her name is Crystal Summers. She and her friend, Stacy . . . Riddick or something like that, were waiting when I got back from an appointment."

Jared's fist tightened around the phone receiver.

"Stacy said Crystal had just moved to New York and wanted some decorating ideas. When I told them I didn't have time until after the holidays, Stacy got in my face."

Jared rubbed his forehead. He knew without asking for a description that Stacy had gone to New York, dragging her friend Crystal with her. "Is that all they wanted?"

"Crystal asked a lot of questions. Did I ever get home to Texas? Was I married? The whole thing seemed weird. Stacy flashed the *old friend* card, but Crystal and I were never friends, old or otherwise."

Jared sat back in his chair. He never imagined Stacy would travel to New York, but he should have. He wouldn't put anything past her.

He'd tell Cecelia about Stacy the next time he saw her, which would be soon. "I'm coming to New York on Thursday. Can we do some sightseeing if you're free?"

"I'll see if I can rearrange some things on my schedule," she said softly.

He didn't care much about sightseeing. Other than work, he wanted to spend time with Cecelia. He already asked Windy if she could manipulate Cecelia's schedule a little, and she'd promised to work on it.

He didn't know if anything could be salvaged from the

feelings they used to have for each other, but until she signed those divorce papers, he wanted to explore the idea.

*L*ate the next day, Jared smelled steaks grilling as soon as he got out of his car. He followed the mouthwatering smells through the side gate of Knox's four-bedroom rambler, situated in the cove of a nice, older neighborhood.

Something most people didn't know about Knox. He was loaded, but, like Jared's grandparents, he didn't flaunt his money. Stacy had no idea, or she would have treated Knox much differently.

After his phone call with Cecelia yesterday, Jared felt confident about seeing her again, but at some point during the night, doubts crept in through his subconscious. By the break of day and many sleepless hours later, he knew, even if the consequences were disastrous, he had to try for this second chance with her.

The summer they spent together was the happiest time of his life.

In hindsight, he wished he'd done so many things differently. He should have taken Cecelia to California with him. He should have tried to transfer to a law school closer to her. He should have tried harder to find her.

Before he signed those blasted papers, he should have found her and insisted she tell him why she wanted a divorce. He'd given up too easily. Finding out they were still married was a sign—at least to him—that they might still have a chance for a future together.

Booger Red, Knox's Irish setter, came barreling toward him.

"Hi, boy. How're you doing?" He scrubbed Booger behind the ears.

"About time you got here," Knox called from the patio. "These steaks are almost done."

"Sorry. Got caught up in something at work."

"There's beer in the fridge. Grab one for me. Oh, and can you get the potatoes out of the oven? There's a bowl on the counter."

Jared let himself in through the sliding glass door and stopped. Placemats and a vase of white daisies graced the table, the barstools were covered with checkered fabric rather than their usual black leather, and a new picture hung on the kitchen wall.

He grabbed two beers out of the sparkling clean fridge and popped the tops. Turning off the oven, he forked the two baked potatoes into the bowl. Outside, the patio table had also been arranged with a woman's touch.

He set the potatoes and Knox's beer on the table and took a swig from his bottle. "Your house is showing signs of an invasion."

Knox chuckled. "Yeah, Abbey is trying to domesticate me."

"Looks like she's succeeding."

Jared got the design magazine out of his back pocket and set it next to his plate while Knox removed the steaks from the grill.

After garnishing potatoes, buttering corn on the cob, and cutting into the steaks, Knox motioned to the magazine with the tip of his knife. "You bring that for me?"

Jared opened it to the picture of Cecelia and set the magazine next to Knox's plate.

"That's the basketball player who left the Mavericks a couple of years ago," Knox said.

"Look who's with him."

Knox leaned closer. "That's Cecelia."

Jared nodded. "Stacy flipped to that page Friday night at

Granddad's birthday party. Susan recognized Cecelia and brought it to everyone's attention. Stacy started barking questions while Dad glowered and Susan's husband drooled."

Knox laughed. "Sounds like a typical night at the McAlister household. Stacy always barks. Charlie always glowers. And I can see why Tim was drooling. Ce's hot."

"Exactly what Tim said."

Knox tapped the picture with his index finger. "What did you tell Stacy?"

"The truth. Well, after we left Susan's, I told her the truth. That Ce and I got married, she filed for divorce, but it was never finalized, and that I've taken Cecelia to dinner twice." Jared took a big bite of sweet corn. "She's convinced Ce and I are sleeping together."

"Are you?"

"Come on, Knox. No. I do have a few morals left—more than you ever had. I can't believe you'd even ask."

"Just wondering, buddy. It's not like you aren't married," Knox replied with a grin. He picked up the magazine. "It's kind of weird to see Cecelia dressed so professionally."

"I told you she looked great."

"How are things going with her?"

"We talk on the phone. She's . . . skittish, and I don't understand why. She'll answer questions about her work or New York but clams up when I mention the past. We haven't discussed the divorce much. I dropped new divorce papers at her office, but she hasn't sent them back to Connor yet."

"Maybe she doesn't want a divorce."

A shimmer of hope moved through Jared.

"Where do things stand with Stacy?"

"I called off the wedding, told her I couldn't marry her."

"Oh, to be a fly on the wall," Knox said, spitting corn when he laughed.

"She doesn't want kids."

Knox's you're-an-idiot smirk appeared before he looked up from the magazine article. "And this is a surprise to you?"

"Strange as it sounds now, realizing did surprise me. I thought everyone wanted kids—eventually. You want kids, don't you?"

"If you'd asked me that question six months ago, I'm not sure how I would have answered, but now, with Abbey? Yeah, I want kids."

Knox cut a bite of steak. "Breaking off your engagement is the smartest move you've ever made. Hope you got the ring back."

"I didn't ask for it. I don't even care." The weight he'd been carrying around on his shoulders felt lighter every day.

Jared held a small piece of steak under the table. Booger snatched it, then licked his fingers in thanks.

"Will you quit doing that? Abbey thinks it's me."

Jared patted the dog's head.

"So, what's your plan with Ce?"

Jared took a minute to look around Knox's backyard. Mature trees shaded the pool and most of the patio. Huge planters held tall grasses rather than girly flowers. He wanted this—with Ce.

Except her business was booming in New York. She'd never want to come back to Texas. As comfortable as her apartment was, Jared didn't think he'd be happy living in that concrete jungle.

"I don't know. I'm going to New York on Thursday, and Ce's agreed to show me around. We haven't discussed a future together, but I'd like to see if one is possible."

Knox sat up a little straighter. "You love her?"

Jared paused a moment before nodding. "I still love her."

Pushing away from the table, Knox went inside. He came back a minute later, holding out a black velvet ring box.

"Is this what I think it is?" Jared took the box, lifted the lid, and whistled. "This is some rock, buddy. Congratulations."

"Don't congratulate me yet. Abbey might take one look and run for the hills."

"If she were going to run, she would have done it by now."

Knox pointed at his chest. "Would you marry this?"

"No, but for some reason, Abbey seems to like you. Does she want kids?"

"Yeah, the subject of kids has come up."

Jared set his plate aside, feeling satisfied and lazy. He and Knox didn't get to spend much time together anymore, so he appreciated when their schedules meshed for these rare dinners or Sundays on the lake.

The only thing missing was Cecelia by his side.

CHAPTER 22

*C*harles McAlister stopped in front of Grant Stern's
assistant. "Is Grant with a client?"

"Not at the moment. If you'll take a seat, I'll see if—"

"He'll see me." Charles pushed through Grant's door. He
caught the moment of surprise, then irritation, that crossed
Grant's face, which he did nothing to hide.

The assistant came through the door behind him. "I'm
sorry, Mr. Stern."

"It's fine, Anita. Please hold my calls." Grant stood. "Hello,
Charles. Two visits in a month. I'm starting to feel special."

"Well, don't. You know why I'm here."

"Can't say that I do." Grant indicated a chair in front of
his desk. He didn't wait for Charles to sit before taking his
chair.

"Jared broke off his engagement with Stacy."

Grant didn't respond, which infuriated Charles. "I believe
his trips to New York have something to do with it."

"As I've told you before, if Jared were to come to me
about personal matters, he knows I would keep our conversation confidential."

"So he has talked to you."

Grant rested his elbows on his desk. "I've known Jared his whole life, Charles. He's a good man who knows his mind. I'm sure he had his reasons for breaking his engagement."

"His reason is—" Charles stopped himself. Grant and his wife had liked Cecelia, so he'd get no support from him.

"My wife happened to see Stacy with another man two nights ago. Based on her description of the encounter, you're more upset over the broken engagement than Stacy appeared to be."

"I want Jared's trips to New York to end."

Grant studied him for a moment, which stoked Charles' rage even more. "Jared is the next junior associate in line to make partner, Charles. If his trips to New York end, so does the partnership. Do you really want that for your son? We need team players now we've opened the New York office, and Jared showed initiative by taking the bar exam. Beyond that, he's well-liked by both our clients and his peers, and his reputation is exemplary. The other associates are scrambling to catch up."

"If Jared wasn't offered the partnership, maybe he'd rethink his career choice. McAlister Industries is a much better fit." Charles stood and drove his index finger into the top of Grant's desk as the image of Cecelia ran through his mind. "I don't want him in New York. If that means losing out on a partnership at this firm, then so be it."

～

*O*n his way past, Jared set a stack of files on Violet's desk. "I need copies of these too."

She held up the copies she already made. "Mr. Stern is in your office."

Jared nodded and thumbed through the stack of papers

Violet handed him. "After you make these additional copies, will you send the entire file over to Stan Thorpe's office for me?"

"Give me two minutes," Violet said over her shoulder, already heading for the copy room.

Jared stepped into his office. "Morning, Grant."

"Sorry to come at a busy time. I only need a couple of minutes."

"Have a seat," Jared said, rounding his desk. He unbuttoned his suit coat and sat in his chair. "What can I do for you?"

"Your dad visited me again this morning. He told about your broken engagement and demanded that I put a stop to your trips to New York."

Cold fury swamped him. How would he ever escape his father's long arm of interference? Grant would tire of dealing with Charlie's intrusions, and Jared would lose his job. Unless he left Dallas. "I'm sorry, Grant."

"Don't think his visits reflect badly on you, Jared. Your dad popping in doesn't bother me. I think his hostility stems from me offering you a job after law school. He feels I stole you away from your family's business."

Jared shook his head. "I wouldn't have worked for Dad even if you hadn't offered me a job."

"He doesn't see it that way. I just want you to be aware that he's determined to stop you from traveling."

Grant looked down at his hands and flexed his fingers before meeting Jared's gaze. "Jessie and the girls were in Fort Worth two nights ago. They have a girls' night out once a month with my mother-in-law—dinner and a movie. Jessie saw Stacy at the restaurant with another man. They were in a corner booth, and they weren't just having dinner."

Surprise? Anger? Disgust? Nope. Jared felt none of the

emotions Grant probably expected. Instead, he was relieved. And a little sad that he didn't care more.

Grant cleared his throat. "I'm sorry, Jared. Though Jessie thought you should know, she didn't want me to be the one to tell you. She feels horrible."

Jared knew Stacy wouldn't be alone for long. "Please tell Jessie not to feel bad. I'm glad Stacy has moved on."

"Are you okay?"

Jared smiled. "Actually, I'm great. Kind of twisted, huh?"

Grant shook his head. "No, especially if things between you and Stacy weren't working."

"I can't believe it took me so long to realize how tense and unhappy I've been."

"Does the breakup have anything to do with your divorce not being finalized?"

"I would have broken off our engagement anyway. Stacy and I want different things in life. I feel pretty stupid that I didn't realize we just don't mesh before I proposed. Dad's furious. Mom's upset. The grandparents have my back as usual."

"And the divorce? Does Cecelia know?"

"Yes. I delivered new divorce papers to her office."

"Are you okay?" Grant asked again. Something his dad never asked.

"I'll let you know when I see how things play out."

⁓

After his frustrating conversation with Grant, Charles went back to his office and formulated a plan. James Decker had a female associate call Foster, Stern, and Wallace to request an appointment with Jared to discuss a possible merger between two Colorado mountain resorts.

When the call transferred to Jared's assistant, she said

Jared would be traveling the rest of the week but had some availability the following week. She didn't reveal where, but Charles knew the kid was going back to New York.

"I want him followed twenty-four hours a day, both before and after he leaves. I need a full report daily, and pictures," Charles said when Decker called with the information his associate had gathered.

"I've already booked a flight," Decker said.

After Charles transferred funds to Decker's account, he walked to his office windows. The summer heat finally let up with a slight break in the blazing temperatures. Betsy had planned to send out invitations for their annual dinner party with cocktails on the patio, but all the planned guests would have been wedding guests as well. Betsy, still mortified by Jared's decision to break his engagement, didn't want to field the expected questions, and neither did he.

Jared had made life among their acquaintances very uncomfortable. Because of his immature, rash decision, Betsy had turned down a couple of engagements they normally would have attended.

Charles circled his desk in aggravation. As soon as Decker got back to him with proof Jared was seeing Cecelia, he could set his plan in motion.

~

Cecelia sensed it was Jared calling before she picked up. "Cecelia Chadwick."

"Sorry to call in the middle of the day, but I'm selfish. A day . . . that's as long as I can go without hearing your voice."

You went for twelve years without hearing my voice.

She wasn't sure why he was calling or what they were doing. He asked her to show him New York, but he hadn't said anything about calling every day being part of the deal.

Putting a hand to her chest, she tried to decide if her heart was still shedding pieces or going through the painful process of trying to piece itself back together.

Stepping off the cliff's ledge, she said, "I'm glad you called."

"You are? You're glad, as in you wanted to hear my voice too? Or you're glad, as in, you wanted me to call so you can tell me to quit bothering you."

"I'm glad you called, as in I'm afraid talking to you could be one of the biggest mistakes I'll ever make, but I wanted to hear your voice, too."

"It won't be a mistake, Ce."

"How do you know?"

He didn't answer for a strangled heartbeat. "You used to look on the bright side of things. What happened to your optimism?"

Life. Her heart must be piecing itself back together because it only ached rather than the searing pain she felt twelve years ago. "I'm not the same person I used to be."

"We've both changed, so let's get to know the people we've become. You said we were friends. Isn't that how friends become more than friends?"

Her heart stopped beating altogether. The office really needed a defibrillator for these moments. "How would that be possible? You live in Dallas."

"But I travel to New York pretty frequently."

"Are you dating anyone?" she blurted out. She needed to know but was terrified to hear the answer.

"No, Ce, I'm not dating anyone."

She swallowed hard, trying to ease the catch in her throat. The next question would be the most difficult to ask, but again, she needed to know. "Do you have any children, Jared?"

"No. I don't have any children," he said, his tone gentle.

Honest. She imagined his face, his brown eyes. She loved his eyes.

"Do you have any more questions?"

"No." But she wanted to leave the door open. "Not right now."

"There are some things I want to tell you, Ce, but not over the phone. Nothing bad, but things I think you should know."

Her imagination flew in a dozen directions.

"I plan to come to New York as often as possible. Are you okay with that?"

She touched her chest again. Would the ache never stop? "Honestly?"

"Yes."

"I'm not sure."

"I want to see you, Cecelia, as often as you'll let me." He waited a beat. "Let's get to know the people we are now."

Please don't let me be sorry. "Okay," she said after a moment's hesitation.

❧

*J*ared, still on a high after talking to Cecelia, ended up being lucky enough to golf the afternoon away in a scrimmage with lawyers from several firms. Afterward, the club closed the restaurant to everyone but their group. He enjoyed a steak dinner with all the trimmings while talking shop with other firms.

Just as a server cleared his plate, his cell phone rang. He was tempted not to answer when he saw Stacy's pouty-lipped face, but a niggling feeling told him he should.

Twenty minutes later, he pulled into the parking lot of The Stampede, Stacy's favorite club. Over the phone, he could tell she'd been drinking and knew he wouldn't sleep if he didn't make sure she got home safely.

Inside, the blare of the country band and the stomping of feet vibrated the wood floor. He stood for a moment, allowing his eyes to adjust to the dark. For a weeknight, the place was packed. Didn't any of these people have to work the next day?

He finally spotted Stacy cuddled up to a cowboy. She lifted his hat and set it on her head.

Jared walked over and touched her shoulder. She glanced around, her eyes widening in drunken surprise. Then she stumbled toward him.

"Well, look who's here. Wha'd you want?"

He took her arm to steady her. "I thought you might need a ride home."

"I've gotta ride," she said, looking behind her with an exaggerated wink.

"Stacy, look at me." Jared turned her chin in his direction. "Don't do something stupid just because you're angry at me. Let me take you home."

She wrapped her arms around his neck, leaning into him. "I knew you'd come back, Jare Bear."

"Give the cowboy his hat, and let's get out of here."

∼

*T*he annoying ring startled Cecelia awake. She fumbled for her cell phone. "Hello?"

"Sorry to wake you. I just need to hear your voice one more time today."

"Except it's tomorrow in New York," she said, glancing at the clock.

"Right. Sorry about that, too," Jared said.

Cecelia snuggled back against the pillows. "Bad night?"

"Not great."

"Want to talk about it?"

"Nope. I want to talk about you. I tried to call you earlier but only got your answering machine. Were you out?"

"I went out with a friend, movie, and dinner."

"Woman friend?"

"Yes," she said, smiling at the change in his tone. She put a hand over her mouth to stifle a yawn. "Did you work late?"

"I golfed with some buddies, then went to dinner. Tell me about your friend."

She spent several minutes telling him about Valerie and how they met. Val had spent some time tonight questioning her about Jared, too.

The moon lit a path across the foot of her bed. She remembered moon-watching with Jared many times the summer they were together. "Tell me about your *not great* day."

"Another time. What are you wearing?"

"Jared." He used to ask the same thing before they were married. And after.

"Sorry. I couldn't help myself. Is it sexy?"

"No. I'm wearing one of Derrick's Navy T-shirts."

"That could be sexy."

"It's not. I promise."

They talked for thirty minutes before they both started yawning and apologizing. "I'll let you get back to sleep," Jared finally said. "I'll call you tomorrow. Sweet dreams, Cecelia."

Her breath caught. He used to say the same thing that long-ago summer. Good or bad, they were falling back into their old routines. "Good night, Jared."

CHAPTER 23

*J*ared pressed the intercom button on his phone when it beeped. "Yes, Violet."

"Stacy Richardson is here to see you."

"I'm pretty sure he remembers my last name," came a voice in the background.

Jared blew out a breath. The last person he wanted to deal with today. "Send her in."

Stacy opened the door and stepped over the threshold, then turned to Violet. "If you ever decide to get your hair professionally cut, let me know, and I'll give you my André's number. He loves a challenge."

Jared couldn't hear Violet's response but could easily imagine her eye-roll as soon as Stacy closed the door.

He studied her for a moment, angry that he'd taken so long to come to his senses, yet grateful he'd gone to Connor for his prenup, or he wouldn't have found out he was still married. Believing his feelings for Cecelia were long dead, he wouldn't have tried to find her. But seeing her again reminded him what it felt like to really be in love. She'd awakened long-dormant, heart-pounding emotions. As silly as it sounded, she made him feel like a kid again.

"I hope I'm not interrupting."

Stacy wore a new dress the equal of every figure-accentuating dress she owned, her hair and makeup as perfect as always.

He stood as she walked toward him. "I have a few minutes."

"Something must be wrong with your cell phone. I've left several messages, and you haven't returned any of my calls. I thought maybe you'd taken a little trip to New York to see your wife."

No way would he bite the shiny bait she dangled. Instead, he waited until she sat in a chair and crossed her legs provocatively before he took his chair. "What can I do for you, Stacy?"

"If you'd listened to any of my messages, you'd know I want to take you to dinner to thank you for last night."

He hadn't listened to her messages and wasn't interested in dinner. He sat back and relaxed his jaw, still angry she'd gone to see Cecelia. "Dinner isn't necessary."

"Please, Jared. My treat. For being sweet enough to rescue me."

He'd driven her home, carried her inside to bed, and left. "I just wanted to make sure you got home safely."

"So you *do* care?"

"Of course, I care."

"Tucking me into bed *while I was still dressed* was knight-in-shining-armor gallant. So, dinner?" She tapped her long pink nails on her bare thigh.

His flight to New York was in a few hours. "I have plans."

"You have to eat, Jared. What's the harm in a thank-you dinner? Are you afraid your wife will find out?"

"I'm not doing this with you, Stac."

"Doing what? I'm sure she's thrilled you broke our engagement. Or didn't you tell her about me?"

Stacy was a master at manipulation, but not today. Not ever again.

"You haven't seen her since you broke our engagement, have you?"

"No, but you have."

She quickly masked her surprise. "She told you?"

He didn't answer.

"Well"—Stacy flipped her hand and produced a smirk—"she's a sweet little thing, but not very willing to help a friend."

"You think she should have agreed to help Crystal only to find out Crystal never moved to New York?"

Again, a shot of surprise flashed across Stacy's face. "Discussing her clients with you isn't being very discreet."

"Crystal isn't her client."

She ran her fingertips along the neckline of her low-cut dress in an attempt to draw his eyes lower. She was desperate. Like their chat about having children, she was not only losing the battle but the war.

"We'll go out, and your sweet little wife will never know. Simply an innocent dinner." She batted her eyelashes. "What happens afterward will stay between us."

Jared stood, walked around his desk, and took her elbow, pulling her to her feet. "Let me walk you to the elevator so I can get back to work."

She yanked away from his grasp and stomped to the door, shooting him an icy glare. "I won't be so nice on my next trip to New York."

He caught her arm again before she got to the door. "Stay away from Cecelia, Stacy. I'm warning you."

She stared at him for a split second, then smiled. "You've got nothing on me."

"Try me."

Jerking the door open, she stalked out. Violet glanced at him with raised brows.

Stacy was right. He didn't have any inside knowledge that would hurt her. And he would never use it if he had. But her moment of hesitancy—that tiny flicker of insecurity that held her in place, staring at him—would be enough to keep her away from Cecelia.

⁓

"*J*ared." Windy jumped up and ran around her desk. "Are you here to get lucky?"

Jared hugged the woman he'd been getting to know over the phone. "I certainly hope so. Please tell me Ce is in."

"She is."

Jared touched his pounding heart at the news.

"When did you get here?" Windy asked, releasing her hold.

"Just now. I stopped at the hotel long enough to drop off my suitcase and unpack this."

She slapped his chest playfully. "Another gift? You're spoiling me, and I love it."

"Don't get too excited. It's just a small thank-you."

"For what?"

"Believing in me from the very first day we met."

"Yeah, Ce wasn't too happy when I gave you the name of her favorite café."

He'd wondered if her revealing information would get her in trouble. "Sorry."

She ripped the paper off the bracelet-sized box. "If this is diamonds, I absolutely can't accept—well, I can, but I shouldn't."

"It's nothing that elaborate."

Windy lifted the lid, and her eyes grew wide. "Jared, I love it."

He'd had her name engraved in a matching pen and pencil set.

She hugged his neck. "Thank you. You're so thoughtful."

"You're welcome."

"Does Ce know you're in New York?"

"She knows I'm coming, just not when."

"Come with me. I'll take you up to her office." Windy took his hand and led him up the stairs. In the office at the top, a man sat behind a desk. Windy shushed him when he opened his mouth.

Jared knew from the picture in the newspaper that the man was Cecelia's boss but didn't get a chance to introduce himself as Windy hauled him along behind her. She put a hand on his chest to stop him just short of an open door. "Hey, Ce?"

Jared heard a chair roll over the wood floor. "Yes?"

The sound of her voice made Jared's heart knock harder against his ribs. He'd been nervous about surprising her, but it was too late to turn back now. Maybe he should have mentioned when to expect him the last time they talked.

"Sorry I forgot to tell you, but you have another appointment today."

"I do?"

"Yes. He's a cranky, demanding guy."

"When's the appointment?"

Windy pulled Jared around her. "Right now."

As soon as he saw the shocked delight on Cecelia's face, Jared's unease evaporated.

"Jared." She stood and moved around her desk.

Without stopping to think, he pulled her into his arms. Once he had her tight against him, he didn't want to let her go, pleased when she hugged him back. He leaned back enough to look into her beautiful blue eyes. "I hope I'm not interrupting."

"You're not interrupting," she said breathlessly, which pleased him even more. "I just assumed you'd be busy at your office all day."

"I have to go in tomorrow."

The man from the other office walked in, hands in his pants pockets.

"Jared, this is the boss-man, Arthur Winston," Windy said.

Jared extended his hand. "Jared McAlister. It's nice to meet you, sir. Cecelia speaks highly of you and your wife."

Winston shook his hand. "Nice to put a face with the nickname Windy gave you, Jared."

Jared grinned at Windy. "She and I have become pretty good friends over the phone."

"Windy has that way about her," Winston said. "What brings you to New York so often?"

Jared smiled at the question. From what Cecelia told him, Winston was more of a father figure than a boss, so obviously, he would be curious and concerned. "In Dallas, I'm an attorney with Foster and Stern, and our office recently merged with Kenneth Wallace here in New York."

Winston rubbed a hand over his goatee. "What kind of law do you practice?"

"Mergers and acquisitions."

"You must travel quite a bit."

"Some," Jared said. "Mostly between Dallas and New York."

Winston nodded as if satisfied with the answers. He glanced at Cecelia. "Do you two have plans for this afternoon?"

"Yes," Windy interjected before Cecelia could say anything.

"If Ce is free, I hope she can show me some of the city. I've never had time to do much sightseeing on my previous trips."

Windy clapped. "Fun. What do you want to see?"

"What would you recommend?"

"That you end your sightseeing expedition at my husband's restaurant for dinner."

"Your husband has a restaurant?"

"Kevin is part owner and executive chef at a very nice restaurant not far from here," Winston explained.

"We'll never get in without reservations," Cecelia said.

Windy picked up Cecelia's desk phone. "I'll get you in."

Winston chuckled. "Dinner is hours away. What are you going to do until then?"

Jared held out his arms. "I don't know the city, so I'm leaving the decision in Ce's capable hands."

She smiled sweetly. "Okay, let's see some sights."

Windy hung up the phone. "You can stop by anytime. There's a table with your name on it."

"Thanks, Windy," Cecelia said.

They took a cab to Times Square. After fighting the crowd, they broke free and walked east along Forty-Second Street past Bryant Park, where the leaves were just beginning to turn.

Jared took a chance, reached for Cecelia's hand, and smiled when she intertwined their fingers and smiled back.

They walked past the New York City Public Library Main Branch on their way to Grand Central Terminal. Then they backtracked to Fifth Avenue and Rockefeller Plaza.

Jared enjoyed seeing the landmarks, but he enjoyed spending time with Cecelia more.

Next, they visited a small section of Central Park, where she pointed out a few movie landmarks.

Dusk had fallen by the time they hailed a taxi that carried them back down 5th Avenue, past the Empire State Building on their way to Windy's husband's restaurant, located in the heart of Tribeca. The interior was warm and inviting, decorated with dark wood and earth tones.

Cecelia asked the hostess if the chef had a moment.

A man Jared recognized from one of the pictures in Cecelia's living room came from the back and gathered Cecelia into a familiar hug.

"Kevin Conley, this is Jared McAlister."

Kevin held out his hand, his brown eyes dancing with as much delight as Windy's. "Ahh, my wife's Tall, Dark, and Handsome."

"Nice to meet you, Kevin."

"Show them to table eight, Shawna," Kevin said to the hostess. "You two enjoy your dinner."

Cecelia smiled. "Thanks, Kev."

"If you'll follow me." The hostess led them to a table in a quiet corner. A server appeared immediately after they were settled. He recited the specials along with the chef's recommendations. They both selected Kevin's suggestions, which started with boiled shrimp in a unique remoulade dressing.

"Mmm, this is delicious," Jared said.

"Everything here is delicious. Kevin is an amazing chef."

Salads were mixed greens tossed with artichokes, asparagus, tomatoes, and hearts of palm in a light vinaigrette dressing.

Cecelia ordered trout with toasted almonds and lemon-butter drizzle along with steamed asparagus. Jared had prime tenderloin with Marchand de Vin sauce, diced potatoes, and glazed carrots. Chocolate molten cake with raspberry filling and ice cream for two were delivered without them ordering dessert.

Cecelia stared at the dessert with wide eyes.

Jared held out his spoon with a bite of the decadent dessert.

Cecelia shook her head. "I can't, Jared."

"What do you mean you can't?" Kevin appeared behind Cecelia and rested his hands on her shoulders.

She patted one of his hands. "Kevin, everything was delicious as usual."

"My tenderloin was perfect."

"I'm glad you enjoyed dinner, but you have to try the dessert. We have a new pastry chef, Ce. Her desserts are out of this world."

"One bite," Jared coaxed, wiggling the spoon.

Cecelia leaned forward and ate the bite he held out. He and Kevin laughed when she rolled her eyes.

"Oh my gosh, this is amazing."

"Told you," Kevin said.

When the server passed by, Jared asked for the check.

"It's been taken care of," he said with a smile.

"No, Kevin," Cecelia said.

"Not me." He held up his hands as he backed away from their table. "You two have a nice night."

"Who?" Jared asked Cecelia.

She shook her head. "I'll bet it was Winston, but he'll never admit it."

Jared reached across the table and took Cecelia's hand. "I have a long day in the office tomorrow, but I'd like to meet afterward at that little café where we first had dinner if you don't have any plans."

"I'd like that."

They took a cab from the restaurant to Cecelia's apartment. She argued that they were passing his hotel to get her home, but he insisted. With the cab waiting, he walked her up the three flights of stairs and unlocked her door.

"Thank you for showing me some of the city this afternoon. I had a really nice time."

"Me too," she said. "I'm glad you're in town for a couple of days."

"Me too." He closed the slight distance between them, unable to fight the rare and powerful cord that tugged him forward. Would she hit him or turn away if he tried to kiss her?

Her eyes sparkled. Did she feel the longing as acutely as he did? He stretched the moment out, not wanting to rush. Tonight would be a memory to last him long after he went back to Dallas. A new memory. A New York memory.

He raised his hands to her face and slowly lowered his mouth to hers, pressing lightly. Every nerve in his body hummed with an awareness of her.

She responded by leaning into him, so he tilted his head to deepen the kiss, pulling her closer while they explored each other's mouths like it was their first kiss.

He felt her tremble against him—or was it he who trembled? It didn't matter—he had Cecelia in his arms. He drew back enough to rest his forehead against hers, needing to catch his breath. He opened his eyes. "You taste the same."

She smiled. "So do you."

"How is that possible?"

One of her shoulders lifted slightly. "I don't know, but I'm glad."

He studied her for a long moment. "Happy anniversary, Ce."

Her chest rose with her quick gasp. "You remembered."

He nodded. How could she think he'd forgotten? "Thank you for today. It was the perfect way to celebrate."

"I agree."

He brushed his lips lightly across hers. "I'll see you tomorrow."

"Good night, Jared."

Leaving her standing at her door was harder than Jared could ever have imagined. He climbed into the taxi, fighting the urge to run back and tell Cecelia he loved her, that he didn't want a divorce. He'd move to New York if that's what it took for them to be together.

For the first time in a long time, he felt in control of his life. Tonight had been like a cleansing rain, washing everything clean, clearing his mind of the clutter, removing the blinders from his eyes and his heart.

He loved Cecelia Chadwick, and he wanted to spend the rest of his life with her.

~

*C*ecelia watched Jared disappear into the night before she stepped inside and closed the door. That he remembered their anniversary left her breathless. They'd pledged their love twelve years ago today.

She sank to her sofa with equal amounts of awe and dread. Twelve years ago, she thought New York would be far enough from Texas, but Jared found her. She lived in Manhattan, and his life was in Dallas. Between her mom and Charles McAlister, she didn't think she could ever go back, so how would this work? She had so many clients here. It would take years to rebuild what she had at Winston and Associates.

But everything felt so real tonight, yet so surreal. Jared was back in her life. Whether for good or bad, Cecelia wasn't sure. While sitting across the table from him, looking into his beautiful brown eyes, it seemed like no time had passed. Yet it had. So much in her life had changed, and she was sure his life had changed quite a bit too.

Did she dare risk her heart, now beating true and strong after that kiss? Could she put what happened behind her and finally move forward? Because she still loved him, she knew she had to try.

CHAPTER 24

*W*indy had a whole list of questions for Cecelia as soon as she walked in the next morning. Cecelia answered while collecting her messages.

"Did he kiss you? Oh, I can tell he did," Windy said, laughing and pointing to Cecelia's pink cheeks. "Was it good? Better than when you were eighteen?"

"Both the same and better."

An hour later, she made her final walkthrough with Mr. Basketball amid his enthusiastic thanks for completing his loft ahead of schedule. After she finished there, she stopped to check on the renovations at Mr. and Mrs. Hollywood's place. One set of subcontractors was installing the stairs, and another couple of men were hanging drywall in the master bedroom. When the architect happened to show up, they walked through the space together while he filled her in on how the different projects were timed out.

Back at the office, she'd barely sat at her desk when Winston walked in.

"Hey, sweetheart. How did your final walk-through go?"

"Mr. Basketball is happy with the results." She smiled. "Thank you for dinner last night."

He tried to look confused without success. "Dinner?"

"I know you paid for our dinner, Winston. You shouldn't have, but thank you. It was very nice."

He nodded. "Now you've brought up the subject of Jared . . ."

"I didn't," she said with a laugh.

". . . you looked pretty happy to have him in your office yesterday," he went on as if she hadn't spoken.

"Did I?" She tried for calm when she really wanted to scream and shout her happiness and apprehension at the same time.

He took a seat and folded his hands over his belly. "Will you tell me the story?"

"I've told you."

"Humor me."

"Jared and I dated the summer before I came to New York. His family had money, mine didn't, which meant I was nothing—lower than nothing—to his parents." She looked away. "I was so far beneath them, I glided under their radar for the first month Jared and I dated. I'm sure they thought Jared would come to his senses and drop me. I might have thought the same thing."

"But he didn't," Winston said.

She met his gaze. "No. We dated until he left for law school and I came to New York." Their marriage was still too personal to reveal. "You were here the afternoon Windy told me Tall, Dark, and Handsome had come in. I had no idea who it was until she mentioned dimples. Then I knew. Jared found me after eleven years. Actually, twelve." She blew out a breath and glanced at the ceiling. "Now I ask myself, is our running into each other a mistake? Or a second chance?"

Winston shifted in his chair. "What does your head tell you?"

"Something different than my heart."

"Why the conflicting emotions? Did he hurt you?"

She wished she could brush the question away with a laugh. "Once he got to law school, he . . . started seeing someone else while I thought we were still together. I was a naïve, inexperienced eighteen-year-old, just out of high school." She felt her smile wobble. "Jared was my first love."

"And now?"

Cecelia shrugged. "He lives in Dallas, and I live here."

"He said the firm he works for merged with an office in New York, so maybe—"

Cecelia held up her hand to stop him. "It's way too soon to start thinking beyond today."

"Is he seeing someone in Dallas?"

She was embarrassed that she'd asked Jared the same question. "He said he isn't."

"I've been the one saying you need a nice man in your life. Now I'm worried. I don't think I could bear to see you hurt."

"And I don't want to get hurt." *But how will I ever fall in love if I don't take the risk?*

❧

*J*ared had been waiting at their table for twenty minutes when Cecelia rushed in. He'd barely made it through the day. He'd been so distracted with thoughts of her. The fact that they'd fallen back into such a comfortable norm after so many years amazed him.

He stood when she approached the table and kissed her cheek. "I couldn't wait much longer to see you. I thought about coming to your office and dragging you away."

Cecelia glanced at her watch. "Am I late?"

He held her chair. "I didn't say you were late. I said I couldn't wait much longer to see you."

Pink misted her cheeks.

Lonnie stopped at their table. "We missed you last night, Ce."

"We ate at Kevin's restaurant."

"Ahh, so you're slumming it tonight."

Cecelia laughed. "Not at all. You know I love Rosemary's cooking and your wonderful hospitality."

Jared watched the interaction between Ce and Lonnie and wondered how long they'd been friends. She'd changed so much since she was eighteen. Back then, she'd known what she wanted and had a determination he admired. Now she was a beautiful businesswoman who exuded confidence and poise.

And in spite of all that, the kind, gentle part of Ce hadn't changed. As he listened to her and Lonnie talk, he could tell she still cared about the people in her life.

After dinner, Jared walked Cecelia home. At her door, he pulled her close. "I have to fly back to Dallas tomorrow afternoon. Please say you can meet for lunch before I go."

"I can meet."

He loved her smile; he loved her voice; he loved her blue eyes—he loved everything about her. For fear of scaring her, he worked hard to contain the feelings overwhelming him. But he couldn't wait another minute before kissing her. Gently, he lowered his mouth to hers. Her fingers touched his jaw, then his earlobe, sending goosebumps down his arms. She felt so good against him, exactly where she belonged. He leaned back to see the warmth flood her blue eyes. "I'll pick you up at your office at noon."

"See you then. Good night, Jared."

On the way back to his hotel, Jared felt the negativity and

discontent slipping away from his life. Like a slow leak, it was seeping out of his soul, being replaced by pure joy.

How long had it been since he'd felt this satisfied with life?

So long he'd forgotten how good a simple smile felt.

~

*W*indy, Winston, and Jared were chatting in the reception area when Cecelia came down the stairs at noon the next day. Seeing him in her world, joking with coworkers like he'd known them forever, was jarring.

"Hello."

"Hi." He reached out and took her hand. "Winston was just telling me about his annual Halloween party."

Cecelia felt a moment of self-consciousness as both Winston and Windy's glances dropped to her and Jared's linked fingers. She nodded. "Everyone looks forward to Winston and Maria's Halloween party. It's quite the event."

"We were just discussing what Jared could come dressed as," Windy said.

Cecelia turned to Jared in surprise. "You'll be back in town that weekend?"

He nodded. "Want to be my date?"

She couldn't think of anything she wanted more . . . but was she ready to be a couple in a huge group setting? The thought kind of terrified her.

She hadn't been able to sleep last night thinking about the divorce papers she still hadn't signed. Where did she and Jared stand on the matter, and should she mention the divorce at lunch?

"I'd love to."

He narrowed his eyes. "You hesitated. If you'd rather I didn't come—"

"No. No, not at all. My mind flitted somewhere else for a moment."

"You sure?"

"Absolutely. Winston's Halloween party is always amazing."

*A*fter lunch, Jared kissed her goodbye under the autumn leaves. How could something feel so right so quickly? Jared had wedged himself into the crack in her heart that felt like it was mending itself one piece at a time. Not quite as fragile anymore, its beat became stronger every day.

He ran his thumb across her cheekbone. "I don't want to leave you, Ce."

She swallowed her fear and stepped into eighteen-year-old Cecelia. "I don't want you to leave me."

His lips met hers. "I'll be back next Monday. I can't stay away from you for long."

A voice whispered, *divorce papers.*

"I miss you already," he said before kissing her again.

She'd forgotten how much she liked this kissing part. "Call me?"

"Every single day."

She watched the cab drive down the street, Jared waving out the back window. She put a hand to her stomach as emotions clashed against each other. Giddy happiness. Panic and trepidation.

She told Winston it was too soon to think beyond today, but she couldn't help thinking about the future. They'd tried once and failed. Did she dare risk another attempt? Normally too organized, too methodical to live with uncertainty, she'd found herself changing her schedule around to accommodate his visits.

She shook her head to clear her thoughts. They hadn't made any commitments or promises.

The cab turned the corner, and she lowered her hand.

He called much later that night, waking her with a start. "Hi."

"You know the reason I call you so late is to hear your soft, sexy, full-of-sleep voice," he said with a chuckle. "Sorry to wake you."

"It's okay. Did you make it home safely?"

"I did." He waited a beat. "I'm still thinking about that moment of hesitation you had about the Halloween party."

She turned on her side and pulled the comforter up to her chin. "I'm sorry. It just seems so weird to be seeing each other again. It takes me by surprise sometimes."

"It surprises me too, but it feels good, doesn't it? It seems so effortless and right to me."

She felt the same way about seeing him but didn't have the courage to tell him just yet.

"Even though you've changed in some ways, Ce, you're exactly the same in others. You feel the same when I hold you. You kiss the same. I know when I take your hand, you'll squeeze mine back."

"I didn't realize I did that."

"Always," he chuckled. "But you look different, and you certainly dress differently. You've changed your hair. Even your perfume is different, but you still smell the same—fresh, like a summer field of flowers and sunshine. And your heart is the same, Cecelia."

No, my heart has had reconstructive surgery.

"Are you sure you're okay with me coming for the party?"

"Yes."

"You'll have to give me some ideas for a costume. I haven't dressed up for Halloween since . . ." He laughed. "I can't remember when. Maybe when I was twelve."

"I'll get you fixed up."

"No silly elf nylon-y things on my legs."

His comment made her smile. "Nothing involving tights."

"Are you going to make me look weird?"

"Absolutely, but only because you'll look weird if you don't look weird. Everyone goes all out for Winston and Maria's party."

CHAPTER 25

*C*ecelia and the Hollywood couple finalized the last of
the renovation details Monday morning. Then she
and Peaches, the nickname Windy gave her client because
the woman smelled like a fresh peach, shopped for a traditional table to fit the Norman Rockwell Thanksgiving she
had planned. Her last stop was the office.

After checking with Windy, she ran upstairs to her desk.
Just as she sat, her cell phone rang, and Jared's number lit the
screen.

"Hi. It's me," he said when she connected the call.

She wished she could see his smile rather than just hear it
in his voice. "Hi, me."

"I thought I'd give you a quick call before I board my
flight."

"I'm glad you did."

"Guess what?" he asked.

"What?"

"Just hearing your soft voice is like rain during a drought,
a cool, welcome relief. I can't get you off my mind. It doesn't
matter where I am or what I'm doing, I'm thinking of you."

"I'm having the same problem."

"Oh, great," he said with a laugh. "You think of it as a problem, and I love that you're everywhere I look."

"I didn't mean it like that."

"How did your weekend go?"

"Wonderful. I spent two days in the country with no work." She walked to the window and looked at the tree just outside their office. The leaves were changing to a pretty shade of orange.

"Who did you go to the country with?"

"My friend Valerie. Her parents live on a farm about an hour north of the city, and Val has a house on their land. How was your weekend?"

"Uneventful. I did have brunch with my family yesterday."

"That's nice."

"Not too bad. I told Grammy that you and I had dinner together a few times. It got me thinking about the day I met you."

"I've thought about that day myself recently."

"I told myself I wasn't interested in a high school girl until you looked at me with your beautiful blue eyes. Then I heard your soft voice and was completely hooked. Do you remember later, when we walked along the beach? Man, I wanted to reach out and touch your hair, feel your skin, kiss your lips."

Just listening to his sweet words had her heart pounding. "Why didn't you?"

"Because I promised if you'd take a walk with me, I'd keep my hands to myself. Plus, you were an Ice Princess. I was scared you'd freeze me to death with your frosty glare."

"You said my eyes are beautiful."

"They were that night, too, after I warmed them up. I wish I could gaze into them right now." He paused a moment.

"You have no idea how many times I reached for your hand when we were walking to your apartment that first night in New York. I wanted to touch you that night, too."

"Why didn't you?" she asked again.

"For fear you'd haul off and punch me in the nose. You were very wary that night, and I didn't want to take the chance that you would refuse to see me again. In a round-about way, I kept trying to find out if you were seeing someone, but you wouldn't come out and say yes or no. I didn't know if you were married or living with someone, although I hoped it was neither. Especially since I had divorce papers in my hotel room."

"We should talk about the divorce papers."

"No," he said abruptly. "Let's talk about anything but the divorce papers."

"Okay." She searched for a topic. "Tell me about where you live in Dallas."

"I live in a condo in a suburb with a pretty view of a golf course with lots of trees. It's a guy's place, drab and boring, and in desperate need of your expertise to brighten it up. I don't have many pictures on walls that are painted—I'm not sure what color to call it—condo drab."

She tried to imagine his living space.

"Actually, I don't want you to see it. You'd run screaming in the other direction."

"I'm sure it's not that bad."

Zack climbed out of a cab in front of the office and waved up at her.

"Do you know how I knew Knox was getting serious about his girlfriend?" Jared asked.

"Knox! How is he? You two must still see each other."

"He's exactly the same. He owns an import business and is doing extremely well. We still hit the lake when we can.

"That's good to hear. So how could you tell he's getting serious?"

"He has placemats on his kitchen table."

"She's domesticating him."

"That's what I told him," Jared said on another chuckle.

"Do you like his girlfriend?"

"Abbey is perfect for him. You'd like her."

Cecelia wondered if she'd ever get the chance to meet Abbey.

"I can't wait to see you. Can we meet for dinner?"

"Come to my place. I'll cook."

"No, Ce, I don't want you to go to any—"

Cecelia sat at her desk. "Jared, you've bought my dinner every time you've come to town. Let me make dinner tonight . . . unless you object to home cooking?"

"If you cook anything like you used to, I'd be a fool to object."

"Then it's settled. Dinner at my place."

"I'm not sure when I can get there."

"Don't rush. It'll be ready when you arrive."

As soon as she disconnected the call, Windy walked into her office. "So, you're cooking dinner for Jared tonight?"

"Yes," Cecelia replied without looking up.

Windy plopped down on a chair in front of Cecelia's desk. "Mind if I ask why you two stopped dating—and don't give me that *we lost touch* stuff. I'd like to know, Ce, because you two seem fabulous together."

Cecelia opened her laptop. "The summer we dated came to an end, Jared went away to law school in California, and I came to New York. I heard he started dating someone else. The end."

Windy rolled her eyes. "Maybe him dating someone else was just a rumor. Did you ever ask him?"

Cecelia looked down at her desk. "I was told by a *reliable* source."

"Still—"

"We come from very different backgrounds. His family is rolling-in-money rich. According to his parents, my family came from the wrong side of the tracks. His family owns McAlister Industries—which is a multi-billion-dollar company. My father works in a hardware store, and my mother—"

"That wouldn't matter to Jared."

Cecelia smiled. "You're right. It didn't seem to matter to him, but it did matter to his family, especially his father. Charles McAlister saw me as a threat to Jared's future. Jared and his father fought a lot that summer, all because he was dating me." Cecelia took a deep breath and exhaled raggedly. "In the end, it was the smart decision."

"How do you know?"

"I know."

"But—"

"Windy, you need to let this go. It's in the past."

❧

*C*ecelia buzzed him through the street level door at seven-fifteen. Jared took the stairs two at a time, anxious to see her. Her apartment door stood open, so he set his briefcase down and turned into the kitchen. She was standing at the sink but glanced over her shoulder and smiled. "Hi."

"Hello." He caught her arm and pulled her close. He'd been thinking of her lips all day and needed to get a kiss out of the way. She delighted every one of his senses. His jittery nerves calmed the moment he heard her soft voice. Her floral fragrance was intoxicating. Her pretty blue eyes sparkled right before they closed for his kiss. The second his lips met hers, he found home.

"I've missed you," he whispered near her ear, delighted by the shiver his words induced.

"I've missed you too."

He smiled down at her, loving her. "Whatever you're cooking smells wonderful."

"Roasted chicken." She stepped out of his arms.

He shrugged off his suit coat, pulled his tie free of his collar, and rolled up his sleeves. "What can I do to help?"

"Everything's almost ready. There are drinks in the fridge." She turned back to the sink.

At the fridge, he noticed the photo strip of Ce and the man was gone. For a brief moment, he thought to say something about it but changed his mind when an image of Stacy flashed brightly. They both had pasts. Now wasn't the time to delve into them.

He grabbed a soft drink from the fridge and leaned against the cupboard close to her while she washed a couple of tomatoes. "I was so impatient to get here. The flight seemed to last an eternity."

When she smiled, every part of his body responded. He needed something to do with his hands. "How about I slice those tomatoes?"

Dinner was delicious. Cecelia had always been a good cook, and that hadn't changed. They talked about their day over salad, roasted chicken, rosemary potatoes, and fresh green beans, just like an old married couple. She asked about the merger he was working on and then listened, following along, and interested enough to ask more questions.

While they were clearing the table and cleaning up afterward, he couldn't help thinking how great it felt to be working side by side with Cecelia. Stacy left him with the cooking and the cleaning, never offering to help. He could get used to this domestic harmony very easily.

They went into the living room, and he pulled her onto his lap. Before he could get to the business of making out like a couple of teenagers, she scooted free.

"We need to talk."

She'd done this a lot the summer they dated. Ce was a thinker and wanted to discuss—overanalyze—what he might have said or how his dad had looked at her.

"Okay."

Her thumbnail went between her teeth, so he snuggled her into his side and tipped her head, so their eyes met. "What is it, Ce?"

"We need to talk about the divorce papers."

This night could end very well or very badly for him. He could beat around the bush or go for broke. Either way, this would be a defining moment for them. The elephant in the room took a seat on his chest.

He ran his fingers along her jaw and decided to go for broke. "I don't want a divorce." He waited a beat, giving her time to pull away. She didn't. "Do you?"

She shook her head so slightly he wouldn't have noticed if he hadn't been touching her.

The elephant got up so he could suck air into his lungs. He'd hoped for a somewhat stronger response, but he'd settle for what she offered. "Good. That takes care of the divorce papers, but I can still see the wheels turning in that pretty head. Tell me what you're thinking."

"I'm nervous."

"I'm nervous too." But his excitement overshadowed his fears. "Let's take things a day at a time. Get to know each other again."

A tiny smile tipped up the corners of her mouth. And he kissed those corners.

"I know logistics are involved, but let's not worry about that for now."

She snuggled a little closer. "A day at a time sounds good."

Jared released a long-held breath. The night would end on a positive note, after all.

CHAPTER 26

*C*ecelia hated being the center of attention, but Windy always insisted on rolling out the red carpet for everyone's birthday. She'd decorated the conference room, so Cecelia tried to act surprised, even though she knew exactly why Winston called her downstairs for a consultation with an "unexpected" client. But she didn't expect to see Jared among the other guests yelling, "Surprise!"

"Thank you." She put a hand to her heart before going around the room, hugging each person individually. When she got to Jared, he wrapped her in his arms.

"I thought you had a busy day at the office."

He held his thumb and index finger apart by an inch. "That might have been a tiny lie."

"Did Windy tell you it was my birthday?"

His brows came together in an instant frown. "No, Ce." He took her hands in his. "Do you remember when my birthday is?"

"March twenty-second."

"If you remember mine, why would you think I don't remember yours?"

Cecelia was very aware of the watching eyes. Even though she and Jared hadn't been together for any of his birthdays, she always thought about him on that date.

"Uh, Ce?" Zack pointed at the cake. "You might want to blow out the candles before they melt into puddles."

"Do you need help, old lady?" Windy teased.

She scanned the cake covered with candles. "I might."

Maria put a gentle hand on her shoulder. "First, make a really good wish."

Cecelia closed her eyes and wished. Then, with a deep breath, she blew out every candle. Jared pulled her into another hug as her friends cheered.

Her birthday had always been bittersweet. Derrick was the only family member who ever remembered. She never received a call or card from her mom, dad, or sister—but her coworkers never forgot, and Valerie always came uptown to join the celebration. Even the man she married for a brief moment in time remembered.

"Did you wish for something wonderful?" Jared asked.

"Yes."

"Okay, time to cut the cake," Zack said, holding out a plate.

She picked up the knife Windy provided. "Jared, have you met everyone?"

"I introduced him around before you came downstairs," Winston said.

"He's gorgeous!" Val whispered in her ear when Jared turned to talk to Maria.

"I know."

Val glanced at Jared. "Looks like things are getting cozy."

Cecelia didn't try to hide her smile because things had

gotten very cozy last night, despite their agreement to take their relationship one day at a time.

While everyone sat around the conference table, eating their cake and ice cream, Windy moved Cecelia to the head of the table where gifts were stacked. The crazy-paper-wrapped first box had to be from Windy and Kevin. She worked the tape free and opened the box to reveal a winter scarf, hat, and gloves.

"Windy says you walk to work most mornings, so that'll keep you warm," Kevin said

"I love them! Thank you so much."

She opened a beautiful shawl from Zack and his wife, Anna, and two framed school pictures of their kids for her desk. Mia gave her a gift certificate to one of her favorite boutiques, and Val scored two books signed by one of her favorite authors. She received an opal ring, her birthstone from Winston and Maria.

"Jacques said to bring it in for sizing," Maria said.

She slipped it on her finger. "It's beautiful and fits perfectly. Thank you."

"There's one more," Windy said, handing her a pink velvet box. "It's from Jared."

Cecelia glanced at him.

He smiled and gave a slight shrug.

Her hands shook slightly as she untied the white ribbon and lifted the lid. Inside was a diamond bracelet. "Jared"—she shook her head—"I can't—"

"Yes, you can." He took out the bracelet and fastened it around her wrist before she could object further. "I bought this for your nineteenth birthday, a day we didn't get to celebrate."

"That's the sweetest thing I've ever heard," Maria said with a sniffle, dabbing at the corners of her eyes.

. . .

*J*ared took her out for a lavish birthday dinner. Afterward, they rode through Central Park in a carriage with Jared holding her close. Emotions were on the edge of overflowing as she stole glances at his handsome face. She loved the man he'd become. Sweet, strong, affectionate, tender, with a maturity that he wore well.

As he walked her up to her apartment, she ran a finger over the diamond bracelet, wondering if he really bought it all those years ago.

How could she accept such an extravagant gift and not get her hopes up? What did Jared expect from her? What should she expect from him? Would he just pop in for occasional weekends? If so, would she be okay with that?

She'd told him the truth when she said she didn't want a divorce, but a tiny place inside her was still unsure how things could work.

"What are you thinking?"

She met his intent gaze and shook her head.

"Talk to me, Ce. What put that pensive expression on your beautiful face?"

"Did you really keep this bracelet all these years?"

His dimples winked with his smile. "I can bring the receipt if you'd like proof."

"If you had the receipt, why didn't you return it?"

He took her wrist in his hand and fingered the bracelet. "Do you remember the day we drove to Waxahachie to pick up something for Grammy? I can't remember now what we went to get."

"We picked up a mosaic heart she made for your grandpa for their anniversary."

He touched his forehead. "Oh, that's right. Do you know they still have that mosaic in their backyard?"

"Really?"

He nodded. "After we picked it up, we walked down Main Street to get some lunch and passed a jewelry store. I glanced in the window, spotted that bracelet, and imagined you wearing it. I found myself thinking about that bracelet all the next day, so I drove back, bought it with your birthday in mind, and put it away. I forgot I had it until my attorney told me we were still married. I went through a box where I put our divorce decree and discovered the bracelet. After all these years, it's finally where it belongs."

His sincerity touched her so deeply, the last pieces of her damaged heart slipped into place, making it beat fully for the first time in years.

"Were you checking the divorce papers for signatures?"

"Yep. I can't believe neither of us noticed, but I'm glad we didn't."

She smiled up at him. "So am I."

⟳

*S*tanding at the railing of the ferry, his arms wrapped around Cecelia, her back tucked against his chest, Jared experienced another surreal moment. One he thought he'd never have.

Other than the short three months he spent with Cecelia, he couldn't remember a happier time in his life. Maybe happier wasn't the right word. He couldn't remember feeling more content, more intact, more complete. With Cecelia, he felt like a piece of him that was missing had been returned.

He kissed the side of her neck and watched her face light up with a smile. They'd spent the morning at the Statue of Liberty and the afternoon wandering through the Immigration Museum on Ellis Island. He knew he wouldn't be able to get enough of her on this short visit. Being here would only make him want her more. "Where would you like to have dinner?"

"My place." Before he could protest, she looked over her shoulder. "Jared, you're spending too much money when you come to New York. Please, let me cook dinner."

"On one condition."

She turned to face him. "What condition?"

"You have to kiss me."

She wrapped her arms around his neck. "I can do that."

He immediately felt the difference in this kiss compared to her others. Cecelia's walls were crumbling. She gave in to her desire, building his to a boiling point, and at the same time triggering a silent appreciation for that day in his attorney's office.

Cecelia was back in his life, and he loved her.

He leaned back slightly. "You know you're amazing?"

"No." She kissed his chin. "I'm just me."

"Thanks for being just you."

$\sim$

When Jared got to Cecelia's apartment Sunday morning, he found her in the kitchen packing a big picnic basket. He'd invited her to spend the night at the corporate apartment last night.

"We are still married," he said, lifting an eyebrow.

"That wouldn't be moving slowly."

"No, but we could see if we're still compatible in the bedroom and in the kitchen, or any of the other places we dubbed *our spot*." Two days and nights of wedded bliss in a buddy's apartment, that's all they had before he left for law school.

She'd shaken her head at him.

"What's this?" he asked, nodding toward the basket.

"We've been running around the city for the past couple of days. I thought you might like to relax and enjoy the sunshine. New York won't have many more warm days."

Making new memories he could take back to Dallas with him. "I'd like that a lot."

They found a spot of grass in Central Park and spread out a blanket. While he lay back and closed his eyes, Cecelia read to him. He thought of all the times he'd imagined this exact scenario. The sun on his face while listening to the sound of her soft Southern drawl flooded his mind with memories. He reached out and rested a hand on her leg. She never faltered as she continued to read.

"Are you falling asleep?" she asked a few minutes later.

He squeezed her thigh. "No. Just trying to remember the last time I've enjoyed myself this much." He opened his eyes and smiled up at her. "I like myself when I'm around you. I can't say that about very many people."

"Why?"

"As an attorney, I find myself looking for loopholes that I shouldn't be looking for to help a client. And I certainly don't like who I am around my parents. I turn into a different person when I'm with them. I do have friends like Knox who I can be myself around, and of course, Grant and his family."

He closed his eyes again. Time to tell Cecelia about Stacy. Even though she had no relevance to his life anymore, she'd played a major role in it for a long time. "My life was very messed up two months ago. That night at Market City Cafe changed everything." He looked at her again. "I'd become a person I barely recognized, and I didn't even realize how unhappy I was until I saw you. Does that make sense?"

She set the book aside. "I don't understand how you lost yourself so badly. You've always been so sure of who you are and what you want out of life."

"No. I usually did what was expected. What my father expected."

Cecelia laughed.

"What's funny?"

"You did what was expected except when you were with Knox. And me."

Jared chuckled. "My two favorite people in the world. I escape to the lake with Knox as often as possible. Escaping is the perfect word. Running from the reality of what my life was and just being me. The real me."

Cecelia intertwined their fingers. "I'm sorry."

"Don't be. It was my own doing. I allowed things to get out of hand."

"Has your opinion of New York improved?"

"Dramatically." He got up on an elbow and ran a lock of her hair through his fingers. "There is something I should tell you."

She wrinkled her nose. "Will it ruin the day?"

"It's a part of my past, but you should know—"

"The past is called that for a reason, so let's not talk about it."

He certainly didn't want to bring Stacy into their nice afternoon, and Cecelia knowing about her wouldn't change anything between them. He wasn't sure he wanted to know about the men Cecelia had dated. "Okay. We'll let the past go."

He leaned forward and gave a mental sigh of relief when she met him halfway for a sweet kiss.

She leaned away. "Are you ready to eat some lunch?"

"Read to me with that sexy voice of yours for a while longer." Settling back, he closed his eyes.

She began reading where she left off.

～

*S*ix days later, Jared stared at himself in Cecelia's bathroom mirror, amazed at the transformation the makeup artist had accomplished. His own family wouldn't recognize him. His cheeks and eyes were hollowed out, making his face look skeletal. His hair was ratted and powdered and sticking up everywhere. He walked out, rocking his jaw and laughing. "This stuff itches."

Cecelia grinned. "You look hideous."

She had the same hollowed-out cheeks and gray lipstick. Her antebellum evening gown was powdered and cobwebbed in the same way as his nineteenth-century frock coat, complete with cravat and vest. Gene, the makeup artist who worked on them, had grayed her hair and piled it high, with ringlets cascading down around her face and back.

"We make a gruesome pair," he said, pulling her into his arms.

"No kissing!" Gene commanded, clapping his hands with authority. "You'll ruin your walking-dead lipstick."

"Wait. We can't kiss at all?" Jared asked.

"No." Gene's brows wrinkled in a frown. "At least not until you make your grand entrance, which will be epic."

"Thank you for doing this, Gene. You're amazing."

"Anything for you, my darling Ce," Gene responded, air-kissing both of her cheeks. "Let me take a quick picture for my portfolio."

Jared and Cecelia posed close together while Gene snapped several pictures.

"I've got to get out of here. I have my own party to get ready for," Gene said, grabbing his makeup case and coat.

"I'll get the costumes back to you by Tuesday, Gene. And tell your parents I'll call next week to make an appointment."

"Thanks, Ce, darling. My mother will be thrilled."

"So you trade jobs? He does our makeup, and you do what for him?" Jared asked after Gene left.

"He wants to give his parents' living room a makeover for Christmas."

"Why don't I just pay for this?"

"I could have paid him, Jared, but Gene wants to do something for his parents, so we agreed on a trade."

An hour later, Jared was shocked and impressed by the people Cecelia introduced him to at Winston and Maria's party. He knew his share of influential people in Dallas, but he'd never met a famous novelist before. He and Ce had read a couple of his books their summer together. He also met her seven-foot Mr. Basketball, a couple of movie stars, a national television reporter, a governor, two NFL players and their wives, and a country singer who attended with her rock star boyfriend.

Winston and Maria's brownstone had been turned into a haunted mansion. Cobwebs draped everything, pictures hung crooked, and candelabras held dripping black candles. Witches and goblins carried trays of hors d'oeuvres, and drinks were being served at several makeshift bars by Dracula, Frankenstein, and Cruella De Vil. Jack-o'-lanterns lit tables, spiders dangled from the ceiling, and bats roosted in dark corners.

Several times during the early evening, Jared slipped his arm around Cecelia's waist and hoped she felt as comfortable with it as he did. They were among her friends, clients, and colleagues. He didn't want her to feel anxious, but she eased his worry when she took his arm or his hand while introducing him around, and she went out of her way to include him in the conversation.

He hated all the cocktail parties and social events that Stacy dragged him to for the sole purpose of posing for pictures to be splashed over Dallas society pages.

This party had nothing to do with who wore the most expensive dress or whose shoes were from Milan. Winston and Marie's guests were here to have fun, and he could honestly say he was having a great time.

After tasting a variety of finger foods, Jared pulled Cecelia to the dance floor and tucked her close.

She ran a finger around the curve of his ear before gently tugging on his earlobe. "Do your parents know you're here with me?"

"No. At least not yet, but they will."

She pressed her lips together.

"What are you thinking?"

"I don't see how this can work, Jared."

When Cecelia looked away, Jared pulled her chin back so he could see her eyes because if she was about to say, *"I can't see you anymore,"* he wanted to know now. His heart needed to know what her next words were going to be before he fell any deeper in love with her—if that was even possible.

"Finish what you were going to say, Cecelia. I want to hear what you're thinking."

"You live in Dallas, and I live here. Are we just going to have random weekends?"

"I have more in mind than random weekends. Let me take care of the little details."

"The distance between Texas and New York is *not* a little detail."

"We'll figure it out, Ce."

"I've built a life in New York, and you've got your life, your home, your work in Dallas."

"I know you're happy here, and you have a successful business—"

"So do you. I don't understand how you can call that a little detail."

He stared into her worry-filled eyes for a moment. "I've talked to Grant about transferring to the New York office."

"But you hate the city."

"I won't hate anywhere if you're there."

Tears pooled in her eyes. "I can't ask you to do that. You'd be leaving your family."

"You didn't ask me. I don't like spending a couple of days here and then leaving you. I want more. I want it all. I want you. I love you, Cecelia."

More tears pooled. "Please don't say that."

Not the response he hoped for. "Why?"

"Because it's too soon."

He shook his head. "It's not too soon for me. I gave you my heart a long time ago, and I've never asked for it back. I never stopped loving you, Ce."

He waited for what seemed an eternity, thought his heart would splinter before she looked up with love shining right back at him.

"I love you too, Jared."

CHAPTER 27

ecelia and Jared talked every day since he returned to Dallas, at least two times, usually three. She looked forward to his morning calls because he'd tell her how much he missed her. His afternoon calls were usually brief, just to say he wanted to hear her voice, to tell her once more how much he loved her. Their night conversations were long and full of anticipation of when they'd see each other again.

She'd told him the past is called that for a reason, but she knew it wasn't completely true. They wouldn't be able to move all the way forward until she told Jared the reason she filed for divorce.

She was guilty of disappearing without an explanation, but he wasn't innocent either. She knew he'd cheated, and he didn't seem to know that she knew. Telling him the whole truth would cause more friction between him and his father. She hated to add to their discord, but it was the only way to make him understand why she disappeared.

The bell over the front door jangled, bringing her mind back to work. Winston was with Mia and Zack checking on a joint remodel they were working on, and Windy had a dentist appointment, so she was in the office alone this morning. Cecelia had moved her work to the conference room so she would be close to the front door.

She put on a smile and walked into the reception area, smoothing her skirt. When she looked up, her greeting lodged in her throat, and a loud buzzing blocked out all other sounds for a long moment.

Charles McAlister stood at Windy's desk, his spine ramrod straight. He glanced toward the stairs, and Cecelia noted changes, gray threaded through his once dark hair, deeper frown lines. He was impeccably dressed as always, a black pinstripe suit under a charcoal gray overcoat. When he turned toward her, his lips thinned to a white line, his idea of a smile that never reached his eyes. His gaze was steady and stone cold.

"What an enchanting little office, Miss Chadwick. Or should I say, Mrs. McAlister? It seems you've done well for yourself. Much better than I anticipated."

Cecelia carefully tamped down any reaction. She longed to press a hand over her pounding heart but wouldn't give Jared's father the satisfaction of knowing he terrified her. This man was her Achilles heel—her kryptonite. Despite her success, just seeing him catapulted her into the past, making her feel eighteen and inferior all over again.

She clasped her hands together to keep them from shaking and attempted to keep her expression as unreadable as possible, refusing to allow him to see the power he still wielded over her.

Stay calm. He's just a man and can only hurt you if you allow it.

"I must admit I'm surprised at how successful you've become in such a short time." He walked around Windy's desk, his gaze traveling from her face to her toes. "And look at you, my dear. You've grown into a beautiful young woman, very beautiful indeed. How old are you now, thirty, thirty-one?"

She didn't answer because he didn't care. He only wanted to rattle her, make her succumb to his bidding.

Instead, she waited with her shoulders back and her head high because Charles McAlister wouldn't be here if he didn't want something. She fought the urge to do anything but stand perfectly still and watch him eye her from the high and mighty throne he'd perched himself upon.

She didn't have to wait long before his false smile disappeared.

"I hear you've taken up with my son again."

Jared must have talked to his parents. Did he know his dad was in New York? She doubted it. Jared would have warned her. "That's none of your business, Mr. McAlister."

"You're wrong. You made it my business twelve years ago."

"No, you're wrong. I didn't make it your business. My mother did. And what happened twelve years ago doesn't matter anymore. I'm no longer eighteen years old, and your son is a grown man who's capable of making his own decisions."

He slowly walked toward her, meticulously pulling off his gloves one finger at a time, folding them, and pushing them into the pockets of his overcoat. The cold, cruel expression she remembered so well fell into place. He stopped in front of her and drew a large envelope from under his arm, holding it out. "Maybe you'd like to see some of the decisions Jared *has* been making."

He wants to stay married. He talked to Grant about moving to the New York office. "I know about the decisions he's been making."

His harsh laugh echoed through the quiet building. "Oh, I

don't think you do, Cecelia. Please, take a look because these decisions will affect you."

When she didn't move, he opened the flap of the envelope and slid out a glossy eight by ten photo. He held it up for her to see. "This is Jared and his fiancée, Stacy Richardson. I'm surprised a resourceful woman like you didn't think to pull up the Dallas Society Pages on the Internet. Jared has made quite a name for himself in Texas and is in the paper often. Along with Stacy."

Cecelia's gaze shifted from his face to the picture he held. Her heart dropped from her chest and hit the floor, shattering into a million irreparable pieces. Against her will, her shaking hand took the picture from him.

Jared with his arms wrapped around a beautiful blonde woman.

A beautiful blonde Cecelia recognized because Stacy Richardson had been here, utilizing the same intimidation tactics Charles used.

The buzzing in her ears grew louder. He thrust another photo into her view. "What do you think of Stacy's beautiful engagement ring?"

The ring sat in a pink box like the one containing the bracelet Jared gave her for her birthday. As this information slammed around in her head, searching for a place to land, the next picture appeared. Jared kissing Stacy. Another, them standing outside of a building.

"That's Jared's townhouse where they live. Together."

"But he told me—" *his condo is drab and needs my touch.*

"I'm sure he did," he said in his condescending tone.

Jared was not only engaged but living with gorgeous Stacy. His fiancée. Cecelia shoved the pictures at Jared's dad while trying to suck air into her lungs, so light-headed she was afraid she might faint.

"Oh, we're not finished." He slipped another picture out

of the envelope and placed it on top of the ones he wouldn't take. "A couple of weeks ago."

The eight by ten had a picture of Jared carrying Stacy into a building. She had her arms wrapped around his neck.

"And this was taken last night."

Jared sitting in a chair, his fiancée standing behind him, her red lips pressed against his cheek. Jared was smiling, his dimples deep. The date and time were imprinted on the bottom right corner, confirming that the shot had indeed been taken last night.

Cecelia slowly closed her eyes as she started to tremble. She couldn't be this blind. Not twice. She'd believed Jared. Trusted him. Given him her heart.

A clammy wave of nausea swept over her. Everything within her periphery faded to black. She clenched her tingling fingers. The empty cavity in her chest ached clear through to her backbone.

She was so gullible. Jared had easily fooled her again. He told her he loved her just an hour ago and, giddy with happiness, she'd told him she loved him more.

Charles slid a white envelope out of his inside coat pocket. He set it on the stack of pictures in her hands, which were shaking like leaves in a breeze. "This is the last check you'll receive from me. I will have divorce papers sent to this office. Sign them and send them back immediately." He bent close enough that she smelled spearmint on his breath. "Then stay away from my son."

When he straightened, he brushed his hands together as if ridding them of dirt. Which is exactly how he always made her feel. Like a clod of mud on the bottom of his shoe.

"I don't want your money," she said, finally finding her voice.

"You've already benefited from the McAlister wealth, Miss Chadwick," he said with a snarl. "Do you think you ended up in New York without money changing hands? There was never a scholarship. I made everything happen. You are bought and paid for. You and your mother both."

His eyes narrowed with loathing. "Now you owe me because you wouldn't be where you are today without McAlister money. Stay out of my son's life, or I'll not only destroy you. I'll bring this pillow-fluffing company to its knees."

He turned his back on her and stalked out the door, his heels clacking against the wood floor.

Cecelia stumbled to Windy's chair and covered her mouth as bile rose in her throat. Charles McAlister had paid for her education to get her away from Jared. He'd planned it all, made it happen.

The scholarship in New York never existed. She questioned it at the time, but the woman in the admissions office reassured her—a woman who'd probably been paid off as well.

She should have known. Everything had fallen into place too smoothly. But everything made perfect sense now. How had she been so blind, so trusting? So stupid?

She'd called her mother for advice, and Marybeth turned around and struck a deal with the devil for money. Days later, her mom produced the envelope with the New York scholarship. Sure, she'd applied, but without a full ride, Cecelia would never have been able to afford her top pick. Her mom encouraged her to take advantage of this golden opportunity. New York would be a once-in-a-lifetime chance.

How much money had her mother been paid to sell her daughter out?

She looked down at the picture of Jared and Stacy taken last night. His dimples winked mockingly as Stacy kissed his cheek.

The bile rose faster than she could stand. She leaned over and vomited in Windy's wastebasket.

～

*C*harles climbed into the limousine waiting at the curb. "Back to the airport."

He methodically pulled his gloves on, satisfied he'd put enough fear into Cecelia to resolve another of Jared's messes.

His plan fell into place after Stacy came to his office to tell him she'd seen Cecelia. James Decker provided proof with more than a hundred photos from Jared's week in New York. His irresponsible kid was indeed seeing Cecelia again.

Charles knew he had to move fast. With a wave of his wallet, he reassured Stacy that things would be back to normal soon. She'd been more than happy to show up at the country club last night to pose for the picture the club photographer snapped.

He wasn't fooled by Stacy. He knew she could be bought. Almost anyone could, for the right price. Jared had shown suspicion when Stacy apologized, saying all was forgiven, and she hoped they could be friends. She leaned down just as the photographer said something to coax a smile from Jared. Stacy's kiss on his son's cheek couldn't have been more perfectly choreographed. Stacy was a professional when it came to setting up the perfectly timed picture.

The limousine arrived on the tarmac near the McAlister Industries Learjet. Charles didn't wait for the chauffeur to open his door but climbed out and signaled the pilot to start the engines.

Cecelia looked very polished this morning—nothing like that white trash mother of hers, with her crude vocabulary and brash hair color. No, Cecelia was the top designer at Winston and Associates, and, according to the reports he'd been able to get his hands on, the design firm was doing extremely well.

He wondered what she'd done with the last check he gave her, besides disappear. Not only had he paid for her tuition, books, room, and board, but he'd given her fifty thousand to vanish and was surprised when she kept her part of the bargain. The cost to keep her away had been fifty thousand dollars twelve years ago and another fifty thousand today, but it would be money well spent.

This time she *would* stay out of his son's life, or he'd follow through on his threat and find a way to ruin her.

He climbed aboard the jet and ordered a drink. Jared had cost him more money in private investigators than in schooling. If a PI hadn't been following the kid in college, he wouldn't have had those first pictures he showed Cecelia years ago.

He knew the first time Jared brought Cecelia home that she would be a problem. She and Jared spent every free moment together. After a month, Charles was convinced their relationship was different. He'd hoped Jared would get bored and move on the way he usually did, but his son cared about this nobody who he tried to pass off as one of them.

Charles never thought he'd have an ally in Cecelia's mother until Marybeth Chadwick marched into his office one morning to announce that Cecelia was "knocked up" by his son, and what did he intend to do about it? His attorney found out Jared had secretly married that teenage tramp before he left for law school, compounding the mess.

He'd had divorce papers drawn up, then reached a quick agreement with Marybeth. Charles would cut Marybeth a fat check, but only if she could get Cecelia to sign the divorce papers and disappear.

Next, he flew to New York City, secured Cecelia's place at

NYU, and paid for everything in advance, while Marybeth traveled to Arizona to work her magic.

Initially, Cecelia turned the offer down, saying she wanted to talk to Jared. He should know about the baby immediately so they could make plans. Charles stepped in again, paying Cecelia a visit with the pictures of Jared taken almost three years earlier in bed with a little freshman he'd been dating. Charles handed the photo to Cecelia much as he'd done today. "Jared has moved on, and you need to do the same."

His flight attendant brought Charles his drink, and he took a celebratory swallow.

After he convinced Cecelia to pack, got her signature on the divorce papers, and told her a plane ticket to New York would be waiting at the airport. He paid off Marybeth, but she'd been cheap. Ten thousand dollars and her promise not to tell Jared where Cecelia went were all it took.

Charles removed his cell phone and scrolled to Stacy's number. He only had to wait for one ring before Stacy answered.

"Cecelia is out of the picture," he said. "I'll deal with Jared tonight. After that, the rest is up to you."

He hung up and relaxed in his seat as the plane glided down the runway. In a few hours, he'd be back in Dallas, and the ball would drop.

CHAPTER 28

*J*ared was beginning to worry. Zack answered when he called Winston and Associates yesterday and said Cecelia went home early. She didn't answer her cell or home phone and didn't return any of his calls.

He called this morning with the same results. When he reached Windy at Winston and Associates, she said Ce had taken an *unexpected* day off.

During his busy day, he tried to reach her several more times, but with no luck. Grabbing his phone from the center console of his car, he placed one more call as he pulled through the gates of his parents' house. His father had left a message with Violet demanding Jared come over immediately after work to discuss an urgent matter.

"It's me again," Jared said to her answering machine. "I'm getting worried, Ce. Please call me. I love you."

Climbing out of his car, he shoved his cell in his pocket. He hadn't hit panic mode yet because Windy, though surprised because Cecelia rarely took time off, didn't seem nervous. Maybe she'd gone to the country with her friend.

He rang the doorbell, something he never did at his grandparents' house. Here it was expected.

The McAlisters' housekeeper opened the door and offered a smile.

"Hi, Dorothy. How are you?" He bent and kissed her soft, worn cheek.

"Just fine, Mr. Jared."

Mr. Another expectation, he thought ridiculous. Dorothy had known him since he was a toddler.

His mother appeared in the foyer. "Jared. We didn't expect you."

"Dad does. He insisted he has some important matter to discuss that couldn't wait."

She looped her hand through his arm. "He's in the sunroom. Dorothy, tell cook Jared is staying for supper."

"No, thank you, Dorothy. I can't stay tonight."

When they entered the sunroom, his dad stood behind the bar mixing drinks. The French doors were propped open, showing the cobalt-blue of the swimming pool sparkling in the early evening light.

"What'll you have, Jared?"

Though being around his father made him crave alcohol, he declined. He hadn't had a drink in weeks and felt much better because of it.

Charles held out his wife's martini.

"Stacy has been seeing Jensen Williams," his mom blurted, watching him closely.

"Jensen's a good guy"—*with lots of money*—"I hope she's happy."

Charles walked around the bar and pinned him with cold, expressionless eyes. "Are you, Jared?"

"Am I happy?" Jared asked. He waited for his mother to sit, then took the other end of the sofa. "As a matter of fact, I am."

"Are you seeing anyone?" Charles chose a wicker chair to Jared's left.

"Yes."

"What?" Betsy wailed. "You're already dating someone else?"

Charles took a sip of his drink and set it on a side table. "So, this breakup between you and Stacy had something to do with another woman?"

"I would have broken my engagement with Stacy anyway." Jared looked from his mom to his dad.

He didn't want to tell them about Cecelia yet, knowing how they'd react, but he might as well get the fireworks over with while it was just the three of them. He was done trying to evade the subject. He loved Cecelia and felt happier than he had in years. His life finally seemed to be moving in the right direction.

"I'm in love with someone."

Betsy's mouth formed a perfect O. "Not only are you seeing another woman, but you're already in love with her? What about Stacy?"

"Mom." Jared released a tired breath. "Stacy and I are finished. We were finished long before either of us were willing to admit it."

"So, you think you're already in love with Cecelia Chadwick?" his father sneered in the tone he used when speaking of someone he deemed lower class.

"Cecelia Chadwick?" his mom squeaked.

Jared glanced at his father, his mind racing. Only two people knew he was seeing Cecelia—Grant and Knox. Neither one of them would have mentioned her without giving him a heads-up warning. "How do you know about Cecelia?"

Charles picked up an envelope and pulled out some

pictures. He leaned forward and flicked them down on the coffee table one at a time.

His mom scooted close to Jared and picked up one of the pictures. "Where is this?"

He and Cecelia sat on a blanket in Central Park. She held a book. His hand rested on her thigh. The perfect, private moment had been stolen from him by his father. His mom picked up another photo. He and Cecelia were coming out of her apartment building in their Halloween costumes. The next picture showed him climbing into a cab, Cecelia at the curb. Another, him kissing Cecelia's neck on the ferry ride from Liberty Island. He looked at his father. "You had me followed?"

"Charles, what's happening? Where did you get these?"

Jared answered for his dad. "They were taken in New York City. I was there last weekend with Cecelia. We went to a Halloween party at her boss's house." He tried to rein in the rage flooding through him, from burning face to shaking hands. "How long have you had someone following me, spying on my private life?"

Betsy continued to pick up photos—them walking down a tree-lined street holding hands, another taken through the front window of Market City Café—them having dinner together at "their" table. The last one showed Cecelia wrapped in his arms, him kissing her.

"Charles, you've had Jared followed?"

"I did it for the boy's own good."

Betsy turned to Jared, her perfectly arched eyebrows drawn together. "You lied to me. You lied to Stacy. You said you weren't having an affair while you were engaged to her."

"I didn't lie. I only saw Cecelia a couple of times—in public—before breaking up with Stacy."

"But how did you find her?"

Jared stared at his mom. She used almost the exact same

words Cecelia used the first night he met her at the cafe, and it dawned on him that perhaps Ce wasn't supposed to be found. Alarms sounded in his head.

But before he could ask the questions tumbling over each other, his dad unfolded a piece of paper and held it out.

His mom took the paper before Jared could. "What is this?"

Jared studied a bank statement. A date, highlighted in yellow, from twelve years ago. Two more highlighted lines ran across the page marking a fifty-thousand-dollar withdrawal and a ten-thousand-dollar withdrawal.

"Charles?" His mother looked at his dad with concern etched across her features.

"It took ten thousand dollars for Cecelia's mother to sell out her daughter and fifty thousand for Cecelia to sign divorce papers, get an abortion, and disappear."

"What?" Jared grabbed the paper out of his mother's hand. He studied the highlighted areas.

"What divorce?"

"Jared and his tramp got *married* at the courthouse before he left for law school. A month later, she told her mother she was pregnant. Fifty thousand dollars is what she took in exchange for signing the papers I had drawn up and moving to New York."

Ce was pregnant?

He couldn't breathe. He couldn't believe Cecelia would divorce him for fifty thousand dollars. She wouldn't—

Jared closed his eyes to flashes of red. "You're a liar," he ground out.

"She couldn't have gone to college if I hadn't set everything up. The transaction is in front of you. Look at the date."

Charles picked up his martini, leaned back in his chair, and took a sip. "You spent last weekend in New York. Did you see a child? *Your child?*"

His mother frowned. "You told me you paid Cecelia to leave town, Charles. You said she took the money to go to school."

Jared turned to his mom. "You knew about this?"

"As your father said, it was for your own good. But Charles, you didn't tell me Jared and Cecelia had married or that she was carrying his baby." She touched Jared's knee. "Where is your child?"

"Along with the check, I gave Cecelia a list of clinics she could visit in New York."

"You paid to have what would have been our first grand-child aborted?" his mom asked, her voice shaking.

"No." Jared shook his head. Suspicion on the heels of questions raced through his mind. Money, New York, baby, he couldn't separate them enough to focus on just one. His spinning thoughts were making his stomach lurch. "Cecelia wouldn't have done that."

Would she?

His dad smirked. "Maybe you don't know Cecelia as well as you think you do."

"Cecelia would have told me if she was pregnant, and she would *never* abort a child—mine, or anyone else's."

His mom stood and paced to the French doors, rubbing her temples. "Charles, please tell me you didn't do this."

"Jared was dating a *nobody* who he recklessly married after only three months. They kept it a secret because they knew they'd be ridiculed for their stupidity."

He glanced back at Jared. "Cecelia told her mother it was your baby. I didn't believe her, but I also didn't want that floozy running around telling everyone her daughter was carrying a McAlister baby. Do you have any idea the damage that would have caused your career? Cecelia is *still a nobody*. Do you know how I know that? Because *a nobody* can be bought, and I bought her again yesterday. Fifty thousand dol—"

Jared felt his dad's cheekbone under his fist, heard the crack before he realized what he'd done. The martini glass shattered across the tile floor. The shock on Charles' face before he tumbled backward, taking the chair with him, would be forever burned into Jared's memory. His mother's scream registered before he stalked out the front door.

Jared jumped into his car and gunned the engine. Gravel shot out from beneath his rear tires when he cranked the wheel and sped down the long drive, through the front gate, onto the road beyond.

Two miles away, he skidded to a stop on the shoulder, and a cloud of dust blanketed his car. He had to get a grip before he ran himself or someone else off the road. He had to think. He had to talk to Cecelia.

She wouldn't do this. She wouldn't do this.

He lowered his forehead to his hands, clutching the steering wheel. His groan sounded animalistic to his ears. "Cecelia, please, tell me you wouldn't do this."

He yanked his cell phone out of his pocket and scrolled to her number. Her answering machine picked up for the umpteenth time. "Cecelia, I know you're there. Pick up the phone!"

"Jared."

His breath caught when he heard her soft voice, his heartbeat pounding erratically.

"I know about Stacy. I know you spent a weekend with me and told me you loved me while you were engaged to someone else."

She was speaking so quietly he strained to hear her over the roaring in his ears. "Ce—"

"Everything makes sense now. Stacy coming to my office to see who you were cheating with. She should have said something," Ce said as if talking to herself. "I also know about the other girl from law school. You can thank your dad for that piece of information. Yes, he came to see me again, filled in all the blanks. Everything, my whole adult life has been a lie. I don't even know how to fix . . . I don't know where to start."

"What do you mean again? What girl?"

She inhaled deeply. "Don't ever call me again. Do not come to my apartment or my office. I overnighted the divorce papers this morning. Your attorney should receive them tomorrow."

"Cecelia, listen to me."

"I'm through listening. Stay out of my life this time, Jared. I don't ever want to see you again."

"Don't you hang up, Ce!"

The distant click was as loud as a metal door slamming shut forever.

~

Shaking violently, Cecelia sank into a chair. She put her head in her hands, fighting waves of nausea, wishing she could erase the past two and a half months.

No. If she could erase, she'd go all the way back to that hot spring day at the lake. She wouldn't have read aloud or stayed for dinner with a boat full of college boys or gone for a walk with Jared.

Her whole grown life, she'd believed she got that scholarship on her own merit, only to find out there'd never been a scholarship. Now that she looked back, things had aligned too perfectly. The pain of seeing those pictures of Jared in bed with another woman had blinded her. All she could think of was escape, and there was Mr. McAlister, offering her a way out. She'd grabbed it with both hands.

I should have confronted Jared rather than run. All this would be in the past if I hadn't been so naïve.

Glad Jared hadn't tried to call back, she set her phone aside. She'd said what she wanted. Now she was done with him and his *crazy* family. After protecting her heart for all these years, she'd lowered her guard and fallen for Jared's lies a second time.

Fool me once . . . What a droll but true cliché.

She pushed to her feet and walked to the window, looking out into the night. A cold rain pelted the glass, coming in waves through the darkness. The weather matched her mood, dismal and bitter. She usually loved the sound of rain, but tonight it grated on her nerves, sounding like pebbles being thrown against her windows.

Tracing a finger over her distorted outline, she fought tears. Her internet search through the Dallas Society pages last night produced image after image of Jared McAlister and Stacy Richardson. Spanning a year of time, their smiling faces covered her computer screen. They'd attending fundraisers and gallery openings, and numerous parties. Stacy, in dazzling gowns, was always cuddled up to a tuxedoed Jared.

He must have had a great laugh at the costume party she dragged him to.

Stupid, trusting woman.

Yanking the curtains shut, she turned toward her bedroom. She'd take the weekend to cleanse Jared from her system once and for all. Then she'd go back to work with a vengeance.

She'd been through this before and survived. She would do it again.

CHAPTER 29

*J*ared rolled over in bed and punched the air with a fist. The incessant knocker wouldn't give up. He threw back the covers, staggered through the living room, and yanked the door open.

His mother lowered her fist. "Why would you keep me waiting so long?"

"I can't do this today, Mom."

She pushed the door wider and shouldered past him. "I called your office, and that assistant of yours told me you called in sick."

He didn't respond, wishing she'd go away. To him, she was as guilty as his father.

"I see you slept in your clothes," she said, looking him up and down. "That's unacceptable, Jared, no matter the circumstance. Please go change. I'll take you to breakfast."

"I don't want breakfast." He shoved the door shut.

She crossed her arms. "If you won't go to breakfast with me, I'll have to tell you goodbye here."

"Where are you going?"

"To stay with your aunt in Austin. I need time to think

this fiasco through and decide if I can stay with your father." She glanced out his living room window. "I didn't realize you have such a nice view."

"You're leaving Dad?"

"Go change, Jared. Quickly, please. I didn't have dinner last night, so I'm cranky. And you know I hate to eat alone."

Jared changed into jeans and a polo, brushed his teeth and hair. Half an hour later, they were seated in a booth at a little café with steaming cups of coffee in front of them.

His mom poured a generous amount of cream into her coffee. "None of this is your fault."

"How can I not feel responsible? You're leaving Dad because of what happened with me."

"No. I'm leaving because of your father's actions." After stirring the creamer in, she tapped her spoon on the side of the cup.

"I didn't tell you about Cecelia because you're both so narrow-minded about her." He shook his head, physically sick. Emotionally drained. "Who I see is none of your business."

"You're right."

He glanced up in surprise. "That's a first."

"Don't be smart." She picked up her coffee and took a sip. "I sat up all night thinking about our whole horrible conversation."

"Join the club."

"I don't know if I can get beyond what your father did," she said as if Jared hadn't spoken. She twisted her cup on the saucer. "I don't think I can ever like Cecelia for doing such a thing. I know I haven't been the best grandmother to Susan's children, or the best mother to you and your sister, for that matter. But to think money and position would mean more than holding a sweet baby you helped create."

He slumped back in his seat.

"I'm sorry." She put fingers to her lips. "I shouldn't have said that."

"I don't believe Cecelia did that. She *wouldn't*." He wrapped his hand around his coffee cup, more for warmth than to drink. "I can't believe she was even pregnant. We were only together two days—two nights before I left for law school."

He glanced down, embarrassed to face his mother's judgment. "I pressured her to get married." *So much like Stacy. Exactly like Dad.* He met his mother's gaze. "I loved her. I didn't want anyone else to have her."

"We do stupid things when we're in love." His mom touched his bruised knuckle. "You gave your dad a black eye."

"After what he did, he's lucky I only gave him one."

His mother exhaled and took a sip of coffee. "Where do you and Cecelia stand?"

Jared ran fingers through his hair, feeling it stand on end and not caring. "I have no idea what Dad said to her, but she won't take my calls. Says she never wants to see me again. Dad must have convinced her that Stacy and I are still engaged."

He leaned forward, making sure he had his mother's full attention. "I love Cecelia, Mom. I'm sorry if you have a problem with that, but she's the only woman I've ever loved. The minute I saw her in New York, I knew I couldn't marry Stacy. Things hadn't been right between us for a while, but seeing Cecelia reminded me how it felt to really be in love, to really, truly care about someone."

Betsy tapped her coffee cup with a pink fingernail. "What are you going to do about it?"

"I don't know. When I called her last night, she also said she knew about the woman in law school, but there wasn't another woman."

His mom looked out the window. "I feel partly responsible for Cecelia disappearing. I knew your father offered her money to go away, and I agreed with him at the time. I thought Cecelia would hold you back. She was so different. I didn't think she would be a good choice for you, or for our family. I had no idea you felt so strongly." She offered a tight smile. "Or that you'd gotten married."

Anger rocketed through him. "I was twenty-three years old. What gave either of you the right to interfere?"

"Jared," his mom admonished, glancing around at his outburst. "We thought we were doing what was best at the time. After Cecelia left, you got right back to your life and studies."

"I looked everywhere for her, Mom." He looked up at the ceiling, trying to calm the acid churning in his stomach. "Did you know where she'd gone?"

"No. Your father didn't say, and I never asked."

"Cecelia's mother wouldn't tell me. Now I know she and Dad were working together." He looked out the window. "Isn't it ironic? You and Dad didn't like Cecelia because her family didn't have money, and her parents didn't like me because mine did. Dad and Mrs. Chadwick both meddled in something that was none of their business, and Cecelia and I were the ones to pay for it with twelve years of our lives."

"So Cecelia has been in New York the whole time?"

"She told me NYU offered her a scholarship, and she thought the opportunities would be better there."

"Jared, maybe your father's right when he said you don't know Cecelia as well as you think. She went to New York to start a new life with the money your father gave her. You said yourself she didn't have money. Fifty thousand must have seemed like a million to her."

"Ce's not like that."

"Then why did she disappear with the money? The bank statement is proof. She cashed the check."

"There's an explanation. If you and Dad had taken five minutes to get to know her, you'd know Cecelia would never take Dad's money. Dad said she's a nobody, but at the costume party, she introduced me to movie stars, an NBA player, and a famous author. They called her by name. A New York senator is on a first-name basis with Cecelia."

He shook his head. "And her apartment— She probably makes more money than I do, but you'd never know it. She actually traded services with the guy who did our Halloween makeup rather than pay him or let me pay him. She doesn't expect anything from me. She cooked dinner and packed a picnic. Do you know how many times Stacy cooked while we were together? Not once."

"You're not being fair to Stacy, Jared. She wasn't raised to cook."

He rolled his eyes. "You're missing my point. Cecelia's not after my money. She wants me for me. Or did until Dad interfered."

"Maybe she was looking at the big picture. She knows your grandparents have money. Surely she understands you'll inherit a large fortune."

Jared groaned when what he really wanted to do was yell at the top of his lungs. "Mom, Cecelia doesn't need Dad's money or mine. She has her own. She is *very* successful. She is a good person who helps others. She's kind, sincere, and— up until yesterday—she loved me completely."

Betsy shook her head. "Can you get past Cecelia terminating her pregnancy?" she asked without looking at him. She held up a hand before he could answer. "And if she didn't terminate the pregnancy, where is your child?"

He stared down at the coffee in his cup. "I don't know, but until I hear Cecelia's side of the story, I have faith in her. I've tried to put myself in her shoes, to look at her situation objectively. What would I have done if I was eighteen, pregnant, and didn't have any family support?"

"She had fifty thousand dollars." His mom sat back with a loud sigh when their breakfast arrived. "I thought we'd been forgotten."

Jared ignored his mother's jab at Cecelia and smiled an apology at the waitress.

Betsy picked up the salt shaker. "When is your next trip to New York?"

"I can't go until the end of the week."

$\approx$

The buzzer at the street level door sounded. Cecelia considered not answering. When she glanced out the kitchen window, she spotted Maria's car—someone she couldn't ignore.

She pressed the intercom to release the door lock, then opened her apartment door and waited while Maria climbed the stairs.

"Hi, sweetheart. I hope you haven't eaten yet. I brought lunch. Yummy salads from Antonio's."

Cecelia pasted on a smile. "Lunch sounds great."

In the kitchen, she got plates, napkins, and silverware while Maria unloaded a bag with enough food to feed an army.

"Winston and I are worried about you," she said as soon as they sat down. "We both think you took two days off because something happened between you and Jared. I'm not here to pry, but to listen if you want to talk."

Cecelia looked down at her salad, unable to see because of her tears.

Maria took her hand and squeezed lightly. "Please, tell me what happened. Maybe I can help."

You can't.

Cecelia dabbed at her eyes with her napkin and told Maria about the day she and Jared met, about his sweet courtship, how he'd pursued her until she finally said yes to his invitation to dinner. She explained how she fought her feelings at first, but Jared persisted.

"He was irresistible." Embarrassed she'd been duped a second time, she forked an olive. "We got married a couple of days before he left for law school."

"Oh, my goodness," Maria said with raised brows.

"It gets better." Cecelia set her fork aside and crossed her arms on the table. "I found out Jared had been cheating, so I filed for divorce. The problem is, the divorce was never finalized."

This time "Oh, my goodness" was said in a whisper.

"That's the reason Jared came to New York. He had new divorce papers drawn up. Instead, we went to dinner a couple of times and kind of started up where we left off. He said he didn't want a divorce and . . . well, neither did I. He planned to transfer to the New York office." She met Maria's gaze. "He said he loved me, and I believed him."

She wiped fresh tears away. "Jared's father came into the office Thursday morning and showed me pictures of Jared with his fiancée."

"Oh, Cecelia." Maria covered her mouth. "Are you sure Jared was in the pictured? He seemed so sincere on your birthday and at the Halloween party. I can't believe he'd do something like this. He kept your bracelet all those years. That's the kind of thing only a man in love would do."

"Jared *said* he kept the bracelet all those years." Cecelia pushed away from the table and picked up the pictures Charles McAlister left.

Marie spent two hours trying to come up with different

scenarios that might change the situation Cecelia knew couldn't be changed.

After she left, Cecelia felt better for having told Maria. The part of her story she didn't tell was that she had been carrying Jared's baby when she moved to New York. To her knowledge, only her mother and Charles McAlister knew.

~

Knox answered the door wearing a ripped T-shirt and a pair of gym shorts. "Hey, buddy? What's going—?" He narrowed his eyes. "You look like a train hit you."

"Yeah, thanks. Can I come in?"

"Sure." Knox opened the door wider. "Want some lunch?"

"No, I had a late breakfast with Betsy."

Knox ruffled a hand through his already disheveled hair. "Breakfast with Betsy? Something is definitely up."

Abbey came out of the kitchen. "Hi, Jared."

"Hey, beautiful." He returned her hug.

"Can I get you something to drink?"

"No, thanks. What I need is advice."

"Sit down." Abbey pulled out a dining room chair, then disappeared into the kitchen.

Knox sat across the table from him. "What's going on?"

Abbey came back with three glasses and a pitcher of iced tea. Jared didn't need any more caffeine. His hands were already shaking from the three cups of coffee he had with his mom.

Jared unloaded the story of him and Cecelia from beginning to end, with only little gasps and an occasional "Oh!" from Abbey. When he finished, he looked at Knox. "So you were right. My father had everything to do with Cecelia's disappearance."

"That's unbelievable, Jared," Abbey said.

"Not if you know good ol' Charlie." Knox draped an arm over the back of Abbey's chair. "I don't think Ce would take any money from your dad, and I don't think she'd terminate a pregnancy, even if she'd been backed against a wall." Knox shook his head. "That's not the Cecelia I remember."

"I'm glad to hear you say that." Jared ran both hands down his face. "Between my mom and dad, I was beginning to doubt her."

"Maybe she had the baby and put it up for adoption," Abbey suggested.

Jared leaned back in his chair and shook his head. "I've done the timeline in my head a dozen times. That article in the magazine I showed you said she's been working at the design firm for over nine years, which means she finished school in three. There is no way she could have done that and had a baby, even if she'd given it up for adoption."

"Sure there is," Abbey said. "She could have taken extra courses online, and there isn't much of a recovery period after having a baby nowadays. But if you and Knox are right about Cecelia's character, she wouldn't have given up your baby without discussing it with you."

Knox shook his head again. "I don't believe Ce would have done any of this, Jared." He swirled the iced tea in his glass. "Do you think Marybeth told Charlie that Ce was pregnant when she really wasn't?"

Jared snorted. "You know my dad. He would have made certain before he gave Marybeth a dime."

"True," Knox agreed.

He held out his hands, palms up. "What should I do?"

"You said Cecelia mentioned another woman. What happened to her?" Abbey asked.

"There was no other woman. I have no idea what Ce's talking about."

"Another thing good ol' Charlie probably told Ce so she'd leave town," Knox said.

An epiphany jolted through Jared's mind. He stared at Knox with an open mouth. "That's how he did it. He wanted Ce to believe I was seeing someone else. That's how he got her to go to New York."

Knox sat back, lacing his fingers over his stomach. "I haven't told you this because it's business. I called Ce after you showed me that article. I'm going to New York next month to sit down with her and Arthur Winston to discuss importing some furniture items for a few of their clients."

"Why didn't you tell me?"

"Like I said, it's business. Anyway, Abbey's coming with me. We could take Ce to dinner and try to talk to her."

"No, I've got to do this myself. I just can't get away from the office until the end of this week."

"Maybe that's a good thing," Abbey suggested. "Give her some time to get past the initial hurt and anger. She's probably too mad to listen to you right now."

"I can't give her too much time. I don't want her disappearing on me again."

"She has a life in New York, Jared. She's not going to disappear." Knox ruffled his hair. "I wasn't going to tell you because I thought Cecelia would want to, but she's buying half of the design firm. By this time next week, she'll be Arthur Winston's partner."

Jared hated himself for thinking it, but he knew he wasn't the only one in the room wondering if fifty thousand dollars was playing a part in that business deal.

CHAPTER 30

Cecelia walked into the office and picked up her messages. Flipping through them quickly, she saw she needed to return three calls and set up another appointment with the Hollywood couple. They'd be in town for a few days close to Thanksgiving.

Windy came out of the conference room as Cecelia headed for the kitchen. "Good morning, Ce," she said hesitantly.

"Hi, Windy." She set the top message on Windy's desk. "Will you set up an appointment with the Oakleys? It needs to be at least three hours. See if they can meet here in the conference room. I'll call Mrs. Hollywood and let you know what day we plan to meet."

"Sure."

Cecelia put her lunch in the fridge and headed past Windy's desk for the stairs.

"Cecelia?"

She knew what Windy wanted before she turned toward her, one foot on the bottom stair.

"Jared called Thursday and Friday. He said you aren't returning his calls."

"Jared is engaged. He's living with his fiancée in Dallas." She waited a moment to see if Windy had any other questions rather than standing with her mouth open. "Will you let me know when the Oakleys want to meet?"

"Yes," Windy whispered.

"Thank you." She jogged up the stairs.

~

"Hi, Windy. It's—" Jared pulled his cell phone away from his ear and stared at it. Windy had hung up on him. He hit the call icon for Cecelia's office again. When Windy answered, he quickly said, "Please don't hang up, Windy. I need you to listen to me."

"You lied to me, Jared," she said, her voice low.

"I didn't lie to you—or Cecelia. I can't explain everything right now, but I need to make sure she's okay."

"No, she's not okay!" she said an octave higher.

How could he convince Windy, who'd become a friend, that he was telling the truth? "I promise I did not lie to either of you. It's important that you believe me."

"You're engaged," she whispered harshly.

"No. I was engaged, but I broke it off three weeks after I met you. My dad lied to Cecelia."

"Why would he do something like that?" From miles and miles away, he could hear the disbelief in her question.

"He's angry. He hoped to grow McAlister Industries through the connection with my fiancée's family." That was all the explanation he was going to give. He didn't want Windy telling Cecelia how Charles felt or that he had them followed and photographed.

"I'm not sure I believe you, Jared."

Jared sighed. "I probably wouldn't believe me either. I'm just concerned about Cecelia and want to make sure she's okay."

"Are you going to tell her the truth?"

Jared looked up when someone tapped on his door. Violet pointed to her watch and held up both hands, fingers splayed, signaling he had ten minutes before meeting with new clients. He nodded. "Listen, Windy, I have to go. I want to talk to Ce face-to-face. I thought I could get to New York this week, but something has come up. Don't tell her I called. I don't want to upset her. I just wanted to make sure she got to the office and that she's okay."

"She's here, but she's not okay. Your dad is a horrible person, Jared."

"He always has been." Jared ran his fingers through his hair in frustration. "I'm sorry I disappointed you, Windy. I wish I had the time to explain everything, but I'm due in a meeting. I know I promised I wouldn't hurt Cecelia."

"Yeah, well, you did."

"I know. I'm sorry," he repeated. "Please, take care of her until I can get there."

                      ~

Cecelia waited in her office until she heard Winston come in. He greeted Windy; then their voices moved away from the reception area. They'd probably gone into the kitchen or the conference room so Winston could ask how she was doing. She waited until he came up the stairs and settled at his desk before she went into his office. "Good morning."

"Good morning, sweetheart." He flashed a sad smile. "How are you?"

"I'm fine. Thank you for sending Maria over to babysit me."

"You know that's not why she came over."

She did know. "Do you have a few minutes?"

"I have as much time as you need." He sat back and laced his fingers over his stomach.

Cecelia shut the door. "I'm sure Maria told you everything."

"Yes, and I'm sorry I left you alone in the office that morning."

"You couldn't have known."

"No, but I won't be leaving you, Mia, or Windy alone ever again." His exhaled loudly. "I'm also sorry Jared hurt you."

Cecelia slipped into one of the chairs in front of his desk. "There were a couple of things I didn't tell Maria."

Winston waited.

"Remember, I told you I had a full-ride scholarship in Arizona, then suddenly another at NYU was offered?"

"Yes."

"While he was here, Jared's dad told me that, with my mother's help, he set up the other scholarship. He paid for everything. He wanted to get me as far away from Jared as he could." She swallowed the threatening tears. She was so tired of crying.

"Oh, sweetheart." Winston moved around his desk and sat in the chair beside her.

"I can't be in debt to Charles McAlister. I was stupid to believe I'd been offered a scholarship to NYU after the semester started."

"He took advantage."

Cecelia looked down at her clenched hands. "What I'm trying to tell you, in a very roundabout way, is that I can't buy into Winston and Associates yet. I need to use that money to pay back Mr. McAlister."

Winston planted his palms on his knees. "You are like a daughter to us, Cecelia. Let Maria and I pay for your education. We'd love to do that for you."

She put her hand over his. "You are the sweetest man, and I appreciate the offer, but this is something I need to do myself. Mr. McAlister thought I'd never make anything of my life, and I'm going to prove I have.

"I called the University Friday and got an approximate total. The loan I took out to buy into Winston and Associates will easily cover the amount. I want to write one check to show him I can pay my own way. I've already visited the bank, and everything is set."

"I understand," Winston said. "Let me lend you the money to buy into the business."

She laughed. "You'll lend me the money to buy half of your business from you? I don't think that's the way it works, Winston. Just give me a couple more years. I'll get the money."

"There's no rush, sweetheart. I didn't offer you this opportunity because I'm financially strapped. I don't have anyone else who could take over when I retire. Maria and I discussed this, and we want you to be a part-owner because we knew you wouldn't accept an outright gift."

Of course, she cried. How could she not?

❧

"Come in," Charles barked when his assistant knocked. How many times had he told her he didn't want to be disturbed at this time of day?

"I'm sorry, Mr. McAlister." She peeked around the door. "A certified letter just arrived."

"Sign for it."

"It's a restricted delivery that requires your signature."

He blew out an impatient breath and beckoned for the delivery man to enter. He half expected news from his stubborn wife, who had decided to stay with her sister in Austin and had refused his calls, but she hadn't refused the diamond necklace he sent.

A slim young man in a black uniform eyed Charles's black eye before he held out the cardboard envelope. Charles pulled the card off the front, signed, and handed it back. Waving away his assistant and the man, he waited until the door closed before he opened the envelope, but the name on the front stopped him. Cecelia Chadwick.

He ripped the tab open and dumped the contents onto his desk. A handful of donation slips paperclipped together, a check, and a folded piece of hand-cast ivory linen stationery. He opened the letter.

Mr. McAlister,

Enclosed are copies of the donation slips from the nonprofit organizations your fifty thousand dollars helped to support twelve years ago and again on Monday. I'm sure all those that benefitted from your generosity are extremely grateful.

You'll also find a check enclosed for the amount of my education, all expenses included, plus the interest that money would have accrued in the past twelve years.

I am no longer bought and paid for.

Sincerely,

Cecelia Chadwick

CHAPTER 31

The morning was beautiful, the air crisp—a perfect fall morning. Cecelia pulled the collar of her coat tighter under her chin, then waved to a shop owner putting a sale sign out on the sidewalk.

Last week Mia had announced she planned to leave Winston and Associates to go out on her own at the beginning of the year. Yesterday, Winston, ever resourceful, hired her replacement. Kayla, who was energetic and had a fabulous eye for design, would fit into the office perfectly.

Cecelia pushed the elaborate wood door open. "Good morning, Windy."

"Morning, Ce," Windy chirped.

After peeling off her coat, scarf, and hat, she walked over to the reception desk for the pile of messages Windy held out. The top one said, Tall, Dark, and Handsome called.

Cecelia hadn't spoken to Jared in two weeks. She assumed he understood she wasn't interested. Obviously, she hadn't been clear enough. She put a hand to her stomach, hating her impulsive reaction. "When?"

Windy feigned surprise. "Oh, did I forget to write that down?"

"Yes, you forgot the when *and* the why."

"The when was about an hour ago." Windy lifted her shoulders and her eyebrows. "I thought you'd know the why."

She hadn't heard anything from Jared's attorney, but she knew about the sixty-day waiting period for divorces to be granted in Texas. That left six more weeks before she was a divorced woman.

"Did he tell *you* why he called?"

Windy shook her head. "He asked *me* to tell *you* to call his cell phone when you get in."

Fat chance. Cecelia went to the kitchen and just about threw her lunch in the fridge. She should have known he couldn't let this go. He wasn't finished with her yet. As part of some sick mind game, he clearly intended to extract her soul along with her heart.

"Maybe you should call Jared, find out what he has to say," Windy said as Cecelia passed her desk.

"You need to stay out of this, Windy." Cecelia stopped halfway up the stairs. "I don't mean to snap at you. I'm sure Jared has sweet-talked you into believing him. He can be very persuasive, but you don't know the whole story, so please mind your own business."

She dropped her briefcase near her desk and went to the window, pressing a palm against the cold glass. She'd felt ill ever since Charles McAlister's visit but only allowed herself three days to mourn before burying herself in work.

How pathetic that she'd fallen for the same scenario all over again. Except, the first time she'd been carrying Jared's baby while he'd been in bed with his next conquest. She'd been a young, trusting fool back then. She had no excuse this time around.

Trusting her heart to anyone was now a thing of the past.

The tree out front had dropped its leaves. The bare branches stark against the pretty blue sky. Cecelia fought the tears burning the backs of her eyes. *No more tears for that man.*

Glancing at the message she still held in her hand, she walked over to the trash can and let go, watching it flutter to the bottom.

She was finished with Jared McAlister. She was finished with the whole McAlister family. She was finished with Texas and her mother, who played a huge role in Charles McAlister's plan.

She reached for her phone and pressed Windy's extension.

"Yes?"

"If Jared calls, again, tell him I can't talk. Do not transfer his call to my office."

"Okay. What if he comes by?"

"Is he in town, Windy?"

"Yes."

"Tell him I can't see him either."

~

*J*ared saw Cecelia coming down the sidewalk before she noticed him. He'd been sitting on the front steps of her apartment building for more than an hour while the temperature plummeted. He stood up and stomped his feet to warm them.

He was afraid she wouldn't let him in if he arrived after she got home. Determined not to leave until they both told their side of the story and all their questions were answered, he waited. Windy had been kind enough to call him when Ce left the office for the day, so he had an idea when she might be home.

He knew the minute she spotted him because she stopped, her lips forming his name. They were close enough that he could see her breath, a soft cloud of white under the streetlight. He half expected her to turn around. Instead, she came toward him, her eyes as icy as the first day they met.

"Hi," he said when she stopped in front of him.

She didn't respond.

"I know you don't want to see me, but I have some questions. I can't go on without knowing the truth. No more secrets and no more half-truths. We need to clear the air."

Her chest rose and fell with her heavy—probably anger-driven—breathing.

He held up the manila envelope she sent to his attorney. "If you don't want me around after everything's out in the open, you won't see me again. You have my promise, Ce. I'll sign these and go away forever."

She climbed the steps and opened the door to her building. He followed her up the three flights of stairs to her apartment.

"Have you been waiting long?" she asked as soon as they stepped inside.

"Yes. I would have arrived closer to the time you got home if you'd called me back."

She surprised him by taking his hands in hers then frowning. "Jared, you're frozen. Come sit down." She slid his coat off his shoulders and flipped on the gas fireplace. He sat in the chair she indicated, and she wrapped a throw around him. "Have you eaten?"

"I'm not hungry, Ce. I want to talk."

"I made some chicken soup last night. It'll only take a minute to heat up." She disappeared into the kitchen. "I don't have coffee, but I can make some hot chocolate."

As angry as he felt at the moment, her offer made him smile. Only Cecelia and her nurturing ways would make this so difficult. He dropped the throw, got up from the chair, and followed her into the kitchen.

Cecelia dumped soup from a leftover container into a pan and lit a burner. Though hurt, a tender protectiveness enveloped him. If his dad had told the truth, Cecelia was pregnant with their baby. He walked up behind her and slipped his hands over her hips to her stomach.

"Don't touch me," she wheezed out on a whisper.

"Tell me about our baby."

She turned and tried to push past him, but he caught her arm.

"I have the right to know."

She turned to him, her eyes shimmering with tears. "I-I lost our baby," she choked out. "I mi-miscarried at ten weeks."

He felt like he'd been punched in the gut. In the same instant, his heart broke for her. She'd been alone in a strange city. He gently placed his arm around her shoulder, and when she didn't pull away, he tucked her close and smoothed a hand over her back. "I'm sorry, Ce. I wish you had come to me. Why didn't you tell me you were pregnant?"

She clung to him until he pulled back enough to take her face in his hands and tried to dry her tears. Suddenly, she wrenched free. "The soup is ready."

"I don't want soup, Ce. I want answers. I want to know why you tried to divorce me. I'm tired of wondering why you disappeared without a word. Why would you run away, especially knowing you were carrying our child? If my dad was involved, I want to know how."

She swiped tears away, and her glacial eyes narrowed to slits.

"Why didn't you tell me you were pregnant?" He tried to suppress the anger that surged through him. "If you hadn't miscarried, what were you planning to do? Raise our baby without ever telling me? Put our child up for adoption?"

She stepped to the stove and flipped the burner off, then shoved past him. He followed her into the living room to the bookshelf, where she picked up an ornately carved wooden box. He'd noticed the workmanship the first time he visited her apartment. She flipped the lid open and shuffled through the contents. Pulling out a photo, she held it out to him.

Jared took it and studied the picture for a moment before he realized he was looking at a fuzzy image of him and a girl having sex. Shame washed over him when he couldn't remember the girl's name. Kathy. . . No, Kelly something. He'd dated her for a few months when he was a sophomore in college.

Then she disappeared. Much as Cecelia had.

Suddenly realization crashed over him like a huge wave, crushing the air from his lungs. He closed his eyes and groaned. "Please, tell me this picture isn't the reason you disappeared." When she didn't answer, he opened his eyes. "Is this who you meant when you said you knew about the girl twelve years ago?"

The anger around her eyes dissolved, replaced by doubt. She nodded.

"Did my father give you this picture?"

She nodded again.

Rage, more ferocious than any he'd ever experienced, slammed through him, his pulse racing so fast his head spun. His father had him followed even before he met Cecelia. Good ol' Charlie had stolen twelve years away from him and Cecelia, and there was nothing he could do to get that time back.

He ripped the picture in half and threw the pieces on the floor. "I dated that girl when I was a sophomore in college, two and a half years before I met you."

Bewilderment crossed Cecelia's face. He saw the moment the truth hit her.

She opened her mouth, closed it, and swallowed while a lone tear trailed down her cheek. "Your father told me you'd moved on, that you only married me to get me into bed." She looked down as her voice broke. "He said you realized as soon as you got to school that you made a terrible mistake and wanted out."

"Cecelia, I loved you then, and I love you now. I've never stopped loving you." Jared reached for her, but she stepped back and pulled more pictures out of her box.

Jared didn't need to look to know they were pictures of him and Stacy. "I was engaged to Stacy Richardson. I broke the engagement the weekend of my grandfather's birthday dinner. I tried to tell you about her that day in Central Park, but you wouldn't listen. The minute I saw you, I knew I couldn't marry Stacy because I still love you."

Jared took another step toward her, but she backed away again. She pulled out another picture and held it up. Him carrying Stacy into her condo the night she called him from the bar.

"By the date, this was taken after your grandfather's birthday."

"Stacy called me from a bar, and I could tell she'd had too much to drink, possibly because of our broken engagement, so I picked her up. She passed out in the car, and I carried her into her condo. Nothing happened."

"Your dad told me you live together."

"Another lie. She lives in the heart of Dallas. I have a condo outside of the city."

Cecelia whipped out another picture of him at the country club. Stacy's arms were around his neck. Instantly, he knew he'd been set up.

"When this photo was taken, Stacy had just finished

telling me she was over the breakup and all was forgiven. I wondered about it then, but now it makes sense. Dad must have set this up too." Jared shook his head. "My mother left my father over all of this. He showed us bank statements…"

Cecelia handed him an envelope filled with donation slips. Jared hated himself for doubting her but couldn't stop his smile. His father would cough up a lung if he knew Cecelia Chadwick had given a hundred thousand dollars to charity.

Jared looked from the slips to Cecelia, but she wouldn't make eye contact. "Where does this leave us, Cecelia? Will you talk to Knox? He'll tell you the truth—the whole story. I want you to believe me."

He pulled out his cell phone. "Will you talk to him? You can ask him anything about me and the past twelve years. He knows me better than anyone and will answer any and all of your questions."

She glanced from him to his phone.

"I am guilty of being engaged when we went to dinner those first two times. And I'm guilty of calling you before I broke up with Stacy, but I never kissed you, and I never told you I loved you until after she and I were no longer together." He held out his phone. "Will you talk to Knox?"

She shook her head. "I believe you."

"You do?"

She nodded, but just barely.

He slid his phone back into a pocket before taking a tentative step in her direction, afraid to move too quickly. "Have you got anything else in that box?"

She pulled out a stack of letters tied with a blue ribbon. The letters he'd written to her after she disappeared from his life. "Why didn't you read them?"

"Because I thought they'd be filled with lies."

"I've *never* lied to you, Cecelia." He took the letters from her. Bound by the knot of the blue ribbon was the delicate gold wedding band he'd given her when they exchanged vows. Taking another step, he leaned down, and he put the pictures back in the box, but held onto the ribbon-wrapped letters. Afraid she'd escape if he gave her the chance, he took the box and set it on a chair, then took her hand. "I told you I gave you my heart a long time ago, and I've never asked for it back."

He watched as another tear slid down her cheek. He slowly drew her to him, wrapped his arms around her, holding her close. "I'm sorry for the damage my dad did. I'm sorry you were hurt. I'm sorry that we lost so many years of our lives when we could have been together."

He took a shuddering breath. "And I'm so sorry about our baby. I'm sorry I wasn't here for you, but I want you to know I would have been if I'd known because I loved you then, and I love you now. I should have taken better care of you. I should have taken you to California with me, Ce."

"I'm sorry I doubted you."

Jared's heart broke as he listened to her tortured voice. He would forever hold his father responsible for all the heartbreak and anguish he caused. "I don't want a divorce. I want to spend my life with you." He lifted her chin enough that he could look into her eyes, relieved the ice was gone. "I want to wake up next to you every morning, and I want to hold you every night as you drift off to sleep. I want us to be together forever."

"I want the same thing," she whispered in that soft Southern voice of hers.

He kissed her then, with tenderness and love, thrilled when she returned his kiss.

"I don't want to live away from you," he said.

Her first smile, slight but there, appeared. "Okay."

"I want to start our life together as soon as possible."

At her nod, he backed her to the sofa and pulled her down onto his lap. They sat like that for a long time, saying nothing, just holding each other close and matching breath for breath, warmed by the fire and their love.

"Knox told me you're going to buy half of Winston and Associates."

"I was, but some unexpected expenses came up, so I had to put it off for a while."

"Unexpected expenses?"

She fidgeted with a button on his shirt.

Jared lifted her chin, kissed her lips. "No more secrets, Ce."

"I don't think you've heard this part of the story."

Jared rested his chin on the top of her head, blowing out a tired breath. "Tell me."

"The scholarship at NYU wasn't a scholarship."

"What do you mean?"

"Your father set the whole thing up. He paid to get me into NYU. He paid for everything."

"To get you as far away from me as possible," Jared finished as another piece of the puzzle fell into place.

"I didn't know, or I would never have accepted."

His dad had destroyed any trust Jared would ever have in the man. "What does that have to do with you not buying into Winston's business?" he finally asked.

"I used the loan I took out for Winston to pay your father back. I sent him a certified letter with a check enclosed last week."

"I wish I could have seen his face when he opened that envelope," Jared said with a laugh.

Cecelia smiled.

"Grant said I could transfer to the New York office as soon as I finish the merger I'm working on. Two weeks at the most." He untied the blue ribbon from the letters, slipped her ring off the loose end, and held it out. "Think you might like to put this on anytime soon?"

She held out her hand, and he slipped the ring on her finger, then kissed it.

"Do you think there's enough room for both of us here in your apartment?" he asked, running knuckles over her upturned cheek.

She smiled. "I think there's plenty of room . . . until we have a baby."

If possible, his love for Cecelia deepened. "We should start working on that immediately."

CHAPTER 32

*J*ared looked around the room, a vision in navy blue and white. Cecelia had outdone herself on her last project before taking maternity leave.

He felt a touch on his back and turned.

"Thank you for picking up the rocking chair. I love it."

"The whole room is perfect. You're amazing at what you do, Ce." He pulled her around so her back rested against his chest and his hands cradled her very pregnant tummy. He thought his happiest days followed moving to New York, but this moment topped that. Their little guy should make his appearance in three weeks.

They found a house forty minutes from the city. It was situated in a wooded area, so it felt far from the bright lights. Ce had worked like mad to get the place just right before they moved in, and the house was homey and comfortable—and theirs, with plenty of room to grow.

Ever since moving in, they'd hosted many guests.

His grandparents came first. The four of them had a wonderful visit. When he decided to leave Dallas, he knew he'd miss his sister, her family, and his grandparents, so he enjoyed every minute of their time together.

Susan, Tim, and the kids had also visited, and just as Jared suspected, they all loved Ce. Especially the kids. And she loved them back. Watching Ce and Susan get to know each other had warmed his heart.

Ce's brother, Derrick, also came to stay for a week. To Ce's surprise, he brought his fiancée, a sweet girl from California. Jared didn't use the word adorable often, but Derrick and Kayleigh were an adorable couple.

"Your mom called," Cecelia said. "She wants to come to visit after the baby is born."

Jared hadn't forgiven her as easily as his wife did. His mom quickly learned that if she wanted information, she should call Ce. He still wasn't ready to answer her calls. His dad hadn't even tried, and Jared didn't expect him to. Charles held grudges long past their expiration date, so maybe he was a little like his dad after all.

The doorbell chimed through the house. Jared bent to kiss Cecelia's neck. "Our visitors are here."

"Let's go greet them."

He and his wife walked down the stairs to the front door, and he pulled it open. Knox and Abbey stood on the porch. "Welcome," Jared said.

Of course, Knox went straight for Ce and pulled her into a tight hug. "Hey, beautiful."

Knox and Abbey came to New York several times a year now that Knox imported furniture and other household goods to a store Winston had opened featuring unique antiques. Jared and Ce had attended their wedding in Dallas six months earlier.

Knox put both hands on Ce's belly. "How are you holding up?"

"I'm okay," she said.

He turned to Abbey with wide eyes. "Holy mackerel, the baby just kicked!" He looked back at Ce. "Does that feel weird?"

"Weirdly wonderful," Cecelia said, her blue eyes glowing.

"You look gorgeous."

Jared had to agree. Cecelia had stopped straightening her hair and looked radiant as an expectant mother. He'd enjoyed every single step she went through, from their excitement over the positive home pregnancy test to their most recent doctor visit. She craved grilled cheese, and he happily went to the kitchen to make her one, even at two in the morning.

"You always were an impressive fibber."

He laughed. "Who but Cecelia Chadwick uses the word, fibber?"

"That's Cecelia McAlister," Jared said, hugging Abbey. "Speaking of gorgeous."

"Notice that pregnancy glow?" Knox asked.

"What?" both Jared and Cecelia asked at once.

Abbey nodded, rubbing a hand over her flat tummy.

Cecelia hugged Knox, then Abbey. "Congratulations."

"When are you due?" Jared asked, thumping Knox on the back. He didn't get to see his best friend as often as he used to, but the times he and Abbey came to stay were sweet.

"February fourteenth."

"A Valentine's Day baby." Cecelia clapped her hands. "Do you know if it's a boy or a girl yet?"

"We find out next week," Knox said.

"Come into the kitchen and relax." Cecelia beckoned them through the living room.

Jared picked up their suitcases. "Babe, if you'll get them a drink, I'll put these in their room."

Cecelia turned to their guests. "I hope you're hungry.

Dinner will be ready in about thirty minutes, but Jared made some yummy appetizers."

He walked up the stairs and turned toward the guest room, glad to escape for a moment. He wasn't sure why the news of Abbey and Knox having a baby made him so emotional. They'd been friends for so long. He couldn't imagine his life without Knox nearby.

In the guest room, he opened the closet and set the suitcase on the luggage rack. When he went back down the stairs, he heard laughter and let it fill him, along with the mouthwatering aroma of Ce's cooking.

In the kitchen, the three of them sat at the island, scooping the vegetables he'd sliced earlier through an herb dip. He walked behind Ce and slipped his arms around her shoulders. She leaned back against him like he knew she would.

If the judge had signed those divorce papers all those years ago . . .

He didn't even want to think of where he might be right now. Cecelia was his life, and every day he said a prayer of thanks for the way things turned out, and for the blessings they enjoyed.

Life was good.

∼

If you enjoyed *When You Love Someone*, I hope you'll continue reading! The other books in the Second Chance Romance Collection are *Endless Love* and *Rhythm of Love*.

To keep up to date on new releases join my newsletter at TinaNewcomb.com.

Following is an excerpt from *Endless Love*.

EXCERPT FROM: ENDLESS LOVE

CHAPTER ONE

Lori Maguire shook out her umbrella under the overhang of the office building. Taking a minute to calm her nerves, she pulled out her silenced cell phone and scrolled through the two good luck messages her kids had left. The last time she interviewed for a job happened so long ago, she couldn't remember the kinds of questions they asked.

Inhaling deeply, she entered the building and smiled at a young security guard. "I'm looking for the *Star's* offices."

"Who are you here to see?"

"Dave Stephens."

"His office is on the second floor. Take a left after you exit the elevator."

On the second floor, she opened one of the double doors with *The Seattle Star* etched in the glass.

"Can I help you?" asked a receptionist.

"I have an appointment with Dave Stephens. I'm Lori Maguire."

"I'll let him know you're here."

Lori slipped out of her coat and hung it on a rack near the door, then smoothed a hand down the side of her dress.

Should she have gone with a brighter color? Navy seemed safe. Maybe a little too safe. A brighter color might have— *Oh, stop being silly! The color of your dress isn't going to get you a job.*

Or would it?

Taking a seat, she set her purse on her lap, willing her fingers to stop fidgeting with the strap. At approaching footsteps, she glanced up. A man stopped in front of her and flashed a friendly grin. "Lori? I'm Dave Stephens."

She stood and shook his extended hand. "It's nice to meet you, Dave."

He tipped his head. "Let's go into my office."

As he led her down a hall, Lori's skittery heart settled slightly. His smile and thoughtful dark eyes matched the voice she'd become familiar with over the phone. After they received her resume, she'd had three phone interviews. One with the HR director Pamela East, one with Dave, the deputy managing editor, and the last one with the executive editor, Leland Jensen.

"Please, have a seat." Dave indicated one of two chairs as he rounded his desk. "I have an advantage over you. I brought my wife to one of your book signings here in Seattle last year, which gave me a face to put with the voice on the phone. My wife and daughters love your books."

"I'm glad they enjoy them."

Seven years ago, she decided to follow a teasing, daydreaming fantasy to write women's fiction. To her surprise, her books took off. She now had nine in print, one being released next week, and another with her editor. Still, writing a column for newspapers had always been her first love.

"You didn't mention your books in your resume."

"I try to keep my day job separate from my night job." She folded her hands in her lap to keep them still.

"When is your move to Seattle?"

She smiled. "Last week."

"You've already moved?" he asked with a raised brow.

"The couple who bought my house wanted to move in over Thanksgiving weekend, so I shifted my moving date up a couple of weeks."

"That was nice of you."

She shook her head. She wanted to be settled in her little house before Christmas. "It worked out for everyone."

"I have a couple more interviews." Dave tipped his head from side to side, seeming to weigh his thoughts. "If hired, would you be able to start the first Monday of January?"

Her heart did a little flip. It couldn't be this easy. "Yes."

"Do you have a few minutes? I'd like you to meet the editor."

Don't get your hopes up yet, she told her racing heart. "I have time."

∾

Matt Kelley had been holed up in his office all morning helping his assistant finalize plans for the office Christmas party which was less than two weeks away. Leland hadn't finalized many details before resigning for another job. Matt didn't feel right about dropping the ball on anyone else's shoulders this close to the date, so he and Denise ended up taking over.

When Dave called to see if he had time to do a quick interview, Matt jumped at the chance to escape for a few minutes. Denise was more than happy to take a break. She'd been complaining all morning that she hated party planning.

He and Dave had already eliminated two candidates for the columnist job. Though well qualified, they hadn't been quite what the newspaper needed. They were looking for a fresh perspective for this particular column. Dave mentioned this interviewee was a woman who'd just moved back to Seattle after living out of state. New blood might be good, and female blood might be even better.

Matt took the stairs down two flights and tapped on Dave's door before walking in. "Hey." And then everything stopped while his heart slammed into his ribs. Sucking in a quick breath, he blinked to make sure his eyes were working correctly while adrenaline flashed through him, leaving him light-headed and hot at the same time.

Lori Maguire, someone he never thought he'd see again, stood up from her chair, her mouth open and her eyes wide —obviously as shocked to see him as he was her.

"Lori." He wanted to say more, to say anything, but nothing came to mind. Instead, he stood, staring like an idiot. A pink blush washed across her cheeks, and memories hit him harder than a three-hundred-pound linebacker.

Dave stood. "You know each other?"

"Lori and I—"

"We went to college together," Lori filled in quickly.

Dave looked from him to Lori. "Small world."

Matt could hear the smile in Dave's voice. He finally willed his feet to move. Ignoring the hand Lori held out, he wrapped her in a hug. The scent of her perfume catapulted him into the past a second time.

She stepped out of his embrace. "I didn't realize you work for the paper." She glanced at Dave and her blush deepened.

"My fault," Dave said. "I forgot you did a phone interview with Leland. He took a job in Atlanta last week. Surprised us all—especially Matt, who was suddenly promoted to executive editor."

Matt stared at Lori, catching only bits and pieces of Dave's explanation. The girl who captured his heart in college was now a beautiful woman. She wore her strawberry blonde hair shorter now, but her green eyes were just as bright and vivid as they were twenty-four years ago.

A breathless "Oh," escaped her.

"Matt?" Dave cleared his throat. "Would you like me to give you a few minutes in private?"

I want more than a few minutes.

Matt shook his head and gestured to her chair. "I'm sorry. I'm just so surprised to see you. Please, have a seat, Lori." He reached for the resume Dave held out and sat in the chair next to her.

"I attached the letter of recommendation sent from Lori's Chicago editor," Dave said before taking his chair.

Matt flipped to the last page and skimmed the letter, smiling at the editor's comments, then turned to Lori's resume, noting dates and places. His smile dropped away. Both the letter and her resume listed Lori's maiden name at the top.

"So . . ." Dave said, followed by a what's-the-holdup look.

"You've been with the Chicago paper for . . ." His muddled mind couldn't do the simple math.

"Sixteen years," she filled in for him.

"That's the only job you have listed."

"It's the only job I held in Chicago, although I've written articles and columns for other Illinois newspapers and magazines. I can supply those editors' names if you need them."

Matt nodded as he kept his gaze on Lori. She caught her full bottom lip between her teeth and his heart kicked hard. Those lips had first tempted him then, driven him beyond reason many times in college. His attention moved up to the green eyes she often used to warn him when he was about to step over the line. Sometimes he stepped over anyway, just to see that flash of emerald.

Dave cleared his throat, and Matt mentally shook himself.

He was gawking. Again. He smiled. "Dave mentioned you moved back to Seattle."

"Yes. Right before Thanksgiving."

He quickly turned a page to see her Seattle address. "Are your parents still in Snohomish?"

"Yes," she said after a pause.

"How are they?"

A slight frown appeared. He'd veered from interview to personal, which seemed to make her nervous. "They're doing well. How are yours?"

"Great. Still in Astoria."

Used to being in control of most situations, he was botching a simple interview, thanks to a thumping heart and sweaty palms. Dave would probably fall off his chair if Matt asked how long she'd been using her maiden name.

Going through the steps of this interview was a waste of time. He already knew that if she met the qualifications they were looking for—and she did, or Dave wouldn't have called him down here—they would hire her. Which meant she'd be invited to the newspaper's Christmas party. He'd make sure Denise got Lori's invitation in the mail along with the others.

His thoughts jumped ahead. He assumed she was divorced, but maybe she'd moved back to town to be with someone. He couldn't think of a way to reword an interview question to get the information he wanted without seeming too obvious.

Dave tapped a pencil on his desk, giving Matt a what-the-heck-are-you-doing? signal.

Matt asked a few questions about her Chicago column, and she answered each with a confidence she didn't have in college. She'd never fully believed in herself or her potential while they dated. Clearly that had changed in a big way.

Dave leaned forward, resting his forearms on his desk. "I

told Lori we have a couple more interviews to conduct before we decide."

None of the resumes he'd looked over matched Lori's experience. "I think we have everything we need." Matt stood.

Lori did the same, and held out her hand, careful to keep her distance—no farewell hug. "Thank you for your time."

He held onto her hand longer than he should have. "It's nice to see you again."

Dave came around his desk and shook Lori's hand. "I agree with Matt. It's great to see you again, Lori."

Matt opened Dave's office door. "Give your parents my best."

She offered a tight smile and walked out. He leaned out into the hall and watched her until she disappeared around the receptionist's desk. When he turned back into the office, Dave grinned.

"When did you meet her before?" Matt asked.

"I took Mary to one of her book signings."

"Her book signings?"

"She writes novels." Dave folded his arms and leaned against his desk "What do you think? She's got a notable resume and the letter of recommendation from her Chicago editor is impressive. She's won several awards for her writing, which he mentions, but she doesn't."

"Lori wouldn't mention awards." Matt glanced at her resume and then the recommendation.

"My wife and daughters rush out to buy her novels as soon as they hit the shelves. She doesn't mention those in her resume either."

Matt walked to the window and peered down just as she pushed through the street-level door. *Is she as rattled as I am?* "She has another source of income."

"Does that matter?"

"Not as long as it doesn't interfere with her job."

"It didn't seem to interfere with her column in Chicago."

"Right."

"What do you think?" Dave asked lowering his hands to the desk.

Matt turned back to the window and watched Lori until she crossed the street and turned a corner, disappearing from view. "I think it would be a shame to let her get away."

Dave snorted. "The newspaper or you?"

Had he been that obvious? Matt dropped into the chair Lori sat in. Her perfume lingered.

"How well did you know Lori in college?"

"Well enough that I wanted to marry her."

"What?" Dave choked out. "I didn't know you'd ever come close to marrying *any* woman."

"Just one. A long time ago."

"What happened?"

Matt leaned forward and set Lori's resume on Dave's desk. "She moved to Chicago and married someone else." He frowned at Dave. "Would have been nice if you'd dropped a name when you called me to come down. I could have been a little more prepared."

"You being tongue-tied was pretty entertaining." Dave pushed off the desk. "If it makes you feel any better, she looked as shocked as you did. In fact, I worried that she might be sick."

Matt frowned. "Yeah, making a woman sick when she sees me makes me feel all warm and fuzzy inside."

Dave laughed.

"Pull up the Chicago newspaper so we can take a look at a couple of her columns." Matt wanted to get this taken care of so he could tell Denise to send out the Christmas party invitation.

"So we're going to offer her the job?"

"Yeah. If she just moved back to town, she may have submitted her resume at other area papers. Let's nab her before someone else does."

Dave circled his desk while Matt picked up Dave's phone and punched in the number for Lori's Chicago editor.

~

Lori was shaking so violently; she could barely open her car door. Falling into the seat, she slammed the door shut and dropped her forehead to the steering wheel.

Matthew Jefferson Kelley still lived in Seattle after all these years, and was editor of the newspaper she wanted to work for. She never imagined he would still be in the area. Why hadn't Leland mentioned he was leaving during their telephone interview?

She took a deep breath and let it out slowly. Okay, so Seattle was out, but there were other newspapers in the area. She'd just have to drive a little farther. Maybe *The News Tribune* or *The Olympian* were hiring. She'd find something. If not, she'd venture into writing fiction full time.

Her thoughts tumbled to the first day of her freshman year at the University of Washington. She walked into her Creative Writing class hoping to recognize at least one person besides the professor, who was an old family friend.

High school AP classes, the three prerequisites she'd taken over the summer, plus a few nudges from her adviser had gotten her admitted to this class, which wasn't usually open to freshmen.

Her hopes were dashed when she stopped just inside the door and glanced around. She'd chosen to go to college close to home, and yet she didn't see one familiar face.

Only the guy sprawled in his chair like a cat in the sunshine noticed her walk in. He fixed his gaze on her, and she could see the intense blue of his eyes from across the room.

Before she could blush, she glanced away and spotted an empty desk down the first aisle.

Professor Hill walked in a minute later. Lori hadn't seen him in a couple of years. He wasn't as lean, and his blond hair had turned a soft shade of brown, but she'd always recognize him by his teasing eyes and contagious smile. He greeted the class, told a joke, and then started calling roll. When he got to the Ms, he stopped, looked up, and scanned the room until he caught sight of her. "Lori Maguire."

She groaned inwardly.

The professor leaned against the front edge of his desk and laced his fingers together. This was how she remembered him—relaxed with a friendly smile that held a touch of mischief. Normally she'd smile back, but she had a queasy feeling the mischief would be directed at her.

"I was sixteen when a beautiful redhead moved in next door. She was inquisitive to the point of annoying, yet too adorable to ignore. Every time I walked outside, she was waiting for me, asking question after question, but I couldn't resist her four-year-old charms."

The class laughed at the twist in his story. She glared at Professor Hill, her cheeks blazing.

When she looked at her schedule a few days before classes started, she wondered if knowing the professor would be a help or a hindrance. Professor Hill had just answered that question. If he planned on embarrassing her with childhood stories, it would definitely be a hindrance.

She spent the rest of the hour with her nose in her book.

After class Professor Hill stopped at her desk before she could duck out and opened his arms.

"You're kidding, right?" she asked with a laugh.

He caught her arm and tugged her into a hug. "Sorry, I

shouldn't have done that to you on your first day—*on any day,*" he quickly corrected when she slugged him in the chest.

"Is it too late to transfer to another class?"

"Don't. I promise not to tell any more stories, though we both know I have some doozies in my repertoire."

"I'd like to hear more stories," said a voice behind her.

Lori glanced around at the guy with the intense blue eyes. He moved to her side, close enough that his arm brushed against hers. At least a foot taller, he grinned down at her, and she had a hard time pulling her gaze away. She side-stepped closer to Professor Hill and the guy smiled. Her stomach took a nosedive.

"Lori, this is Matt Kelley. He took a class from me two years ago as a freshman but decided to squander his talent on the football field instead. Matt, this is Lori Maguire."

Which makes him a junior.

"I'm definitely more interested in your class this year, Professor. Hi, Lori."

"Hello." She picked up her backpack and slung it over her shoulder, then glanced at Professor Hill. "I'll see you Wednesday if I don't transfer out." She headed for the door.

"You better not or I'll come looking for you. Remember, I know where you live," she heard Professor Hill shout before she ducked into the hall, glad to be swallowed up by the moving crowd.

She saw Matt twice on campus before her next Creative Writing class. Both times he was in the middle of a small crowd—mostly girls. Both times he went out of his way to say hello. And both times she nearly went into cardiac arrest. When she arrived at Professor Hill's class on Wednesday, she found Matt waiting at the door.

"Hi, Lori."

"Hello." She hurried past and took the same seat she sat in on Monday. Matt took the desk beside her. When she turned a questioning eye his way, he raised a brow and flashed a devilish, completely heart-stopping grin. "I can see much better from here."

She looked down as her cheeks heated.

"You do look pretty in pink," he said on that long-ago day.

Lori lifted her head from the steering wheel and started the engine. She'd been able to shove memories of Matt aside for years, but he'd be front and center now.

Her mind was so busy going over her interview that her ten-minute drive home flashed by in a blur. Disappointment hit her harder than she thought it might. She hadn't expected to get the job, but she'd hoped her experience would help her be a top contender.

Not likely now.

Okay, not a problem. Newspapers, magazines, fiction—she had plenty of other options. A laugh erupted that sounded a bit on the maniacal side. Had she actually thought things had gone too easily thirty minutes earlier?

And why did Matt have to look so great? At six four, he still had a commanding presence. His wheat-colored hair was a little darker and a lot shorter than he wore it in college. He was clean-shaven when they dated. Now he wore several days' worth of stubble, which looked nice, but hid the dimple in his chin. His eyes were still striking blue and his shoulders still football-broad. Twenty-four years, and he could still unnerve her with a look. He'd always been good at that. Among other things.

She wondered if he ever married.

Turning right, she took the driveway around the side of her house and parked near the back deck. Moving from an eighty-two hundred-square-foot house on the shore of Lake Michigan to a twenty-four hundred-square-foot house in Seattle had been quite a change. She'd planned to buy some land close to her parents' house and build something, but after she happened upon this quaint little place, she wasn't so sure she wanted bigger and newer.

She opened her car door just as her cell phone rang. The number wasn't familiar, but she recognized a Seattle area code. "Hello?"

"Lori, Dave Stephens."

That didn't take long. They must not have wanted her to get her hopes up right before Christmas. *Happy New Year to me.*

"Hi, Dave," she said, dialing her tone to happy.

"I know this is fast, but . . ."

She listened in confused silence while Dave offered her the columnist job. She'd left his office less than thirty minutes before. *What happened to the other interviews?*

"That's a generous offer, Dave," she said when he finished. But suddenly she wasn't sure working for Matt would be wise. "Can I take a day or two to think about it?"

"Sure."

She heard his hesitance. "I'll let you know no later than Thursday morning."

"I'll look forward to hearing from you."

"Thanks, Dave."

As soon as she disconnected the call, she grabbed her purse, searching her wallet for the phone number of *The Seattle Star*, and tapped in the number.

"May I please speak to Matt Kelley?" she asked when the call was answered. "Tell him it's Lori Maguire."

ACKNOWLEDGMENTS

For me, it takes a team of people to get a book ready to publish. First, I send a rough draft to my Beta Readers, Jeanine Hopping, Chris Almodovar, Holly Hertzke, and Marnie Giggey. Since they had all seen an earlier version, I also gave the manuscript to Suzanne Robison, who gave me some great feedback. I appreciate all of them for their time, patience, and talent.

I go over their suggestions, make changes, then send the manuscript to editor extraordinaire Faith Freewoman. She goes over it numerous times for me.

My proofreader comes next. Heidi Robbins caught missing or extra commas and a few misspellings. It's the first time I've worked with her and found her comments invaluable.

I do one more step of editing on my own by listening to the manuscript aloud. My cover artist, Dar Albert is working up a fabulous design while all this is going on. She's a saint for putting up with me and usually knows what is exactly right before I do.

Last, my hard-working, encouraging husband, Rick, formats, makes sure the cover lines up just right, and uploads the manuscript for me.

Then there are you, dear readers, who take time out of your busy days to read my book, send emails filled with sweet comments, and sign up for my newsletter asking for more. I'm still in awe that I have readers!

I have the very best job in the world. Each and every one of you makes it even more so. You all have my forever thanks and appreciation.

xox
　　Tina

ALSO BY TINA NEWCOMB

The Eden Falls Series

Finding Eden

Beyond Eden

A Taste of Eden

The Angel of Eden Falls

Touches of Eden

Stars Over Eden Falls

Fortunes for Eden

Snow and Mistletoe in Eden Falls

Rumors in Eden Falls

Second Chance Romance Collection

When You Love Someone

Endless Love

Rhythm of Love

Second Chance Romance Collection

ABOUT THE AUTHOR

Tina Newcomb writes clean, contemporary romance. Her heartwarming stories take place in quaint small towns, with quirky townsfolk, and friendships that last a lifetime.

She acquired her love of reading from her librarian mother, who always had a stack of books close at hand, and her father who visited a local bookstore every weekend.

Tina Newcomb lives in colorful Colorado. When not lost in her writing, she can be found in the garden, traveling with her (amateur) chef husband, or spending time with family and friends.

Follow Tina on:

facebook.com/TinaNewcombAuthor
instagram.com/tinanewcombauthor
bookbub.com/authors/tina-newcomb
goodreads.com/tinanewcomb
pinterest.com/tinanewcomb

Printed in Great Britain
by Amazon

30425943R00182